AT THE END OF IT ALL

PHILIP MAZZA

Also by Philip Mazza

From Under a Tree
Book One; The Harrow Saga

Shadow in the Flame
Book Two; The Harrow Saga

Children at the Gate
Book Three; The Harrow Saga

The Child of Fire
Book Four; The Harrow Saga
(Coming 2025)

The Neon Hive

The Quantum Gardener

AT THE END OF IT ALL

PHILIP MAZZA

OMNI PUBLISHERS

www.philipmazza.com

Omni Publishers of New York
ISBN 978-0-9977109-5-3
Printed in the United States of America

First Printing: December 2024

To those who cling to the dying embers of this broken world, who dare to dream of a future even as the end may soon come. Whether in infinite mercy or weary frustration, the One above may choose to start anew - may you rise from the ashes of that divine reset, whenever it may come. May the next iteration be kinder. May it endure. But know this: even in paradise, the serpent finds a way to coil.

1 The morning ritual

The clock struck eight. It was a Tuesday morning, just like any other, or so it seemed. But in about thirty minutes, reality would shift, and the world would forever be changed.

With a practiced motion, Professor Thornton North eased himself into his familiar corner booth at the Bookworm Bistro, a small café nestled amidst the bustling campus. A leather satchel stuffed with lecture notes rested at his side, with a cup of coffee, devoid of the sugary frivolities that plagued the palates of the masses, perched before him.

North was a tall, thin man with a receding hairline and a pair of wire-rimmed glasses that sat precariously on his nose. Wearing the customary garb of academia - a worn tweed jacket and corduroy trousers - he mirrored the unassuming demeanor of countless professors who frequented the establishment. Yet, there was something about him, something about his aged face, something in the depths of his clear, blue eyes, that hinted at great wisdom. It was as if he'd seen things that no one else had seen, gleaning secrets that remained hidden from the common gaze.

He peered out through the grimy window, taking a sip of his coffee, a bitter tang that swirled on his tongue. The world outside was going about its routine. Cars and buses crawled along the street like metallic insects. People walked their dogs, their faces etched with the same robotic apathy, their pets the only spark of life in their otherwise monotonous existence. Students milled about the campus, their laughter echoing like the eerie tinkling of wind chimes in an abandoned house. It was a normal day, just like any other.

But this day was far from normal. Little did North know, something strange was stirring, a pawn in some grand cosmic jest. A force was gathering, ready to yank the fabric of his world askew. Had he known, he would've run for his life, that is, what remained of it. But humans are blind to tomorrow's horrors, fated to stumble into the maw of destiny.

He glanced at the clock.

Five past the hour, he thought. *Thirty minutes until the migration.*

He took another sip of coffee, the liquid inferno searing his tongue as it went down. But he didn't care. He welcomed the pain. It was part of his morning ritual, a reminder that he was alive. He winced and put the cup down, his eyes watering.

So it begins.

***

North's mornings unfolded like a well-worn book, pages turning with a comforting rhythm that began with the first whisper of dawn. He would rise, his body stiff and protesting, and shuffle to his office. Words danced before his eyes as he read, his pen scratching across student papers like a mouse scurrying through dry leaves. His latest novel called to him, a siren song of unfinished sentences and half-formed ideas. But time ticked forward, relentless as always. He would march to the bathroom, a soldier answering the call of duty. The shower rained down, a cleansing deluge that washed away the cobwebs of night. He would dress in his familiar attire, a tweed jacket and cotton trousers, and stuff his satchel with the day's lecture notes. The door would creak open, a portal between worlds.

Then, like a pilgrim embarking on a sacred journey, he would set foot upon the path, venturing into the world beyond, to his sanctuary, the café. There, amidst the aroma of freshly brewed coffee and the murmur of hushed conversations, he would settle into his corner booth, a solitary observer of humanity's morning ballet. The cup would warm his hands and soothe his soul, its caffeine a gentle stimulant to his awakening mind. It was a time for him to be alone with his thoughts, to collect himself before the day began, to watch and wait.

***

Curls of steam from his coffee curled and writhed like a spectral apparition, pale, ephemeral, fading into the ether as quickly as it had materialized. He took a tentative sip, the coffee no longer scalding, a reminder of time's relentless march. Staring out the window, his eyes suddenly saw emptiness, but his mind was awash with images, memories of a father long gone, a father whose absence cast a long shadow over his life.

Another part of the ritual.

Memories flickered in his mind like old film reels, each frame a vivid snapshot of his past. His father, a man of quiet strength and unwavering patience, stood at the head of a classroom, a towering figure amidst a sea of squirming elementary schoolers. His voice, a soothing baritone, cut through the cacophony of childhood chatter, weaving tales of history, science, and the importance of kindness. His father was more than just a teacher; he was a mentor, a confidant. He instilled in North a love of learning, a deep appreciation for the world around him.

"Never say you're bored," his father would often remind him, his voice a blend of warmth and playful admonition. "Read whenever you can. Be happy, and feel lucky you're alive." There was a glimmer of mischief in his father's eyes, a spark that suggested adventure lay just beyond the horizon. "And remember," he would add, leaning in as if sharing a secret, "buy the ticket. Take the ride."

In the hushed depths of North's world, his father's presence lingered, an invisible essence that wove its way into the fabric of his existence. It was in the whispering sigh of the summer breeze that rustled through the trees, a caress that seemed to bear his father's comforting touch. It was in the lengthening shadows that stretched like skeletal fingers across the twilight landscape, each one a testament to his father's enduring presence. And it was in the silence of an empty classroom, where the ghost of his father's voice seemed to hover, a gentle reminder that he was never truly alone.

North smiled.

The memories of his father were like a familiar path, carved deep into his mind by years of constant tread. He walked it every day at this time, retracing every step, every turn, every landmark. It was a journey he never tired of, for it led him to the heart of his father's existence, to the essence of the man he had loved and lost.

But his memories of his mother were an impenetrable labyrinth, a dark, overgrown forest where tangled paths twisted and turned, leading to hidden chambers and forgotten trails. He had no recollection of her, no tangible presence in his mind. How could he? After all, she had died shortly after giving birth to him. Yet, there were fragments of her scattered across his consciousness, like pieces of a broken mirror. They glinted in the darkness, casting strange and distorted shadows. Some of the images were familiar, but most remained a mystery.

But there was one memory, a solitary star in the vast, expanse of his mind, that ignited everything off.

***

The cemetery visits were a ritual, as regular and inevitable as the changing of seasons. He would walk beside his father, their footsteps crunching on the gravel path, the sound amplified in the hushed air. The headstones rose around them, not so much menacing as melancholy, each one a story left unfinished. He felt the weight of his father's hand on his shoulder, warm and solid, anchoring him to the present even as the past loomed all around.

Part of him longed to run, to escape the suffocating presence of loss, but the son in him knew that this pilgrimage was as much for his father as it was for the woman beneath the earth. Without a word, he would slip his small hand into his father's larger one.

Standing there among the dead, he always felt the thrumming vitality of his own heartbeat, the rush of blood in his veins. In those moments, surrounded by reminders of mortality, he understood with startling clarity what it meant to be alive.

The grass around his mother's headstone grew with a stubborn persistence that mirrored the ache in their hearts. North and his father would work in a wordless choreography, their hands moving in sync as they trimmed back the green tendrils that threatened to obscure her resting place. The act of planting fresh flowers was both a comfort and a reminder of absence, a ritual that marked the passage of seasons and the endurance of love.

As they finished their task, North would lower himself to the ground, feeling the earth yield beneath his knees. His fingers found the cold surface of the granite marker, and the chill that spread through his hand was as startling as it had been the first time he'd touched it. The stone's unyielding nature seemed to embody the finality of his mother's departure.

With a reverence born of loss and memory, North always traced the letters etched into the stone: Mary Elizabeth North. Each curve and line was a fragment of the woman who he had never known, now distilled into this stark memorial. Kneeling there, his fingertips connecting him to the name that was his mother's, North would feel the complex tangle of emotions that defined his life now - grief intertwined with gratitude, absence wrapped in memory.

***

Then there was that one day when North sat on the porch swing, his legs dangling, not quite reaching the wooden slats below. His father settled beside him, the swing creaking softly under their combined weight. The evening air was filled with the scent of honeysuckle and the distant hum of cicadas.

"Dad," North said, his voice small but determined, "why did Mom die?"

His father's breath caught, a barely perceptible hitch. He turned to look at North, studying the familiar curve of his cheek, the questioning tilt of his eyebrows.

"That's a big question, son," he said finally. "What made you think of it?"

North shrugged, his fingers tracing the peeling paint on the swing's armrest. "I don't know. I just . . . I see other kids with their moms, and I wonder what it would be like. What she would be like."

His father nodded slowly. "Your mom was . . . she was like a summer storm. Beautiful and fierce and unpredictable. She could light up a room just by walking into it."

"But why did she have to go?" North pressed.

"Sometimes," his father began, choosing his words carefully, "our bodies don't work the way they're supposed to. Your mom's heart . . . it was too big for this world, in more ways than one."

North frowned. "That doesn't make sense. How can a heart be too big?"

His father chuckled softly. "I don't mean literally, son. I mean she loved so much, so deeply, that sometimes it overwhelmed her. And her physical heart, well, it had a defect. Something she was born with that the doctors didn't know about."

"Why didn't they know about it?" North's voice held a hint of accusation.

"Because her heart wasn't a problem until it was. When she got . . . sick . . . they tried everything. Believe me, they tried everything they could. Your mom was a fighter, right up until the end. But sometimes, even when we fight our hardest, life has other plans."

North was quiet for a long moment, digesting this. "Do you think she would have liked me?"

His father's arm wrapped around his shoulders, pulling him close. "Liked you? Oh, son, she would have adored you. You have her eyes, you know. And her laugh. Sometimes when you're really tickled by something, I hear her in your giggles."

"Really?" North's face brightened.

"Really. And you have her curiosity, always asking questions, always wanting to know more."

"Like now?"

"Exactly like now." His father smiled, a bittersweet thing. "She would have been so proud of you, of the person you're becoming."

North leaned into his father's side. "I wish I could've known her."

"I know, son. But you know what? In a way, you have her. She's part of you, in your bones and your blood and your beautiful heart."

"Dad?"

"Yes, son?"

"Can you tell me more about her? About what she was like?"

His father took a deep breath, his eyes misting slightly. "Of course. What do you want to know?"

"Everything," North said simply.

The stories his father told of her settled over him like a fine, gossamer web, each strand a memory, each intersection a moment frozen in time. They came to him in the quiet hours when the world outside his window had faded to a soft blue twilight and the crickets began their nightly serenade. His father's words, worn smooth by repetition, painted her in watercolors - the tilt of her head as she laughed, the way her fingers danced across piano keys, the scent of lavender that seemed to linger long after she'd left a room.

"Her voice," his father said, "was like honey poured over warm bread, rich and sweet and utterly comforting. It wrapped around you, holding you close like a favorite blanket on a chilly night, soothing and familiar. You could almost taste the warmth in her laughter, the way it danced through the air, inviting you to share in her joy."

In these stories, she was not so much a person as a feeling, a longing that settled deep in his chest, familiar and aching. He found himself collecting these fragments, these wisps of a woman he'd never known, piecing them together in his mind like a stained-glass window, beautiful but forever incomplete.

Memories are like stained glass fragments, beautiful but incomplete.

***

One evening, North found his father lost in contemplation, his gaze fixed on a faded photograph. A wistful smile touched his lips, a rare softness in his otherwise stern demeanor. The photograph was one of many that adorned their home, each a portal to a moment now gone. North had never seen his father so entranced by a memory. His eyes lingered on the woman's face as if he were trying to memorize every detail, every curve, every nuance. He wasn't merely looking at her; he seemed to be drinking her in, absorbing her essence through his gaze.

North remembered asking, "Is everything alright?" His voice was laced with a touch of curiosity and unease.

His father's face changed, the hard lines of a lifetime softening like butter left in the sun. "Everything is fine, son," his voice carried a tenderness North had never heard before, as if grief had polished away the rough edges of the man he knew. It was the voice of someone else entirely, someone North had never met but instantly recognized.

"She was everything to me," his father continued, each word as carefully placed as a bird building a nest. "My sun, my moon, my stars." He paused, his eyes fixed on some distant point beyond the room. "When she left, it was like someone had snuffed out all the lights in the world." His throat worked, swallowing down what might have been a sob. "Even now, I keep expecting to turn a corner and find her there, smiling at me like she always did."

North suddenly saw his father with fresh eyes. Gone was the stern patriarch of his childhood, replaced by a man who had known love's tender embrace and its crushing absence. He glimpsed the vastness of his father's devotion, a love that had endured life's tempests only to be splintered by an unforgiving twist of fate. North realized then that time would never fully heal this wound; his mother's memory would forever flicker in his father's heart, a persistent flame defying the shadows of loss. It was a revelation both beautiful and heartbreaking, much like love itself.

From that day forward, North carried that memory like a sacred relic, revisiting it each day, polishing its edges with the cloth of his mind, ensuring that it would never fade. There was something about that moment. It brought him closer to the mother he never knew. But still, it wasn't enough. He yearned for more than the image of his father gazing at faded photographs of his mother. He yearned to unravel the mystery that was her, to feel her presence, to understand her.

And so, North embarked on a journey of imaginary conversations with her, intimate dialogues conducted solely within the confines of his mind. He kept these conversations from his father. They were his refuge from the harsh realities of a life lived without her guiding hand.

In these talks with her, he'd made sure to speak only of good and beautiful things, of nature's wonders, of music and poetry, of his plans. In his mind's eye, he saw her. She was beautiful, engagingly witty, a wise woman with a heart as big as the sky. Pretending to talk to her made him feel less alone.

He'd tell her about the things that had happened in his life, even the things he hadn't liked, the things that had made him feel small and insignificant. And in her imaginary response, he'd find solace, a sense of understanding that he craved so desperately.

Sometimes, he'd imagine her laughing, warm, inviting, and contagious, the sound of pure joy. It was in these moments of imagined merriment that he felt truly alive, truly connected to the world around him.

But he knew, of course, that these conversations were nothing more than fantasy. He knew it was just his mind playing tricks on him, that she wasn't really there, but he didn't care. She was real to him, more real than anyone else in his life.

As the years slipped by and time etched its passage on his face, the memories of these imaginary conversations grew fainter, their edges blurring, elusive, and half-forgotten. Still, he clung to these wisps of remembrance, these gossamer threads of a life once lived. They were his anchors in a world that had long since moved on, leaving him adrift in a sea of progress he no longer recognized. In quiet moments, he would close his eyes and reach for these memories, each one a small miracle of preservation against the relentless tide of time.

How silly I was. A rueful smile played on his lips. *But she was always there for me.*

Unlike others, North's obsession with keeping such obscure memories wasn't merely a quirk. It was a compulsion, a gnawing need to hoard every fragment of his past that dealt with his mother and father, every fleeting thought, every inconsequential event, no matter how ordinary or insignificant it might seem.

Memories slowly wilt like petals in the harsh winds of time. But not with me.

2 Carrying the past forward

North often found himself trapped in the sticky web of his memories as if he were a bug preserved in amber, willingly held by a past that would not dim. Beneath the surface of his fixation lay a truth darker and as steady as the pulse in his wrist: his mother's absence. It tinted everything, an imprint on the story of his life, unseen until he looked closely. He carried it with him everywhere, this shadow of loss, shaping his days and slipping into his nights with a gentle persistence that resisted all efforts to be laid to rest.

This obsession carried with it a persistent doubt that nagged at him, a suspicion that his very birth had led to her death. The mere thought filled him with guilt and self-loathing. The weight of it was unbearable, making him yearn for an escape. But there was no escape. He was forever bound to his mother's death, perpetually haunted by the suspicion that he was the cause.

Sure, his father did his best to convince him he was not to blame, but the doubt lingered. The truth was, he couldn't know for sure, and it was this absence of answers, this lack of closure, that was a torture in itself.

"God is fickle," his father told him. "He gives and takes as he pleases, always on a whim, always without warning. We can pray, we can beg, we can grovel at his feet, but he will do as he sees fit, regardless of our pleas."

"Is that true?" North asked. "Is God really that cruel?"

"We're just tiny little specks in his path, caught up in his whimsy, his grand design."

Another sip of coffee.

Tiny specks. Barely visible. Insignificant. How true.

Outwardly, though, North always appeared detached from the memories he held onto, his face an impassive fortress. He would remain strong, a pillar of strength for his father, a bulwark against the relentless tide of grief.

Yet, beneath the veneer of North's stoic composure, there were times when he tried to imagine what it must have been like for his father. It was a morbid curiosity, an insatiable desire to peer into the abyss of his father's soul-crushing sorrow, to understand the agony of losing the one destined to walk beside you till the world's end.

As he tried to fathom the depths of this profound grief, his mind would stumble, teetering on the brink of comprehension. He would become overwhelmed by the immensity of it all. It was like trying to grasp the vastness of the ocean, an endless expanse that dwarfed any human understanding.

It had to be like a monstrous beast chewing at his insides, twisting and turning, refusing to let go. A relentless torment, a constant reminder of the love he had lost.

But his father was a man of untiring strength, a towering figure of resilience, who somehow endured this unimaginable loss. He faltered at times – her birthday, or during the holidays, but he'd never once bowed under the strain. For North, the idea of such sorrow was a void that would engulf anything that ventured too close.

"Life's like a long, winding road," his father would say. "There'll always be hills to climb, valleys to traverse, and storms to weather. But through it all, you must keep walking, son. You must never give up hope."

Hope. It's all we have against God's cruelty.

North clung to his father's words. He admired his father's resilience, the indomitable spirit that had carried him through the darkest of times. He knew that he could never match his father's strength, that he could never hope to endure such a devastating loss without crumbling under the burden of it. Still, he was grateful for his father's example, for the unfaltering love and guidance that had shaped him into the man he was today. He would carry his father's strength with him, as best he could.

There was so much his father taught him about life - countless lessons shaping his understanding of the world in ways both subtle and deep. It was his father who had nurtured his love for literature, fostering a passion that would ultimately inspire him to chase his dream of becoming a writer.

"Write," his father once urged, "write like your life depends on it, for indeed, if it is your passion, it very well might."

And it was his father's hand, gentle but insistent, that steered him towards the ivory towers of academia. There, among the whispering pages and the soft-soled shuffle of scholars, he found his place. He breathed in the musty perfume of old books, and let his fingers trail along their spines, each volume a promise, a secret waiting to be unlocked. The words of the masters became his companions, their voices echoing in his mind long after he'd closed their covers. Years slipped by, marked not by seasons but by semesters, as he climbed the ladder of degrees, each rung bringing him closer to a summit he couldn't quite name but felt compelled to reach.

But life, his father insisted, was not merely about the pursuit of knowledge. It was a tapestry woven with threads of vivid experiences, both joyous and sorrowful, triumphant and fraught with failure.

"Embrace it all," his father would remind him, "savor every moment, for it is in these moments that we truly discover who we are."

So many lessons, each one a precious gem to be cherished.

***

It seemed fitting, a cruel twist of fate, that his father's final lesson would be about death, about the inevitable dance between life and the eternal silence. His passing was a brutal awakening for North, a stark lesson he never sought. The man who had taught him so much was now frozen in time, a poignant reminder of mortality's inescapable grasp.

The world seemed to dim, the vibrant hues of life leaching away, replaced by a monochrome landscape that mirrored the desolation in North's heart. The man who had stood as an unyielding pillar, a source of wisdom and guidance, was now but a series of memories, fragments of images and sounds echoing in the halls of North's mind.

He looked up at the clock.

Just seven after eight.

North remembered that day, that moment, as clearly as if it were yesterday. The phone's shrill ring startled him, slicing through the quiet of his studies. He hesitated, his heart pounding, before picking up the receiver. It was his uncle, and his usually calm voice carried an unsettling urgency.

"Thornton," his uncle began, "your father . . . the cancer claimed him. He fought a brave battle."

North just stood there, stunned. His father had been his whole world, and he couldn't believe he was gone.

"When?" North asked in a whisper.

"Just a few hours ago," came the reply. "He was at peace, Thornton. Don't worry about him. He wouldn't want that."

"I'll come home," North muttered a simple vow to honor his father's memory by returning to the place where their lives had been intertwined.

He hung up the phone, his mind reeling. He could barely catch his breath as he felt a wave of grief wash over him, threatening to drown him. But then his face reddened.

He remembered his thoughts: *First my mother and now my father. Why couldn't someone else have died?*

Fury surged through him like a tempest, a white-hot rage, like a fire in his belly. He wanted to cry, to scream, to rage against the unfairness of it all. But he couldn't. He knew that wouldn't do any good. He'd only end up hurting himself, or someone else.

That's when a childhood memory slithered from the depths of his mind, a dark and ominous creature that had long been dormant, emerging from its subterranean lair.

"Anger, son, is a fire that consumes itself, leaving behind a wasteland of regret and ruin. It's a tempest that howls through the soul, tearing at the fragile threads of peace and serenity."

As the initial shock of his father's death subsided, North found himself standing at the edge of a vast emptiness. His father's absence left a void that seemed to stretch endlessly before him. Yet in that moment of intense solitude, something stirred within him - not the heavy weight of despair, but a quiet resolve. He realized that he carried within him the essence of his father: that steady strength, that unwavering kindness. It wasn't a mantle to be worn, but a seed to be nurtured. In the quiet of his newfound solitude, North made a silent promise to let that seed grow, to become not just a reminder of his father, but a continuation of all that he had been.

He poured his heart and soul into shaping me into the man I became. I couldn't dishonor him by succumbing to the destructive force of my grief.

Another memory wriggled into his mind. He squeezed his eyes shut.

***

He saw himself as a young man standing alone in the funeral parlor, the soft hum of the air conditioning enveloping him. His father lay before him, peaceful in repose, looking more relaxed than North had ever seen him in life. The room smelled of lilies and polish, a scent that would forever remind him of this moment.

He cleared his throat, feeling slightly foolish but compelled to speak nonetheless. "Father," he began with a whisper. "I guess this is it, huh? The final goodbye."

He ran his hand through his hair, a gesture he'd inherited from his father. "You know, I've been thinking about all those times you pushed me, all the talks about hard work and perseverance." He chuckled softly, shaking his head. "I get it. You were preparing me for this, weren't you? For a world without you in it."

His eyes traced the lines of his father's face, memorizing every detail. He paused, swallowing hard against the lump in his throat. "I wish I'd told you more often how much I appreciated everything you did for me. How you were both mother and father to me."

His voice softened, taking on a wistful tone. "You know, I always felt Mom was with us. I could feel her presence in the house. In the way you'd look at her picture, in the little things you'd say about her. I hope ... I hope you're with her now."

He reached out, hesitating for a moment before placing his hand on his father's. "I wonder what she was like? If she would have been proud of me. Of us. I like to think she would be."

He stood in silence for a moment, lost in thought. Then, squeezed his father's hand gently. "I promise I'll keep working hard, keep pushing forward. I'll make you both proud."

Straightening up, he took a deep breath. He could hear people starting to arrive for the service, their muffled voices drifting in from the hallway. "I guess it's time for me to go. But before I do ..."

He leaned in close, his voice barely audible. "Give Mom my love and a hug from me." His voice cracked on the last word, but he managed a small smile. "I love you, Father. Thank you for everything you've given me."

Later, after the services, his uncle asked him what he was going to do. North replied firmly. "I'll focus on my future. That's what Father would've wanted."

North would finish his education and become a teacher like his father. He would carve out a life of success, becoming a celebrated novelist and an admired academic. His proudest achievement, though, he believed, was nurturing young minds, helping them blossom into not just fine writers but better human beings, just as his father had helped him.

I think he'd be proud of me, of what I've become. I'm so grateful to have known him, even for such a short time.

***

A glance up at the clock.

My ritual continues.

Almost ten past the hour now.

Another sip of coffee. It seemed stronger than usual, but he didn't care. He was too lost in thought, thinking of his life without his parents.

A young woman passed by the window, pushing a stroller ahead of her. Marriage, and children – these were concepts foreign to him, mere trinkets of life he had deliberately shunned. There was little time for things like love and parenting. So what if there was no one to share his life with? He had his books. They were his companions, his friends. He'd sit in the evenings, poring over his books, lost in different worlds. He'd read until his eyes burned, and then he'd sleep, dreaming of how he'd share his knowledge with his students.

Solitude didn't trouble him; in fact, he welcomed it. It spared him the entanglements of relationships, the trivial arguments, and the relentless demands for attention. Instead, he immersed himself in his writing, dedicating his energy to becoming the best teacher he could be, finding solace in the quiet pursuit of his craft.

North took another sip of coffee, his eyes darting up again. *Ten past the hour.*

All of these memories were like ghosts, lingering from the depths of his past, conjured every morning by the steam of his coffee. It was his way of paying homage to life, just as his father had taught him. He had survived the absence of his mother, the storm of grief, and the persistent loneliness of his solitary existence. Through it all, these ghosts had been his only solace, his only connection to a time when life was full of color and laughter, when the world was a place of endless possibilities. Yet, North still felt a sense of hollowness. Something always seemed missing. It was as if he were an incomplete puzzle, one missing piece holding him back from a sense of wholeness.

The coffee was cold now, a lifeless puddle in the ceramic womb of the cup. But he brought it to his lips anyway and took a sip, and as he set the cup down, there, in its murky depths, he could almost see an image of his father.

We didn't have much time together. But you taught me so much. One day we'll meet again. It'll be so wonderful to have a conversation with you, this time as an adult.

The image in the cup faded, and North was alone with his memories. He closed his eyes and took a deep breath, savoring the last vestiges of his father's presence.

3 The old man

Continuing his morning ritual, North stole another look at the clock.

A little after ten past the hour.

Sipping his coffee, he'd sit there, watching students pass by the window, each one a fleeting memory, a forgotten name in the vast expanse of his years as a professor. His mind was a crowded filing cabinet, each drawer overflowing with the faces of students.

Some would recognize him, the hint of a smile tugging at their lips as they slowed their pace, a polite nod or a wave acknowledging their former teacher. He'd return the gesture. Occasionally, one would venture into his sanctuary, their eyes scanning the room until they spotted him, a solitary silhouette etched against the backdrop of the window. They'd approach, their footsteps hesitant, their eyes filled with a mix of curiosity and respect.

"Professor?" they would ask, their voices tinged with a hint of hesitation, as if the very act of addressing him required a leap of faith. "How are you?"

"I am well, thank you," he'd reply in a warm and welcoming manner.

Then the inevitable question would follow, a recurring theme in his interactions with these familiar strangers. "How's your semester going, Professor?" they'd ask.

"It's going well, thank you," he'd respond as his mind frantically searched for a name, a course, any flicker of recognition. But everything seemed to blur together into a hazy collage of memories.

He'd force a smile, masking the emptiness within, and ask about their classes, his words echoing the same script he'd used countless times before.

Then he'd say with a trace of cheer, "Well, it's so good to see you. How are your classes this semester?"

The student's response would usually go like this: "So far it's going well" followed up with "I do miss your class" and "It was one of my favorites."

North would take another sip of coffee and smile.

"Thank you for your kind words," he would say, adding sage wisdom like, "Keep on learning," or maybe, "Be happy with what you have as you work for what you want," or even, "Remember to always stay positive because worry is a waste of effort."

The student would always look a bit nervous and give an awkward pause, then smile and say, "Well, it's good seeing you again, Professor. I should be going to class. I just wanted to say hi."

North would smile. "It was good seeing you, again."

And when they left, their footsteps fading into the background noise of his sanctuary, he would be alone once again, staring out the window, watching the endless stream of faces, each one a reminder of his own fading grasp on time.

In these solitary moments, he would fix his gaze on a particular student, following them until they vanished into the blur of the campus. He couldn't explain why he did it, but something drew him in. He'd observe their interactions, the unspoken language of gestures and expressions, their connections forming a web of hidden emotions. Sometimes, he'd catch a glimpse of something deeper - a flash of fear, a bit of sadness, a glimmer of longing. These were the moments that captivated him, moments that whispered stories buried beneath the surface.

So many stories to unravel. So little time. But what is time anyways? A relentless thief mocking my efforts, on its march to outrun my life.

He glanced at the clock.

Quarter past the hour.

"More coffee, Professor?"

It was Margie, the waitress at the café, a young woman with a wiry frame and a brisk step that carried her through the tables with the grace of a dancer. Her smile was quick and bright, but there was always a trace of sadness in her eyes, a flicker of a dream deferred.

"Why yes, thank you," beamed North. "I know I've asked you this many times, but why haven't you studied at the university? Can't work at a café all your life."

She tilted the coffee pot, and the gentle sound of the liquid pouring into his cup was music to his ears.

It doesn't taste good, but it sure sounds nice.

"It's like I told you before, Professor," she began, her voice a blend of resignation and sarcasm. "I can barely afford a babysitter for my girl while I work, let alone afford going to school. Why would I pay to sit in one of your classes and listen to your lecture when I get that for free every morning?" A soft, breathy chuckle escaped her lips, more a sigh than laughter. She turned to leave, but paused, casting a fleeting glance back at him. "And, I like working here, waiting on people like yourself."

A sardonic smile played on his lips as he watched her graceful stride. She was the only bright spark in his sanctuary, an oasis amidst a desert of drabness.

She deserves more, so much more, than the monotonous rhythm of serving endless cups of coffee and humoring the ramblings of an eccentric old man.

North took a sip of the bitter, over-brewed coffee that brought a jolt of unpleasant reality. It was a stark reminder of the harsh shackles that bound Margie to her present. He wished he could offer her more than words of encouragement, more than the fleeting illusion of hope that attending the university provided. But he was just a man of words, not magic, unable to conjure up the means to change her fate.

The sun began to creep through the window, casting a warm glow across his table. He sat there, gazing out at the campus, yet the beauty of the day eluded him. He was oblivious to it.

The next part of my ritual.

***

His mind turned to the day's classes, the same classes he had been teaching for years. Nevertheless, the dread of facing his students never waned. He was haunted by the fear of forgetting something crucial, the fear of boring his students into an apathetic stupor.

A deep breath.

I'll get through it. I always do. Somehow.

Another deep breath.

The aroma of freshly brewed coffee hung in the air, intertwining with the soft hum of conversations. The café was still bustling with patrons, each lost in their own little world. North's eyes swept across the familiar tableau of faces and movements, drawn to a knot of students huddled around a corner table. Hunched over laptops, the glow of the screens casting a sinister pallor on their faces, he watched as their fingers flew across the keyboards, their minds lost in a jungle of pixels and algorithms.

Why do they immerse themselves so completely in such an unreal world, oblivious to the symphony of life playing out around them? Perhaps they don't like the music.

He glanced out the window again, the sunlight now brighter, more intrusive.

Then again, neither do I.

He checked the clock.

Nearly half past the hour. Soon it will begin.

There was a subtle shift in the café's atmosphere, a ripple of anticipation that stirred the crowd. Customers began packing up their belongings, their movements gaining a sense of urgency. The café, once a bustling hub of activity, was about to shed its skin, to metamorphose from a place of chatter and laughter into a haven of quiet contemplation.

At last, the moment has arrived. The migration.

As if responding to an unseen cue, the customers began to rise from their seats, savoring their final sips of coffee, their smiles lingered. One by one, they drifted out the door, casting furtive glances back, as if to ensure they had left no trace of their presence, no forgotten book or stray napkin to mark their passage through this transient space.

The café was slowly emptying, and soon, a place once teeming with life would resemble a ghost ship, its decks eerily deserted. North could feel the air growing still, the silence broken only by the sound of dishes being cleared away, the occasional clinking of silverware, and the distant hum of the espresso machine.

Then, a curious flicker of movement caught North's attention. A lone fly buzzed lazily around the empty tables, its wings creating a dull drone in the still air. He watched its aimless circling overhead, its erratic flight disrupting the otherwise orderly rows of tables and chairs. He followed it with his eyes as it veered past an old man standing against the wall near the door.

I've never seen him before.

The man was fixed on North with an intense gaze, his eyes like two black holes in the universe, pulling everything towards them. His stooped form was draped in a tattered trench coat, its folds hanging loosely over his gaunt frame. He had an unkempt and grimy appearance, his white hair matted, and his face obscured by a scruffy beard. His lips were pursed into a tight, somber line. In one hand he held a dog leash, but there was no dog at the end of it. The leash, worn and frayed, just dangled limp and lifeless, like a dead thing.

Something was disturbing about the force of the old man's stare. North took another deep breath, trying to steady his nerves, but the chill running down his spine was a clear indication that he was failing miserably.

He couldn't look away from the man, even if he wanted to. There was something about him that was unnerving, yet familiar, but North couldn't quite place it. It was as if he knew him, knew him intimately. Yet, there was no name, no face, no memory that could be pinned to this unsettling familiarity.

North felt that he had to say something, anything to break the spell that the old man's gaze had cast over him.

"Lost your dog?" he asked.

The old man glanced down at the leash, then back at North. A cold smile slowly spread across his face, and in a halting voice, he offered, "No, I've lost something else."

North quickly turned away.

He's not part of the ritual. Ignore him. No good can come from engaging with him.

North's eyes darted towards the clock.

A bit past half the hour.

He stared into his coffee, a refuge from the old man's unrelenting gaze that seemed to intensify with each passing moment. Slowly, he lifted the cup and took a sip. Then came the comforting chorus of fresh coffee popping into a pot, a sound that usually filled him with a sense of anticipation. But today, it only served to heighten his growing unease with the old man's presence.

"Making a fresh pot for you, Professor," Margie's voice boomed from the kitchen, her cheery tone jarring against the tension. "And I'll bring your check."

North always had a to-go cup from a fresh pot.

"Thank you," he called back.

Still avoiding the old man's glare, he glanced around the café, seeking shelter in the dull details of his surroundings. But the old man's stare was ever-present. He could feel it, boring into him.

Just ignore him.

A swift check of the time.

Almost a quarter to nine.

Getting there.

He wanted to think of something else, something other than the old man, but he couldn't.

Just ignore him. It's almost time.

He kept his gaze on his cup of coffee, the steam rising like a veil between him and the world outside. He could hear people bustling past the window, their voices a muted hum. Now and then, an occasional laugh would ring out, but North would not look up.

Another glimpse of the clock.

There it is. Quarter to nine.

He heard Margie making her way towards him, bringing a fresh pot of coffee. He knew the sounds of her steps.

A sigh billowed from his lips, not as a lament of fatigue, but an exhalation of anticipation. He knew that the steaming elixir Margie was bringing was the final touch in his meticulously orchestrated morning ritual. And he couldn't wait to escape the old man's presence.

But something strange happened. There was a thud and the crash of glass.

North spun around, his heart in his throat. Margie had fallen. He rushed to her, but as he neared, he stopped short. She lay there amidst a shattered mess of glass, the to-go cup adrift in a widening pool of coffee, her face ashen, her eyes wide and staring. In her hand, his check.

He took a tentative step towards her, a knot of dread tightening in his gut. Something was wrong. Very wrong. She was too still, too quiet.

He reached down, his hand trembling as it brushed against her cheek. Her skin felt like ice, sending a jolt of terror through him that made him pull back sharply. His heart raced, pounding in his chest like a frantic drum, the sound echoing in the stillness around them.

She was dead.

How? Why?

His mind raced, desperately searching for answers, but none came.

He glanced around the room, his eyes darting from object to object, searching for any hint of a clue. But the room was silent, unyielding, offering no answers to her death. Even the fly that had been buzzing around the café was dead, its tiny body lying lifeless on the linoleum floor, its wings spread wide like a fallen angel.

North stood there, frozen in disbelief, his mind struggling to comprehend the horrible scene. Then, a chilling realization dawned upon him.

As he swung his gaze towards the window, his breath caught in his throat. The once bustling sidewalks had morphed into a macabre graveyard, littered with lifeless bodies, their faces frozen in masks of eternal surprise, their eyes wide with a final glimpse of unspeakable terror. Vehicles stood motionless, their drivers eternally stuck in a moment, bodies slumped over the steering wheels. Their skin was pale and lifeless as if drained of all vitality.

The breeze, once a gentle caress, had vanished into an overwhelming quiet, leaving the trees to stand motionless, their leaves curling, shriveling like wilting petals. The sky, once a canvas of boundless blue, had transformed into a suffocating expanse of stagnant, heavy, dark gray clouds, a brooding mantle that pressed down upon the world like a heavy shroud.

Wherever North turned, wherever he looked, there was no life. No life anywhere.

What is happening?

Panic tore at his throat, a suffocating grip that threatened to engulf him.

His stomach churned with an unsettling intensity, wringing with a relentless grip that threatened to turn his insides out. He doubled over, his head spinning, and forced himself to breathe through his nose, trying to quell the rising tide of bile. But his efforts were futile. With a groan, he stumbled to his knees and retched violently, the acrid liquid spewing onto the floor.

He pulled himself up and sank into a nearby chair, his legs buckling under the weight of his dread. His mind was a tangled mess, a frayed web of shattered nerves and fractured emotions. He desperately tried to grasp the vestiges of sanity, to weave them together into a semblance of understanding, but the threads were frayed, the patterns blurred. Rational explanations slipped through his grasp, his mind a captive of the unknown. The reality he had known had crumbled like sand under his feet.

North squeezed his eyes shut, struggling to steady his breath, but his thoughts remained jumbled. The café seemed to shift and waver around him. Reluctantly, he opened his eyes.

The old man. Where is he?

The old man was still standing near the door his gaze fixed and unyielding, gripping the leash so tightly his knuckles had turned pale. With a weary sigh, he let the leash fall to the floor with a muted clatter.

"Now you see what I've lost," he murmured, his voice raw with despair. "I've lost everything. Absolutely everything."

4 At the end of it all

So, North just sat there, his mind a knotted mess, thoughts twisting and coiling like poisonous vines, squeezing the air from his lungs. He felt an overwhelming urge to run but found himself paralyzed. He was at a loss for words with the old man, unsure if speaking was even appropriate. His eyes darted back to Margie, her vacant stare a silent void,

"She won't come back," the old man told him. "None of them will."

North's mind screamed at him to ignore the old man, to refuse to engage with him. But his body remained frozen, his mind caught in a paralyzing web of fear.

His fingers twitched, yearning to resume his ritual, the regular rhythm of his daily actions, a desperate attempt to reclaim some semblance of the familiar.

Maybe if I . . . if I go about things as usual, perhaps everything will return to normal.

But he wasn't sure he could.

The clock!

I'll check the time.

As he looked up, a cold dread took hold of him. The clock's hands remained stubbornly fixed, caught in an eternal pause, while his watch ticked steadily, marking the passage of time.

Ten of nine.

Just go about things. As if none of this ever happened.

North mustered what strength he had, struggling to his feet, his legs wobbling like jelly beneath him. He walked over to the lifeless form of Margie and looked down upon her, her fingers curled around his check, clutching it tightly.

This can't be real.

With a deep breath, he reached out for the check, taking it from her stiffened fingers. He felt nauseous.

"Coffee large $5.25 thank you, Margie," was scribbled, along with a smiley face.

"I've already told you," the old man said. "She's not coming back. None of them are." He made an impatient move of his head towards the door. "Come now. We have a lot to talk about."

Just ignore him.

North walked to his table, still numb. He paused, staring at the check once more. Without thinking, he fished a crumpled ten-dollar bill from his pants pocket, carefully smoothing it out on the table before placing the check on top. With measured intent, he reached for his leather satchel.

Ritual.

The old man spoke. "You won't need it."

North's gaze snapped up at him, then quickly away.

Just ignore him . . . no good can come from engaging with him.

The old man only shook his head. "You won't need it," he repeated. "This was your last morning ritual. Everything is different now."

Just ignore him.

But North's resolve crumbled. He couldn't ignore the old man any longer. There were too many questions, each one more urgent than the last. Who is the old man? What had happened to change everything? How could he know about his morning routine, his private sanctuary?

Before he could voice his questions, the old man spoke again. "The time for rituals has passed, Professor North. It's time to face the new world, to embrace the chaos that lies ahead."

North's face reddened.

Enough with this!

"Who are you?" he snarled. "How do you know my name? What do you mean by a new world? Is this some kind of prank? Because it's not funny."

An ugly twist came to the old man's mouth. "Anger is a fire that consumes itself, leaving behind a wasteland of regret and ruin."

North gasped. "My father's words."

The old man smiled, but it was a cruel parody of human warmth. "I've known you before time started. Your secrets lay bare before me, every twist and turn of your existence, every ripple of your soul. I know everything about everything. This is no mere jest, no childish prank. It is the dawn of a new era, a time of transformation and upheaval. Your rituals, your carefully constructed routines, are mere relics of the past, incapable of shielding you from the chaos that is to come. Now, and for the last time, please, leave your satchel and come with me."

An icy tendril of fear, primal and instinctive, snaked its way through North's veins, a deep-rooted instinct warning him against the darkness. He cast a quick look towards the window, dread swelling in his throat as his eyes took in the devastation. This was the end, a moment of reckoning, a turning point between the known and the profoundly terrifying.

What am I to do?

"You can follow me," the old man told him.

Can he hear my thoughts?

North felt ensnared, a marionette caught in a web of uncertainty, unsure of his next move. Drawn by an inexplicable curiosity, his eyes fixed on the old man, whose presence seemed to pull him along. He observed the way the old man moved, a quiet authority in his gait, and North felt an unspoken invitation to follow.

Against his better judgment, he followed the old man's lead, his steps taken almost against his will as if the very ground beneath him had shifted. The café's comforting warmth faded behind him, all familiar aromas, sights, and sounds, lingering like a memory he couldn't quite grasp. As he stepped into the cityscape, what had once felt like home, with places he had known and frequented, now was devoured by an alien landscape.

Everything had been laid to waste. The air felt heavy and oppressive, like a wet blanket smothering the city. The silence was unnatural, broken only by the creaking of the trees as they continued to dry up and wither. The ground lay barren and cracked, its surface groaning, as long jagged fissures snaked their way about like scars. Dead bodies were everywhere, scattered about like tossed dolls. Some were lying side-by-side, holding hands, while others were still clutching their belongings. They had been caught in the middle of an ordinary day, and then, suddenly, their lives had stopped.

Like flies in amber.

There came the faint sound of a distant wail, like the cry of a lost soul. North stopped to listen, but the sound was gone.

"Don't worry," the old man reassured him as if he had heard the wail too. "There's nothing to be afraid of. This is just the way things are now."

North lowered his gaze. At his feet lay a still form, a young woman with her face turned upwards, her long hair partially obscuring her features. It was one of his students, but he couldn't remember her name.

Poor thing. I am so sorry.

With a gentle touch, he brushed the hair away from her face. Her eyes were open and staring, her skin cold and pale. Like everyone else, she had succumbed to a silent reaper's touch. He started to feel sick again, squeezing his eyes shut, trying to quell his roiling stomach.

Carefully, he walked around the student's body and then stopped at another. There were so many. A hard lump of terror formed in his throat. He tried to swallow, but the dry, parched sensation only amplified his fear. His life had been a predictable melody of routine, a comforting symphony of order. But now, the familiar notes had gone discordant, the rhythm jarring. It was as if reality had been turned on its head, the world he knew twisted and distorted into an unsettling dream.

A bitter, metallic tang clung to the back of his throat like a rancid afterthought. He could taste it, smell it, feel it. It was everywhere. He ran his tongue over his teeth, but it did no good. The taste was still there. He tried to swallow but it only made the taste worse. He gagged and coughed, and tried to breathe through his nose, but nothing would dislodge it. The smell was there too, a sharp, coppery odor that made his stomach churn. He felt dizzy and lightheaded.

The world around him continued its fade into a monotonous gray haze. He fluttered his eyes, in a desperate attempt to dispel the fog of this unreal world he was in. But his vision was clear. The world around was dissolving into an indistinct blur of nothingness, distorted and out of focus.

North lifted his gaze from the gruesome scene, his eyes settling upon his hand. With a slow deliberateness, he raised it, turning it over and back, examining it with a detached curiosity, as if it belonged to someone else. His fingers, curling slightly, moved with a sluggishness that mirrored the decline of his own body. He flexed them, the tendons creaking in protest, the joints aching with the weight of years. A pang of arthritis shot through his wrist, a constant companion and reminder of his mortality.

"Don't fret. You're alive." The old man was a few feet ahead of North. He motioned him on with a wave. "We've much to do."

But North just stood there in shock, silent and terrified, his eyes darting from one body to the next.

I must be dreaming. I must've fallen asleep in the café. Yes. That's it. I'll wake up soon and everything will be back to normal.

North shook his head pushing back tears.

This is a nightmare. This can't be happening.

The old man sighed in frustration and made his way back to North, casually stepping over the bodies. "I know it's hard to accept. But this isn't a nightmare, at least not in the way you might think. There's no waking up from this. Soon enough, the bodies will fade from sight. This is the new reality. Your reality. Come with me. Time is slipping away." He pointed with a skeletal finger at the bodies. "Look. They're just memories now. They've ceased to be real."

North watched in horror as all around him the bodies began to slowly dissolve, leaving behind a trail of discarded belongings. Clothing, shoes, bags, coats, and watches, littered the sidewalks like some macabre game of pickup.

"I don't understand," he said.

"You will," the old man declared. "In time, you will."

He took North's hand, a grip surprisingly firm, and led him away through the campus. The emptiness was eerie, like a dream where you know something is wrong, but you don't know what. Everywhere, the bodies were fading, as if they were being erased from existence.

"The world is not as it seems, young North," the old man began, his voice carrying the weight of untold secrets. "There are always forces at work beyond your comprehension, forces that weave and twist the fabric of reality, bending it to their will."

He paused, studying North with eyes that seemed to hold the depth of ages. "What you see is but a fraction of what truly exists. Behind every shadow, every whisper, there lies a deeper truth, a current shaping the world in ways you cannot yet fathom."

North felt a disquiet rise within him, uncertain of what the old man was trying to say. The old man merely smiled, shaking his head at North as if to say that some truths remain beyond reach.

As they walked, North's eyes scanned the surroundings for any sign of movement, any trace of life. Yet, there was only an overwhelming silence. Everywhere he looked, he encountered sights that would be etched in his memory forever, images that would haunt him for the rest of his days. He grappled with the depth of the terror that surrounded him, unable to fully grasp the horror of the scene.

I feel like a man lost in a waking nightmare.

"Nightmares are mere reflections of the shadows that linger within," the old man said. "You've been chosen to witness these events, to bear witness to the truth of it all," the old man said.

Hearing my thoughts, again.

Finally, North, his patience worn thin, demanded, "Tell me what is going on!" He took a deep breath, his voice softening but still intense. "Enough with the riddles and cryptic warnings. I need to understand what's happening."

The old man regarded him with a faint, knowing smile. "You've been chosen to witness these events, to bear witness to the truth of it all," he said. His gaze was steady and calm, a glimmer of something ancient and profound in his eyes. "In this role, you will come to see not just what unfolds before you, but also the deeper currents that have shaped this moment. Embrace this journey with an open heart, for it is through this understanding that you will find the clarity you seek."

"But why me?" he asked, his voice trembling. "Why am I being subjected to this horror?"

"Some questions are not meant to be answered," came the reply, gentle and resigned.

North was overwhelmed by a deep sense of helplessness. He felt utterly powerless. He looked around, desperate for a way out, but the surroundings seemed to close in on him. The possibility of escape seemed as distant as a forgotten dream, and with each passing moment, the weight of his situation grew heavier.

Trapped.

"There are many things you can't run from, young North," the old man said. "But you can choose how you face them. Why don't we start at the beginning, eh? You want to understand what has happened?"

North nervously nodded and swallowed hard. He was starting to sweat, and his eyes were growing wider. He felt the old man's grasp on his hand tighten.

"I'll tell you then," the old man said. "My dear Professor North, you're at the end of it all."

"What does that mean?" North asked.

The old man smiled gently. "May I answer your question with one of my own?"

North again gave a nervous nod.

"If the Almighty were to come to you and alter your reality, asking you to begin anew, what would you tell him?"

North thought for a moment. "I suppose I would tell him that I'm not ready," he said, the words slower than he expected. "That I'm not sure if I'll ever be ready."

The old man's expression was unreadable, yet something about it felt like understanding. "A fair answer," he said quietly. "But the Almighty - he's not patient. He's not one to wait for you to gather yourself. He'll reshape your reality, whether you welcome it or not."

North's thoughts twirled like leaves in a storm. He stared at the old man in disbelief, the stillness between them growing heavy. "Who are you?" he asked, his voice shaking more than he wanted it to. "Are you - are you God?"

The old man didn't flinch. Instead, he smiled, a soft, almost amused curve of the lips. "That's the question, isn't it? God is a term devised by humanity to grapple with the unexplainable. I prefer truth-sayer instead."

"You did this?"

"I am the one who has come to make the change."

"This? Change? Why?" asked North.

"Do you remember the first class you ever taught?"

North tried to think back, searching through the fog of years gone by. The memories came slowly, slipping away as soon as he thought he had a hold on them. It had been many years ago. "I . . . I think so," he said, uncertain.

The old man leaned forward slightly. "There was a student, one who hardly attended your lectures. He never turned in his assignments. You gave him a failing grade, as you should have. But it stayed with you, didn't it? You couldn't let it go. You went to the Dean and asked if there was anything more that could be done. Do you remember?"

North's chest tightened as the memory came into focus, clear and sharp now. "Yes," he said slowly. "Yes, I remember." He met the old man's gaze, something uneasy stirring inside him. "But how do you know this?"

"I've already told you. I know everything about everything," the old man said. "Do you remember what the Dean told you?"

North nodded slowly, the memory sharp in his mind though his throat felt tight, words slipping out in a hoarse whisper. "He said that I didn't fail the student. That the student failed himself."

The old man held his gaze, eyes steady and piercing, as though searching for something deep within North. "That's right," his words rang in the empty air. "Humanity failed itself. It was given a gift, a chance to rise above its own nature, but instead, it chose to ignore that gift, to turn away from the light."

He paused, the stillness settling between them like a pause in conversation that held far more than words. "There was something you often said to your students," the old man continued, his tone softer now, almost kind. "Do you remember it?"

North closed his eyes for a moment, sifting through the fragments of time, searching for the words that had once come so naturally, so easily.

What were they?

And then, like a distant melody slowly returning to the forefront of his mind, the words found him. "Our choices define us," he said quietly, almost to himself.

The old man's face softened at North's words. He nodded, slowly, his gaze distant as though he were seeing things only he could understand. "Yes," he said quietly, "that's right."

His voice held a quiet sorrow, not sharp with anger or bitterness, but softened by years of resignation. "The world didn't break all at once," the old man said. "It splintered, piece by piece, each fracture a reflection of the choices humanity made. I tried to warn them and spoke until my voice was raw, but it was no use. My words were like drops in an ocean of their ambitions, swallowed up and forgotten. They couldn't hear, wouldn't hear, caught in the hum of their own desires."

North felt like he was standing at the edge of what felt like the end of the world, his eyes sweeping over the lifeless expanse that stretched before them. Under a heavy sky, swollen and gray, the land lay quiet and barren. The wind stirred faintly, carrying with it the sound of something long gone, a whisper of what had once thrived here. The trees, their limbs twisted and bare, reached upwards like broken hands, their desperation etched into the very air. This was a world that had once pulsed with life but now stood in decay, its skeletal trees reaching towards the heavens in a silent plea for mercy unanswered. But in this desolate realm, mercy was a cruel jest.

"No more hatred," the old man said with a smile spreading slowly across his face full of teeth. It was the kind of smile that carried no warmth, just a cold, hollow certainty. His eyes gleamed with something hard and unforgiving. "No more deception. No more puppeteering the lives of others for your own gain. Oh, they hear me now, alright. Every last one of them."

North felt the realization wash over him like ice water, hollowing him out from the inside. It wasn't anger that filled him, nor was it fear - it was an emptiness, a terrible knowing that everything had already been decided. There was no going back from where they stood now.

"Am I the last?" he asked.

The old man's expression seemed to slip away, his features smoothing into an unreadable mask. "There are a few. Very few. But you, North - you are the one they have been waiting for."

"Waiting?" North repeated, feeling the word twist in his mouth. "Waiting for me to do what?"

The old man's eyes met North's. "To save humanity."

A ripple of fear wound its way through North, curling up in his chest like something cold and alive, its weight unfamiliar. He wanted to protest, to say this couldn't be right. He was just Professor North - an old man - how could anyone think he was capable of such a thing?

He looked up again, hoping to find some bit of reassurance in the old man's face, some gentle denial that could release him from this burden. Instead, what he found unsettled him even more: a depth of understanding, a gravity that felt ancient, as though this moment had been waiting for him for much longer than he'd been alive.

"Do I have a choice?" North asked.

"None." The old man shook his head. "Every man has his own destiny: the only thing he can do is to follow it, to accept it, no matter where it may lead him. This is your destiny. To be at the crossroads of reality and the unknown. The ticket's been purchased. All you have to do is take the ride."

Again, words from my father.

North closed his eyes and sighed. "What do I do?"

The old man placed a hand on North's shoulder. "Face your fear and step into the void, even if you're not sure what's waiting for you. That's how you will find your way."

"And if I fail?"

The old man's eyes glinted in the grayness. "Then you fail," he said with no hint of pity, no patronizing condescension. Only a quiet respect, a recognition of the courage it would take to face an uncertain future. "But at least you'll have tried," he continued. "And that's all anyone can ask for. Even the truth-sayer."

***

North and the old man walked across the campus, their footsteps echoing on the empty walkways. Their hands were tucked deep within their pockets, the old man's head hunched low as if evading some unseen specter. The breeze, picking up, carried a bite of the approaching chill.

North cinched his tweed jacket tighter around him and stole a glance at the old man, who seemed lost in thought. He wished he could break through the old man's silence, to unravel the secrets that tugged at him. Yet those secrets remained tightly held, and North feared what might surface if they were freed.

Without warning, the old man came to a halt, turning to face North. His eyes, usually clouded with an air of detachment, glinted with an unexpected intensity. "You've never believed in ghosts, have you North?" he asked with a voice laced with a haunting resonance.

Ghosts? What a strange question!

North felt a tremble deep within him, a primal reaction to the old man's unexpected question. "No," he confessed. "I've never quite entertained the notion. Never encountered one."

"I have," the old man asserted, his gaze fixed on a point beyond North's comprehension. "I see them everywhere I've ever set foot. Even now I see them. They're all over this place. The faces of the students, the teachers, the staff – all frozen in their final moments – even though their bodies have vanished."

"Why can you see them?" North asked.

The old man's gaze fell back to North, his eyes filled with a profound sadness. "Because I am the keeper of everything," he said. "I am bound to every place, in every reality, forever witnessing everything that ever unfolds."

North was curious. "What do they look like?"

"They're all different," the old man said. "But they all have one thing in common."

"What's that?"

"They're all looking for something."

"Looking for what?"

"Peace."

"Can't you give them that?"

The old man's eyes widened. "It's not that easy. There are some things even I can't do. Things that transcend my power, my authority, my very essence. Strange, isn't it? I can create worlds, I can shape destinies, I can breathe life into the barren and lifeless. But there are limits to my power, boundaries that I cannot transgress."

How can this be if he is God or something like that?

North's brow tightened. The old man's words were like riddles, shrouded in mystery and paradox. "Then they're trapped here," he offered, his voice hollow. "Like me."

The old man's gaze dragged him back from the brink of his thoughts. "Yes. Like you."

North's eyes swept across the empty campus. He knew they were there, the ghosts of a now-forgotten age, their spectral eyes following his every move. He could feel their presence.

"They're waiting for me, aren't they."

The old man nodded, his gaze fixed on the horizon. "But we must be on our way. The veil between worlds is thinning, and the forces that lie beyond are eager to make their presence known."

"What forces?"

"Those who dwell in the darkness," the old man replied in a low rumble. "Those who feed on fear and chaos. They are the embodiment of nightmares, the architects of shadows."

The old man's eyes met North's, a spark of determination washing away the North's unease. "You must hold the veil," he declared with conviction. "Standing strong against the encroaching darkness."

His words ignited a spark of courage within North, a bitter taste of hope amidst the ever-present fear. "How?" he asked, eager to learn. "How can I face an unseen foe?"

"They will make their presence known to you in many ways," the old man said. "Sometimes subtle and sometimes overt. But their touch will be unmistakable. You'll feel their pull in the whisper of the wind, and the cold of the night on your skin. But you'll learn," he promised, with a faint, curling smile. "You'll adapt, strengthen, and be a light against the darkness."

Their pace quickened through the campus, the old man leading the way, his gait steady. North was barely a step behind.

Where is he taking me?

They passed the library, the student union, and several classrooms and dormitory buildings. As they neared the edge of the campus, the old man stopped.

"What's this place?" he asked, pointing to a large building.

North turned his attention to the imposing structure before them. It was a behemoth, crafted from reinforced concrete, the building's curved form mimicking the organic shapes found in the natural world, evoking a sense of fluidity. Windows were staggered about, angular slits in the fortress-like façade, while a domed roof, a crown atop this architectural titan, dominated the skyline. It exuded an aura of otherworldly menace, a grim sentinel from some dystopian nightmare.

"Browers Hall," North replied. "The physical sciences building."

"What was taught there?"

"Biology, chemistry, physics, astronomy, and agricultural science. The heart of the university's science programs."

"Tell me. What do you know about it?"

North thought. "Not much. I've only been in it once or twice. It's just a building. Like any other on campus."

"Are you sure about that?"

North shook his head. "No. But, then again, I'm not sure about much anymore."

"Think," the old man insisted. "Think. There's something about it? What is it?"

North's gaze shifted back to the imposing building, its silhouette stark against the darkening sky. He felt the old man was onto something.

What makes it different from the other buildings? What is it?

"I'm not sure," North was nervous. "Just classrooms and laboratories. I'm not sure what you're asking of me."

"Think," the old man demanded. "Think."

Another moment and it came to North. "Sustainable. The building's fully sustainable. There are solar panels on the roof, and there's a rainwater capture system for . . . for . . ." He stopped.

"For what?" the old man asked. "For what?"

North knew what the old man was getting at. "Drinkable water and irrigation. There are greenhouses, fields in the back, a barn with animals, and fenced fields for the animals to graze."

"So, everything about the building and its surroundings," the old man said, "was fashioned with a singular intent - to endure, no matter how dark and twisted the world outside became."

"What are you trying to tell me?" North asked.

The old man turned to him. "I'm trying to tell you that this is your new home. Where you and the others will live."

"Others?"

"I've already told you there are others."

"Yes. But how many?"

"Three. Women. They will come to this place. To you. Each will be with child. You will be a father to the children and help the women raise them. This is where the future of humanity will be born."

North stared at the old man. "What are you talking about? I'm not a survivalist and I've never been a father. I'm a professor of creative writing. What will I do?"

"What you've always done."

"And what is that?"

"Learn and teach," the old man replied, a chilling smile creasing his face. "Learn and teach."

North stared at him, bewildered. "What? Learn what?"

"How to protect the women and the children," the old man said. "And how to teach the children what it means to be human."

"I told you. I've never been a father," North protested. "I don't know the first thing about it. What do I teach them?"

The old man smiled. "What your father taught you. But you start by teaching them about what was. About all the wickedness humanity brought upon itself. You will tell them about how it should be. A world without war, without poverty, without hunger.

A world where everyone is equal, where everyone is loved. A world where people care for each other and for the planet. You will tell them that such a world is possible, but only if they work together. Only if they believe in themselves. Only if they never give up hope. You will tell them that they are the future. That they are the ones who will make this world a better place than the old one. You will look into their eyes, and you will see the hope. The potential. The possibility. You will know that they believe in what you've told them. And you will know that they will succeed."

North stood there, frozen, overwhelmed by the sheer magnitude of the revelation that had just been thrust upon him. Everything he had ever known, everything he had ever held dear, lay shattered in the ruins of a world gone awry. And now, amidst this chaos, he was being told by an old man, a deity of some sort, that it was up to him to protect three pregnant women and ensure the continuation of humanity. Fear was again rising within him, threatening to choke him.

I'm sure of it now. This is a nightmare.

"It's all real. Quite real," the old man insisted.

North took a deep breath. "But I'm merely a man, and an old one, at that."

"You are more than that," the old man countered. "You're a conduit for something far greater than yourself."

"What are you talking about?"

"You haven't figured it out yet, have you? I've given you the power to do something few have ever been able to do."

"What's that?"

The old man looked at him, eyes wide and unblinking. "Shape the world, young North. Now, I ask you: who's the deity here?"

North sighed, a faint hint of a smile touching his lips. But then a thought struck him with cold clarity.

"But will I have enough time?"

"Time is a wonderful thing," the old man said. "It never stops unfolding, bringing all things to pass. It'll be fine. Trust in me."

As North contemplated his own mortality, a profound realization settled over him. The fleeting nature of his days pressed on him, intertwining with a growing urgency regarding what lay ahead. He envisioned the children growing up, their laughter filling Browers Hall, their lives unfolding like a rich tapestry of endless possibilities. Then, the thought of not being there to see their journey into adulthood stirred a deep ache within him.

But maybe my efforts might provide a solid foundation for their futures.

"What about me? How will I know when it's my time?" North mused aloud. The question hung in the air as if waiting for an answer from the boundless, unseen reaches of time itself.

"When the moment arrives," the old man assured him. "I'll be there with you and guide you to a place where you can find rest."

"There are so many questions," North implored.

"There always are," the old man replied, a soft smile brightening his face. With the delicacy of a drifting feather, he began to fade, leaving only the lingering warmth of his presence behind.

North lunged forward, his hand outstretched as if to grasp at smoke. "Wait!" he called out ragged with desperation. "No, please!"

Yet the old man had vanished.

North was alone, surrounded by the vast emptiness, with nothing but his fear and the silence. He didn't know what he was going to do, or even where to start. But he knew he couldn't just stand there and do nothing.

With a slow, measured stride, he made his way to Browers Hall. The fury and despair that had once gripped him had yielded to a weary acceptance. He resolved not to fight the current any longer but to allow it to carry him wherever it would.

What choice is there?

The sky mirrored his somber mood, a canvas of encroaching shadows, while the wind softly stirred the skeletal branches of the trees, adding to the sense of melancholy.

Only a few hours before nightfall. I need a plan. I need a pen and paper.

5   Day one

Time in Browers Hall. No bodies. Empty. Quiet. Lights are on. Whatever system they have is working. Looks like no other building with electricity. Nothing but backpacks and books and laptops strewn about - leftovers from the bodies that are gone. Collected pads of paper and pens and pencils from backpacks. Found pads of paper that fit the pocket in my tween jacket. Turned on some of the laptops. No internet connection. Stacked the laptops and backpacks in a small meeting room.

Browers. Walked all floors. Labs and classrooms. Many labs have refrigeration units. Some are freezers. Will need to clean out the scientific things stored there. Staff lounge - comfortable chairs, refrigerator working. Lunches from staff in the fridge. My lunch and dinner.

!! Student Center - most likely equipment not working there, must get food supplies to Browers !!

!! Toilet paper !!

!! Flashlights !!

Sat down at a table in the staff lounge. List needed.

<u>Gather supplies</u>. Need to gather supplies, food (student center), water, weapons, tools, vehicles. Power systems? Self-sustaining? Is Browers water system self-sustaining? Tools and vehicles (keys) - physical plant? Supplies - paper, medical (campus medical center). Other resources?

<u>Explore the campus</u>. Need to explore the campus to see what resources are available and assess dangers.

<u>Elements</u>. Clothing. Ways to protect everyone from the elements (winter, cold weather, wind). Ways to protect from potential dangers. Old man mentioned darkness. Trust him? (Animals, other people)

<u>Secure immediate safety</u>. Safe place to stay. Security systems? Cameras? Warning system? Should I barricade Browers?

<u>Greenhouses and barn</u>. Take inventory of plants and animals.

Fell asleep at the table.

Breakfast in the staff lounge from someone's lunch in the refrigerator.

Left Browers and walked to the physical plant. No electricity. Doors unlocked. Found toolboxes and other tools on shelves and pegboard. Found nails, bolts, and screws in boxes. Found some old sheets that looked like they were used as drop cloths for painting, and some shop towels made of cotton. Found metal cabinets with reference manuals for many systems. Found a flashlight with batteries. It worked. Put it in my pants back pocket. Found key box. All keys labeled. Saw a key labeled diesel tank. Took it. There was a key labeled truck. Took it. Put all the keys in a bag. Found the truck in the lot. Loaded truck with sheets and toolboxes and nails and screws. Outside saw two large tanks fenced and labeled as diesel.

Only a couple of hours of light remained.

The truck started! Drove to the student center. Empty. Dark. Trays all over with uneaten food. Will clean it later. Made my way to the back. To the kitchen. Knives and utensils about. Two coolers. Opened one. Still cool. Plenty of food. Looked for a cart and something heavy to keep the cooler door open. No electricity but I wasn't sure if I'd get locked in. Didn't want to take any chances. A long metal bench for the cooler door worked. Found a cart. Loaded the cart with several items over and over again and to the truck. When the truck was loaded and put the cart on the back and drove to Browers.

Unloaded the truck. Used a cart to bring everything to the fridges and freezers. Took the scientific items and dumped them outside. Again and again.

Made five trips between the student center and Browers.

On the 6th trip, when I left Browers, when the door closed behind me, it made a strange clicking sound. It was locked. Keypad outside near the door. Will need to somehow figure out how to reset the keypad. Looked at my watch.

!! 7:00 pm !! Security system. Good to know. Will sleep in the truck.

6 Dreams

The wind was picking up, and the temperature was dropping. North knew he would be cold if he didn't find something to cover up with. He rummaged through the truck bed, his movements hurried and jerky, fingers scrabbling against thc cold metal, until brushing against a rough canvas.

Drop cloths from the physical plant. Won't win any fashion contests, but they might be enough to keep the night at bay.

He hefted them out, their weight anchoring him momentarily before he hoisted them around himself, the fabric smelling faintly of dust and paint, remnants of their previous purpose. As he climbed into the front seat, his body trembled, not just from the cold, but from the unnerving silence that pressed in on him like a hungry beast.

Slipping behind the wheel, he locked the door with a decisive click and tried to ignore the chattering of his teeth. He huddled deeper into the canvas and started the engine. It coughed and sputtered to life, a sickly groan.

Just for a while. For a bit of warmth.

He shivered again, the cold penetrating his clothes and settling deep in his bones. He glanced in the rearview mirror. The campus was empty, with only the endless darkness staring back at him. Fear clung to him, its icy grip tightening around his gut. It wasn't the fear of a specific threat, not a bear or a wolf, but something more insidious, lurking in the shadows - a fear of the unknown, of the unseen. The night had become his enemy, and he was trapped, alone and trembling, in its frigid heart.

North killed the engine, letting his head fall back against the seat, eyes squeezed shut in an effort to calm the restless tide within him. The exhaustion clung to his bones, but even in the cramped space of the truck, rest felt out of reach. The night closed in heavy, smothering, wrapping itself around him in a way that made every breath seem harder. His thoughts surged and tumbled, refusing any sense of stillness, each one pulling him further from the peace he sought.

The old man's face floated to the surface of his consciousness, a specter that refused to be banished. North couldn't shake the memory of their encounter, the way the old man's words had sliced through the fog of his disbelief. "The time for rituals has passed," he had said, his voice a low rumble that seemed to reverberate through North's very bones. "It's time to face the new world, to embrace the chaos that lies ahead."

North turned his head to the side, gazing out the window at the darkened landscape beyond. The world seemed to hold its breath as if waiting for something monumental to occur. A sudden chill crept over him, a whisper of foreboding that settled in the pit of his stomach. The old man had known things about North, things he shouldn't have been able to know. He had spoken of the world ending, of a new era dawning, and North found himself struggling under the weight of those words.

He thought of Margie, her vacant stare a silent void that had swallowed his hope. "She won't come back," the old man had said, his tone matter-of-fact, as if discussing the weather. "None of them will." North had wanted to deny the truth of those words, but the evidence was all around him, undeniable and stark.

And the clock - the clock's hands had remained stubbornly fixed, caught in an eternal pause, a mocking reminder of the futility of clinging to the past. North's watch had ticked steadily, marking the passage of time, but it felt like a betrayal, a cruel joke played by the universe. The world had shifted beneath his feet, leaving him adrift in a sea of uncertainty.

The old man's voice echoed in his mind, a haunting melody that refused to be silenced. "You won't need it," he had said, gesturing to North's leather satchel. "This was your last morning ritual. Everything is different now."

North had wanted to ignore him, to pretend that the old man's words held no power over him, but deep down, he knew the truth. The world as he knew it had ended, and he was left to navigate the wreckage.

He squeezed his eyes shut again, hoping the memories would slip away, but they clung stubbornly, just like the old man's face, vivid and inescapable. It was an image that had burned itself into his mind, one that would always remain there.

The old man's words shouted at him, the cryptic message that had been both a warning and a promise. "The world is not as it seems," he had said. "There are always forces at work beyond your comprehension, forces that weave and twist the fabric of reality, bending it to their will."

North felt a shiver run through him, a tremor that seemed to resonate with the very core of his being. He didn't understand what the old man had meant, but he couldn't shake the feeling that his words held a deeper truth, a truth that North was only beginning to glimpse.

The night stretched on, an endless expanse of darkness that seemed to swallow him whole. North lay there, his mind a tangled web of thoughts and fears, unable to find comfort in sleep. The old man's presence just hung there, a ghostly reminder of the world that had been and the world that was yet to come.

North dared to open his eyes, meeting only impenetrable darkness. With a deep breath, he forced them shut again, hoping for sleep to carry him from all this, even if only briefly. At last, he slipped into uneasy dreams, yet even in the depths of slumber, the grip of fear held firm, refusing to let him go.

He woke in a classroom, the sunlight filtering through the dusty blinds, painting long stripes across the worn wooden floor. It felt familiar, the ghosts of a hundred classrooms past lingering in the air. The creak of the old oak door opening was a sound he knew by heart, a sound that promised the comforting routine of another school day. But something was very wrong. The once familiar faces of students were distorted into grotesque masks, their eyes hollow pits staring into an abyss only he could see. They took their seats and just stared at him.

North could feel his heart hammering against his ribs, a frantic drumbeat against the silence of the room. This wasn't just a dream; it was a reflection, a warped mirror held up to the world he now inhabited. He felt a sudden urge to flee, to escape this distorted reality. But his feet felt heavy, rooted to the creaky wooden floorboards. He started to shout out, but the classroom walls closed in, suffocating his thoughts and drowning his voice.

His dreamscape twisted and turned into an endless maze of nightmares. Desperate to escape, he frantically searched for an exit, but the hallways stretched infinitely, drawing him deeper into the abyss. A discordant symphony of whispers echoed through the corridors, each voice an indiscernible murmur.

Going crazy. All alone. Everyone gone.

North forged ahead, the whispers clinging to each footstep like cobwebs. They were fragmented things, these whispers, snippets of forgotten conversations, and laughter that turned to screams in the silence. They hinted at horrors that lurked just beyond the reach of his waking mind. He knew, with a certainty that chilled him to the bone, that he had to face these shadows.

His journey led him to a forgotten library, a crumbling structure barely holding onto its former grandeur, swallowed by the invading night. As he crossed the threshold, the silence was broken only by the sigh of the wind whispering through broken windows. Moonbeams slanted through the damaged roof, illuminating shelves moaning under the weight of leather-bound tomes. He wandered through the tangled aisles, his fingertips brushing against spines that hadn't felt the touch of a hand in decades.

Drawn by an unseen force, he stumbled upon a book nestled at the end of a forgotten shelf. Its cover was faded, and the leather cracked and peeled like sunbaked skin. A single word, embossed in tarnished gold, shimmered on the surface: *Truth.*

His pulse quickened, and his fingers, slick with a cold sweat, reached out to caress the worn leather. Gingerly he cracked it open. Each page was a fresh wound, a gash in the world. The words inside weren't just ink on paper; they were a fever dream, a nightmare given shape. He saw men and women with eyes like hungry wolves, their souls black as coal, devouring everything in their path. He saw cities turned to ash by wars waged in the name of power, leaving behind only the scraps of what once was. And he saw a planet, once green and full of promise, now a dying thing, its skin blistered and scarred, its bones picked clean.

As he read, the world outside the crumbling library walls faded away, replaced by the ghosts of a past he couldn't quite remember. He saw the flames of a million fires, heard the screams of the dying, and felt the cold, suffocating grip of despair. It was a brutal tapestry woven from the threads of humanity's darkest hours, and it chilled him to the core. He had known that the world had been a dark place before it ended, but he had never imagined that it could be so depraved.

North devoured the words, his gut twisting with a sickening certainty. He was unearthing the truth, layer by agonizing layer, and the more he knew, the more the ground beneath his feet seemed to dissolve. Reality, once a solid foundation, was now a shifting sand dune, threatening to swallow him whole.

As he came to the final page, his hands trembled, hesitating before turning it over. The last passage felt like a somber farewell, a chilling epitaph for a world that had vanished. Tears welled in his eyes, blurring the ink-stained words. He understood that he would never be the same after reading what lay before him. The truth, revealed in its stark clarity, was a horror beyond anything he had ever imagined.

He fought back bile rising in his throat. Deep breaths, he told himself, but the images, seared into his brain, refused to be banished. But it was no use. This wasn't a waking dream, a fleeting nightmare that could be dismissed with the dawn. This was the truth. The world had ended, and within the ruins of his mind, so had he.

The silence of the library was suddenly shattered by a deafening roar, so loud that it seemed to shake the very foundations of the building. The bookshelves rattled, and dust rained down from the ceiling. North, startled, jumped to his feet, and spun around, searching for the source of the noise, but he saw nothing. Then, with another ear-splitting crash, the surrounding walls dissolved into thin air.

North found himself standing in the middle of a barren wasteland. The sky was a sickly gray, and the ground was cracked and dry. He was alone. The last man on Earth, standing in the middle of a graveyard of a world. Empty streets stretched out before him, lined with abandoned buildings that stood silent, their windows like vacant eyes staring out at the endless void.

He raised his arms with clenched fists and roared. "Why! Why did you let this happen?"

But there was no reply, only the wind's melancholy dirge. He fell to his knees, burying his face in his hands - his shoulders rising and falling with gut-wrenching sobs.

"Why?" he whimpered. "Why?"

North's eyes snapped open. The view beyond the windshield stretched out, a flat expanse of dull gray, the sky wrapped in a thick blanket that pressed down on everything below.

Was only a dream.

Yet, as he stared at the clouds, he noticed a quiet transformation. The gray tones seemed to stir, slowly deepening, touched with the faintest hint of red.

Sunrise, perhaps.

He scanned the desolate campus, searching for any sign of life. Anything. Any scrap of normalcy.

Normalcy.

The word tasted foreign in his mouth.

But the world remained stubbornly silent, a vast, empty stage waiting for its actors to return.

He worried about losing a grip on reality. He squeezed his eyes shut. Thoughts of him going mad swirled in his head.

"I can't," he muttered aloud.

Must stay focused.

But there were too many fears. What if he was the last man alive? Who was the old man? Can he be trusted? And what about the women? Would they come? Would they find him? Would he be able to create a semblance of life in this wasteland?

Then, a new fear wormed its way into his mind: loneliness.

What if no one comes?

And in that moment, North knew the true challenge.

It's not the unknown. It's facing the silence within.

He started to get sleepy. As he drifted off, he thought of how he would face the silence.

Keep busy. Focus on the job. Fill the day.

But as he closed his eyes to sleep, he could still hear the whispers from his dream, creeping through his mind like a haunting requiem.

7 Dogs

North jolted awake, the guttural barking tearing through his sleep. He sat up, his senses immediately on high alert. There, outside the truck, stood a grotesque caricature of a dog, massive and menacing, a shadow given form, its existence defying the logic of nature. Its coal-black fur, matted and caked in a gruesome mixture of mud and blood, clung to its skeletal frame, each ragged clump shifting with every thunderous bark, revealing sunken hollows beneath. But it was the eyes, burning red embers, glinting with a disturbing ferocity, that was most unsettling.

He knew he should be terrified, should feel the familiar prickle of fear coursing through his veins. Yet, a strange lethargy had settled over him, exhaustion so profound it numbed him to this primal threat. He simply wanted the dog to disappear, to melt back into the pre-dawn darkness from whence it came.

I'll try to scare him away.

As he reached for the door handle, the beast, sensing his intent, reacted with a sudden burst of aggression. It launched itself onto the truck's hood, the sheer force of its leap denting the metal. The guttural barking intensified, a storm of sound shaking the truck beneath him. Razor-sharp claws scraped against the hood, leaving long, jagged scars.

The dog was so close, North could almost feel the heat of its breath, and smell the rotting stench of its fur. He could see the glint of saliva dripping from its fangs, each drop a promise of pain.

"Go away!" North shouted, pounding on the windshield. But it kept barking, its eyes never leaving his face, a relentless predator fixated on its prey. He was trapped in its terrifying grip.

This is no ordinary dog. This is something else entirely. This is a creature born of nightmares. I know . . . maybe if I . . .

North reached for the ignition, but before he could turn the key, a howl echoed - distant but unmistakable. It came again, nearer this time. The dog's ears perked up, its gaze shifting from North to the source of the sound. Then, with a quick, decisive movement, it turned back to North, baring its teeth, in a final, warning snarl before leaping from the truck bed and vanishing into the shadowy embrace of the woods.

There are creatures, dark and deadly. Alive.

The door of the pickup sighed open, and North stepped out and looked around. The dog was nowhere to be seen. Not a rustle in the scrub, not a flash of its black coat against the fading gray of the sky.

Slowly, he reached back for the door handle, his hand shaking. He eased himself into the seat and shut the door with a soft click. For a moment, he sat there, a strange feeling falling upon him. Turning the key, the engine stuttered to life, and he pulled away, yet an unease lingered, refusing to leave him.

I am being watched.

He drove, tires humming against the asphalt, heading towards the English-Philosophy Building, but the distant howl came again as if following him. He glanced around but saw no source for the frightening sound. No dog. He tried to dismiss it, but the howling persisted, growing louder.

"Stay focused. Fill the day," he muttered under his breath.

North slammed on the brakes. The howl, once a faint sound in the distance, was now a deafening roar, pressing against his eardrums with the force of a physical assault. He couldn't see anything. He covered his ears and squeezed his eyes shut, but the sound wouldn't stop. It was like being trapped inside a monstrous beast, its bellowing rage ringing through his very bones.

Then, as abruptly as it had begun, the howl ceased. North, disoriented and trembling, cracked open an eye. The scene before him sent a fresh wave of terror. A pack of dogs, at least a dozen strong, stood near the tree line where the forest met the campus. Their silhouettes were dark and menacing in the dim light, their eyes shining with disturbing intelligence. Each one was as large and imposing as the beast that had jumped on his truck, their powerful muscles rippling beneath their matted fur. North was frozen, his mind a whirlwind of chaos. He knew that he was outmatched, outnumbered, and utterly helpless.

Are they going to attack?

One of the dogs, the largest of the pack, took a step forward. It lifted its head and let out a bloodcurdling howl. The other dogs answered in kind, their cries rising into the morning like a chorus of unholy terror. North felt his skin crawl.

I have to do something. But what?

He was trapped, and he was all alone. But he knew he couldn't stay in the truck. He thought of his list. There was much he needed to do.

What to do? What to do?

The dogs began to move towards him, their lips curled back in snarls. North could see the gleam of their teeth.

I could drive off, but they would only follow.

Suddenly, the dogs came to an abrupt stop, their bodies rigid with intent. A charged silence enveloped the scene as their frigid stares remained fixed on North. Then, just as swiftly as they had emerged, the pack turned and ran back into the shadows of the forest.

It's a message. We're watching you.

North had never seen anything like those dogs before. They were so utterly alien, standing tall, bodies stretched taut over bones, fur the color of storm clouds, with eyes that glowed with an unnatural light, a predatory hunger.

They're not simply dogs. They're born of darkness, something that stalks the fringes of the world unseen.

For now, at least, he knew that he was safe. But he also knew that the dogs were still out there. They wouldn't stay gone forever. They would be back. He would need to somehow protect himself. But for now, he had to keep moving, and he knew where he had to go.

***

The truck's engine rumbled to a stop in front of the English-Philosophy Building, and North stepped out into the silence. The only sound was a breeze whistling through the deserted campus. He looked up at the building, its red brick façade towering over him like a tombstone, its windows like empty eye sockets. The clock tower in the center of the building was frozen at quarter to nine, its hands like a pair of accusing fingers. Oak trees that once surrounded the building had been reduced to shrunken remnants, their leaves sickly yellow and their branches twisted in a sad grimace.

North slammed the truck door shut and reached into the truck bed, sliding a toolbox closer to him. He rummaged through it, his hands shaking, his breath coming in ragged gasps. He had to find something, anything, that would help him.

Finally, his fingers closed around the handle of an old pipe wrench. It felt heavy in his hand, the metal cold and rough against his skin. He hefted it, testing its weight, and felt a surge of confidence.

I can send a message too. It's not much of a weapon against those dogs, but it's better than nothing.

He looked around. There was no sign of them.

The front entrance of the building loomed above North, its granite steps rising like the teeth of a giant. On either side, massive pillars guarded the way to a portico that stretched across the front of the building like a gaping maw. Above, a pediment was carved with the university's seal, a fearsome-looking eagle with its wings spread wide. All of this culminated in two large wooden doors, their brass doorknobs catching the light.

The building seemed to hold an intense silence. A chill inched through him like a cold finger, and he could feel the hairs on the back of his neck rising. He began climbing the steps, the sound of his footsteps piercing in the stillness, and he paused for a moment, listening. A glance over his shoulder to check for dogs. None were seen.

As he continued upward, he reached out, his fingers gliding over the cold, smooth surface of one of the pillars. It felt like an old friend, familiar and reassuring. Though he had touched these pillars countless times before, they always seemed to embrace him anew.

At the top, North stopped at the large wooden doors, the pipe wrench still gripped tightly in his hand. He checked his watch. Six-thirty AM. The building should be locked, but the door swung open easily at his touch. A slight hesitation, and then he stepped inside.

No electricity arming the security system.

The hallway was dark and deserted, like everything else. He could hear the faint sound of his own breathing. The air seemed to be getting colder, and he could've sworn he saw something out of the corner of his eye. It was a flash of something, gone so quickly he could've imagined it.

North walked down the hallway. Shoes, clothing, and other belongings of the dead were strewn everywhere, a reminder of the change that had taken place. He was getting used to seeing all this, stepping around or using his feet to push the things aside.

He slowed as he approached his office. The sign on the door read *Thornton North, Professor of Creative Writing.* He traced his hand over the letters, feeling the raised wood grain beneath his fingertips.

Reaching into his pocket, he fumbled for a key. His fingers were cold and clumsy, and the key felt like a tiny fish writhing in his palm. Finally, he found it and inserted it into the lock. The key turned with a soft click, and the door swung open.

His office was small and cozy, with wood-paneled walls lined with bookshelves, and a large window that overlooked what had been several oak trees. The bookshelves were crammed with books, a hodgepodge of genres and authors, from classic literature to horror to fantasy to science fiction. There was also one shelf dedicated to the books written by North himself, their covers cracked and faded and dog-eared.

In the center of the room sat a large wooden desk, piled high with books, papers, and manuscripts. Behind the desk was a comfortable leather desk chair. The leather was worn as an old glove, and the stuffing, once plump and inviting, had surrendered to gravity, leaving the chair with a resigned slump. Despite its worn appearance, the chair remained inviting, and North had spent countless hours nestled into its embrace, grading papers and composing lectures.

North settled into the armchair, the creak of the old springs like a welcome greeting. He looked over his desk, a mountain of papers and books, each with its own story to tell, seemed to writhe in the dim light. Yet, amidst the apparent chaos, a silent order reigned. He knew where everything was, every volume, every scribbled note.

It was here, in this sanctuary, that his imagination ignited. Here, he listened to the world, the quiet hum of existence that fed his stories. Characters whispered into being, plots unfurled like delicate flowers. So many novels had blossomed from this very spot, each one a child of his heart and mind.

He reached for a pen and a yellow legal pad, and scrawled the words, "At the end of it all." He stared at the words for a moment, then shook his head.

What a great idea for a novel. Too bad no one will read it.

But he wasn't here to write a novel. He was here for something else. Ever so carefully, he pushed aside the clutter of papers on the desk. At the edge of his desk, he found what he was looking for: three framed photos. One was of his mother, another of him and his father, and the last of him and his uncle when he earned his doctoral.

He picked up the pen again and wrote a few more words on the legal pad. "At the end of it all," he then added, "we are left with nothing but the echoes of our choices."

North exited the building. In the truck's bed lay a few boxes filled with books, many of which were his, along with his desk chair. On the seat beside him rested the pipe wrench and the three photographs. He turned the key in the ignition. There was still more to be done.

His father's words scraped through his mind, sandpaper on raw nerves: "Buy the ticket. Take the ride."

8 Cats

The city sprawled empty before North, a ghost town. Time had blurred into the monotonous drone of the engine, the odometer ticking away miles marked not by asphalt stripes but by weaving around hulks of abandoned cars. His foot, a twitchy reflex from a life lived before the silence, hovered over the brake at every intersection, a phantom pressure against the nothingness. It was a foolish habit, braking for ghosts in a city long dead.

No need to stop at stop signs. Just monuments to a vanished order.

Asphalt avenues, once vibrant arteries pulsing with the city's lifeblood, lay silent now, their concrete veins choked with dust. Skyscrapers, now skeletal giants, lonely mourners, stripped bare by the end of it all, cast long shadows across the desolate plains. Yet, amidst the tomb-like stillness, North hummed a Schubert fragment, each note a bold resistance against the quiet, a steadfast refusal to let the silence prevail. He pressed on. The destination: his home.

Reaching his street, he saw the familiar cracks in the pavement. They were like old friends, welcoming him back to a world that no longer existed. He parked the truck, and its engine coughed. The silence was amplified. North grabbed the pipe wrench and stepped into the house. He went straight for his library and a particular bookshelf, his fingers tracing the spines, each touch a memory. As he pulled out a dog-eared copy of Keats along with a battered atlas, a tear escaped, tracing a salty path down his cheek.

But then, a sound drew his attention, a rustle in the attic. His breath quickened as he grasped the pipe wrench, but then he hesitated.

Only the wind.

Then to his bedroom where a duffel bag swallowed up clothes, shoes, and boots; and to the kitchen where he grabbed what he could - a loaf of bread, a half-eaten jar of peanut butter, a chipped mug; and the bathroom, too, snagging some sheets, a pillow, and stripping bare the medicine cabinet.

Next on the list: the grocery store.

He continued his journey, eventually pulling into the parking lot of a Shop 'n Save store. He parked close, in a disabled spot. The reddish-gray clouds were starting to break up, revealing a blood-red sun that hung low in the sky like a malevolent eye. It cast the world in an unnatural, sickly light. He shivered.

Grabbing the pipe wrench and a flashlight, he got out of the truck and stood for a moment. The coppery taste in his mouth, that bitter tang that had been there since the start of the end, had finally disappeared.

Maybe things are returning to normal.

He shook his head.

Normal. There's that word again.

What did it even mean anymore? It used to be the steady rhythm of the day, the predictability of routines, the comfort of the known. But now, normal tasted like ashes in his mouth, a hollow echo of a life that had slipped away.

There will be no more normal.

He surveyed the surroundings, his eyes sweeping the area for any sign of movement. But there was nothing - only the parking lot, empty cars, and the darkened store beyond. With a deliberate pace, he approached the store, yanking at the automatic doors that made a disconcerting squeal as they opened. A rush of air, thick with the stench of rotting fruit, vegetables, and meat, slammed him in the face. He fumbled in his pocket, the fabric rough against his knuckles, and with a muttered curse yanked out a handkerchief. It was a flimsy shield against the assault, but it was all he had.

North paused, letting his eyes adjust to the sepulchral gloom, then flicked on his flashlight. Its harsh beam carved a tunnel through the dimness. Taking a cart, he placed the pipe wrench in the child seat and started down the aisles.

A phantom aroma, a wisp of yeast and warmth, tickled his nose. He froze, mid-stride, eyes searching the air for the bakery that wasn't there.

My mind's playing tricks.

Abandoned carts sat like metal carcasses, littering the aisles. But North, his gaze steady with a quiet determination, pushed his creaking cart through the debris, undeterred. The wheels groaned with each push, grating against the worn linoleum floor, a melancholy wail in the silent store.

He scavenged the produce section, salvaging what hadn't succumbed to the inexorable march of rot. Each rescued item was a small victory in the face of loss. He moved on, his cart growing heavier with the weight of survival, adding potatoes, boxes of pasta, cans of beans and other vegetables, and the reassuring bulk of rice bags. With a practiced eye, he continued to gather necessities from the leftovers of plenty. Surprisingly, some of the coolers had held their chill. Milk, cartons damp with condensation, felt oddly precious in his hands. Eggs, nestled securely in their cardboard cartons, held the promise of renewed life.

With the cart filled, North found himself wheeling to an empty check-out.

A reflex.

He looked at the register where an employee would've stood. The conveyor belt was still, the scanner silent. Standing there for a moment, he reached into his pocket, retrieving a handful of coins, which he placed on the counter. The coins clinked together, sounding weirdly loud in the empty store.

All this was merely the first of several trips that North would make through the store as he tirelessly filled the truck's bed. Yet, with each trip, he felt the silence grow louder and the shadows deeper. The once familiar shelves started to transform into grotesque figures, their contents transforming into twisted faces that seemed to mock his presence.

On his last trip, with the truck filled, he took a deep breath, shook his head, and closed his eyes, attempting to block out the surreal imagery. But he couldn't. The fear of loneliness was still there.

You're back. I've been waiting for you, sinister foe.

It was a living thing, clawing at his insides like a thousand rats. He needed to summon his strength, to steel himself against the encroaching madness that threatened to consume him.

Fighting the rising tide of fear, North pressed on.

He would keep his mind active, throwing himself into the task at hand. He had to, or else he would succumb to the madness.

Keep busy. Focus on the job. Fill the day.

As he was about to drive back to the campus, a sound snaked its way through the silence, coming from behind the store.

It was a subtle noise, barely noticeable, but undeniably present. Then, it came again.

Not my mind playing tricks on me. Not this time.

North grasped the pipe wrench and with the deliberate caution of a predator, he crept towards the sound, listening, straining to hear beyond the frantic thrumming of his pulse. The sound came again, closer this time.

When he reached the corner of the building, he stopped. A brief, intense moment of stillness gripped him as he closed his eyes, silently hoping that the source of the sound might be another human being.

A breath, shallow and quick, escaped his lips. North peeked around the corner and cracked open one eye.

Something shifted there, a hint of movement at the edge of his vision. But he couldn't make out any details. Was it the glint of a feral eye, the twitch of a tail, or something else entirely, something born of nightmares?

He strained to see, his senses on high alert. The shadows morphed and shifted, teasing, taunting, refusing to reveal their secrets. The urge to flee, to melt back into the safety of anonymity, was overwhelming. But something, some stubborn spark of courage, kept him there. He wouldn't run. He wouldn't cower. He would face this, whatever it was, in the dim, flickering light of his resolve.

North straightened his shoulders and tightened his grip on the pipe wrench, the knuckles of his hands white as bone. The thing, whatever it was, moved again, closer, a blur of darkness in the shadows. He took a step forward. The shadows danced, and it was then that he knew. While he might not always understand life's mysteries, he dared to confront them. And that, in this bleakness, was a victory.

Another step into the unknown. North raised the pipe wrench, ready to strike. He held his breath, waiting. Then, from the darkness, a large black cat emerged, staring at him with eyes that were like yellow marbles.

The shadow began to quiver again. More movement as more cats slowly emerged. There were dozens of them, all sizes and shapes, all staring back at him with their yellow eyes. They sat in a circle, their tails twitching.

North swallowed hard. He wasn't sure what to do.

Best to be slow and cautious with my movements.

The cats began to purr, a low rumble that grazed the fringes of his consciousness. The large black one took a sinuous step towards him. North's eyes, wide and wary, held the cat's gaze. He edged back, yet the cat continued to approach, its tail swaying gently from side to side.

"Please," he whispered, the pipe wrench heavy in his hand. "I don't want to hurt you."

The creature paused, its head tilting ever so slightly as if weighing its options. Its eyes held a focused intensity that seemed to demand attention, scrutinizing North with an unspoken challenge.

"You're afraid, just like I am, aren't you?" he ventured. "It's all right. I won't hurt you. I promise."

The cat remained still, a statue carved from shadow. Its glare, penetrating and firm, seemed to pierce through North's defenses, laying bare the turmoil in his own heart. He took a deep breath, stepped forward, and reached out, a hesitant hand hovering over the creature's sleek head. The fur, matted and coarse, met his touch with a soft purr that rumbled deep within the cat's chest.

"There, there," he murmured, his voice softer now. "We're friends now, aren't we?"

He smiled, a fragile thing born of the shadow and the cat's unexpected grace. In the depths of its gaze, he saw not judgment, but understanding, a silent acknowledgment of the shared language of solitude.

"We're both travelers on the dusty path of existence."

The other cats came up to North, and he petted them all. They purred and rubbed against him. He could feel their loneliness and fear, and he knew that they too understood him.

"All lost souls, just like me."

They followed North back to the truck, with some leaping into the bed.

He opened the door of the truck, and the large black cat jumped in, its tail swishing. North got in started the engine and started back to Browers. He could feel the cat's eyes on him, watching him, waiting for him to do something.

"What should we call you?" he asked aloud.

The cat just stared at him.

North thought for a moment. "How about Shadow?" he said.

The cat's eyes widened slightly.

"Shadow," North repeated. "Because you came from the darkness."

The cat purred.

North smiled. "That's right. You'll be my shadow."

9 Day five

So much done!

- ☑ All fridges and freezers filled with food
- ☑ Segmented out 2 labs with medical supplies taken from the campus medical center
- ☑ Stored all tools and things from the physical plant in the basement
- ☑ Went to the back field and barn and inventoried animals: 10 cows, 6 pigs, 15 chickens
- ☑ Inventoried farm equipment and manuals - tractor and several attachments (will need to research) - office in the back of the barn with a refrigerator and freezer, looks like drugs and things in them
- ☑ Inventoried greenhouses: plants (tomatoes, cucumbers, peppers, various flowers, and other plants) - drawers with seeds all labeled - bags and bags of topsoil and mulch
- ☑ Plenty of grazing land for the cows (need to go to other farms for baled hay); pigs will eat most anything, I think
- ☑ Went to dorm rooms and dismantled beds. Brought 5 beds and mattresses with sheets to Browers, in separate rooms on 2nd level
- ☑ My new home in the large classroom - desk, my chair, a few bookcases with books, bed, photos, a comfortable bed and pillows
- ☑ Sundries stored in the several janitor closets

☑ Spent time reading manuals on the various systems (solar, water, septic)

☑ Brought over two additional trucks from the physical plant

☑ Brought over sheets of plywood and other wood and metal scraps from physical plant

☑ Boarded up all doorway entrances with plywood, making small slits as lookouts

☑ Went to the campus security center and found some firearms and ammunition - brought some back with me (will I need to use?) - stored in the closet in the security room

☑ Browers basement, small, full of batteries in metal racking all wired together, must be used to store energy, so many wires and cables and contraptions, found a few manuals, brought them up to the security room

☑ Familiarized myself with security system and cameras in the security room at Browers, in the back 1st level - put system on full alert and set new code

☑ Set new keypad codes for doors and tested

☑ Laptop in security room linked to security system - must be some type of internal wifi - saw what looked like several computer systems in racks in the room - brought the laptop to my room

☑ Brought over clothes from dorms, male and female, and various sizes

☑ Found three sets of unused walkie-talkies in the physical plant along with a box of batteries

Shadow seems to be at home inside Browers. The other cats have found their home in the back barn.

No sign of women or the old man.

10 Alarm

Night consumed Browers, leaving only the faint glow of the hallway lights North kept on as a safeguard. Every evening, he roamed the corridors with Shadow, a whisper of fur brushing against his leg. His notebook and pen were his talismans against the stillness. Meticulously, he combed through his notes, checking each list, seeding them with possibilities, a desperate attempt to keep his mind from unraveling. It was a new ritual, born from the ashes of his old life, a small spark of purpose in the encroaching darkness.

Yet, as he went about his new rituals, there was something always at his side, something utterly maddening – silence. No creaks, no groans, not even the sigh of the wind slipping through cracks. Browers Hall was a tomb of quiet. He would pause, his pen hovering, drawn by a phantom sound, a whisper carried on the still air. But the quiet remained unbroken, a silence with a taste, bitter and dusty, the kind that whispered of secrets and shadows, of stories untold, deep within its walls. North would nod, a silent pact with the quiet, and then continue with his routine.

But one night the routine shattered.

North stood in the hallway, his pen poised over his checklist, when he heard something. The sound was faint but unmistakable. He paused, as did Shadow.

It came again. Soft, yet distinct.

North and Shadow remained still, listening intently.

It came again, louder this time, perhaps because they were waiting for it.

"Did you hear that?" North asked Shadow.

The cat yowled in response.

Again, the sound repeated, with a rhythmic pattern.

"A security alert. The cameras must have caught something."

North and Shadow hurried down a back stairwell to the security room. The faint buzzing grew louder as they descended. They burst through the metal door at the bottom, the security room's fluorescent lights harsh after the dim descent. North quickly scanned the many monitors on the wall.

North pointed. "There!"

The image snapped into focus, black and white turning grudgingly into detail. There, at the door, stood a dog, a shadow against the darkness, teeth bared. Its body was motionless, like a predator on the edge of a strike. Then, two glimmers of red appeared in the gloom, glowing with an eerie intensity. The dog's eyes fixed on North, its silent challenge filling the space with a tension that seemed almost physical.

The dog remained motionless, its attention on the camera.

Shadow growled, her fur rising.

North breathed a silent curse.

The image of the dog on the monitor seemed to pulse with an evil energy, each pixel brimming with malice. North could almost feel its teeth gnashing, the heat of its rage searing his face. Anger, yes, there was anger. But there was something more, something deeper. This wasn't the usual canine fury, the territorial snarl of a guard dog. This was something primal, a bottomless well of hatred that seemed to stare back at him from the screen.

North considered, for a fleeting moment, the primal urge to grab a gun and confront the snarling darkness head-on. But the thought quickly dissipated. He didn't want to take unnecessary risks. There was still plenty of work to be done, and he was safe enough where he was.

The dog growled, a low, menacing sound, that cut through the night, a rusty blade against silk. Then it released a howl, a drawn-out wail filled with sorrow and something far darker, slicing through the night with a raw, unmistakable terror.

Abruptly, it stopped, retreating into the shadows, leaving behind a quiet that felt just as unnerving as the sounds that had shattered the calm. North drew a deep breath, his lungs aching, the metallic tang rising once more on his tongue.

"Not sure what that was all about," North told Shadow.

The cat trilled.

11 Ellie

Forty-two sunrises and forty-two sunsets had passed since North had last encountered another soul, since the world had gone to hell. He didn't rely on a calendar. Instead, he maintained a relentless record, meticulously noting each detail. What he had done each day, the weather's nuances, how the clouds deepened in color with each passing day. The frequency of the wind's mournful cries. And the daily observations of Shadow's behavior.

Time, once a galloping mare, now crawled like maggots on a corpse, each one leaving a slimy trail of despair across North's already frayed sanity. The horizon maintained its greasy dishcloth appearance, smeared with the bloodshot red of a dying sun. But he wasn't fooled by the monotony. The fog still clung heavily to the campus, obscuring the familiar paths and turning the buildings into mournful giants.

It was in this twilight world, where reality blurred with memory, that he first saw her. A sound, soft and subtle, broke the quiet - a figure, vague at first, stepping out of the haze, more wraith than a woman. It was almost as if she had been summoned by the air itself.

But she was no phantom - she was a woman of flesh and blood, marked by her trials, her skin and clothes stained by the road she had traveled. Her clothes were a tapestry of dirt and tears. Her eyes, deep wells of sorrow, seemed to cut through the mist, seeking something elusive, filled with an unspoken plea. Each step faltered, a fragile balance against the pull of weariness.

***

She was a nomad, wandering a world bled of its warmth. She had fled the family farm, escaping its confines, a ghost slipping away from a haunted house. There was nothing left for her in that desolate expanse, no sound of laughter, no scent of life. Nothing. Her family was dead and gone. She watched as they collapsed in death and then slowly faded away. She didn't know what had happened, but she knew it was something terrible. All communication was gone. Electricity was out. None of the farm equipment or trucks would start. She stood in the doorway, looking out at the empty fields.

I'm all alone in this world.

She remembered walking to the nearest neighbor, but their farm was deserted too. So, she returned to her family's farm and stayed there, caring for the animals. She knew she could survive on the farm. She had everything she needed. But the loneliness started to get to her.

At night, she would sit in the living room, listening to the wind claw at the shutters. But the howling wind couldn't drown the questions, couldn't sever the ties that bound her to the ones who were gone. So she sat, alone, fueled by a glimmer of defiant hope, waiting for the day when the darkness might yield, and the dawn might finally paint the sky with answers.

Then, the animals fell. One after another, their life songs snuffed out. She stood in the barn doorway, watching the last of them fade away. Everything was gone. All that was left was her, standing over an empty land, where only dust and quiet reigned.

She remembered dropping to her knees in tears.

When will the darkness come for me? When?

The wind, her tormentor, became a chilling prophecy, whispering through the empty stalls, "Soon, soon."

Can't stay on the farm. The food is running out. I'll eventually have to leave. But where will I go? The darkness is everywhere.

And that's when the dreams began. Each night, they took hold of her, vivid and unyielding. She found herself in a field of cornstalks, the golden leaves slick with an unnatural glow. Her feet pressed into the damp ground, releasing wisps of smoke that clung to her throat like poison. As it cleared, the scene before her unfolded: lifeless animals, torn apart, their bodies marred and swarming. She tried to swallow the panic rising in her chest, the terror sitting deep and ancient within her. She ran, desperate, the cornstalks whipping against her legs like brittle fingers. The stench of decay was suffocating, and it stayed with her, clinging to her skin long after she'd woken in a cold, breathless panic. The dreams grew worse with each night, warping into even darker grotesques.

Then came the dreams of the old man. He wasn't a nightmare, not exactly. His presence flickered in and out, a figure with a wise, weathered face appearing with unsettling frequency. He never spoke, but his eyes held a silent urgency, steering her through the shadows with a steady, unbroken gaze. He stood there, unmoving, his look pulling her forward, drawing her toward something unknown. Every time she closed her eyes, he was there, a steady light in the storm of her troubled sleep.

As the days wore on, the old man began to seep into her waking hours. Far off, she could see a light, his face appearing within it. She didn't fully grasp what it meant, but something deep within her told her to follow. So, one morning, she gathered her strength, packed a pillowcase with keepsakes - family photos, some clothes, bits of food - and set off toward the uncertain.

Atop a rise, she paused, glancing back at the farm as it receded, cloaked in a shroud of crimson and gray clouds. She rested a hand on her belly, silently pledging to the life she carried, yet her gaze was soon drawn back to that distant luminescence. Without knowing where the path would lead, she pressed on, believing that it might connect her with others, with a world beyond her current solitude.

Time flowed in a languorous manner, each day blending indistinguishably into the next. She could no longer remember how many had passed; the sheer volume felt insurmountable. Food and water had long since run out. She was hungry, exhausted, and afraid, with no clear sense of how much longer she could endure. Her legs felt heavy, each breath was a struggle, and her throat burned with thirst. For days, she had traversed wooded paths and rolling hills, drawn onward by that distant glow, as hope began to wane.

But then she glimpsed something ahead, a university campus materializing like a vision, with Browers Hall standing proudly at its center. Above the hall, a solitary light shone steadily. Hope, a delicate ember reignited, sparked in her chest. With a surge of adrenaline, she pressed forward, her legs discovering a strength they hadn't known before. The light grew larger, illuminating the vast campus in an eerie, soft glow. Yet, just as she approached Browers, the light faltered, dimmed, and then vanished altogether.

***

She stood frozen, the campus suddenly feeling empty and forlorn without the light. Drawing a steady breath, she resumed her journey, each step purposeful as she navigated through the shadows of her own doubt. The campus appeared as a venerable relic, its secrets wrapped tightly, just out of reach.

"Welcome," a soft voice floated toward her.

She turned to find North standing before her.

The old man from my dreams.

She felt numb, almost like she was watching a movie, not real life. Disbelief clouded her gaze as she studied him.

Is he real? Or a figment of my imagination? A ghost? A dream?

Her hand trembled as she reached to touch North's face, her fingers tracing the familiar lines of his timeworn features.

"You're real," she breathed, her words barely escaping her lips.

A smile warmed North's expression. "I am indeed."

Relief enveloped her like a warm, gentle wave. She wasn't alone anymore; another person was here, with her, someone to share in her fears and hopes. She could hear his breathing, a gentle, steady rhythm that filled her ears. It was such a beautiful sound. She placed her hand on his chest, feeling the reassuring rise and fall beneath her palm.

North gazed down at her, his expression sharpening. She was small, fragile, no more than five feet tall, dressed in a simple cotton dress, tattered and soiled. Her sandy hair pulled back in a braid, hung in disarray, tangled and matted. It was clear she hadn't rested in days; dark circles shadowed her eyes. Yet, it was those very eyes that drew his attention. Hazel, speckled with gold and green, shimmered with fear, but a strange spark of defiance flickered within them, refusing to fade.

"Thornton North," he said, offering a gentle smile that felt like a warm invitation.

"Eleanor," she started, pausing as if the name weighed heavily on her tongue, "but Ellie..." The words stumbled forth, entangled in the shadows of her grief.

North wrapped her in his arms, a warmth encircling her, though it couldn't quite banish the chill seeping into her bones. She buried her face against his chest, her sobs interspersed with ragged gasps. He felt her shuddering, an aching certainty settling in that she was terrified.

Suddenly, she drew back slightly, her tear-streaked face lifting to meet his gaze. Her eyes remained locked onto his, even as an unsettling sensation crept along her spine. The cold bite of a pipe wrench pressed against her back, North's grip unyielding.

"Shhh," he murmured, his voice a low rumble against her ear. "It's alright, Ellie. It's alright. I'm here. You're safe now."

Safe.

The word lingered, delicate, and all Ellie could do was hold on to it, to North, feeling the steady rhythm of his breath against her own. Outside the warmth of his embrace, however, the world churned with chaos and turmoil.

"But my family," she breathed, her voice rough against the salt of her tears, "where have they gone?"

North wanted to offer answers, promises, anything to chase away the terror dancing in her eyes. But all he could do was hold her, a silent vow to weather the storm with her, one shuddering breath at a time.

He held her for a long time until her sobs subsided. Pulling back, he looked at her. "Come now. We have a lot to talk about," he said, taking the stuffed pillowcase from her grasp.

Then, a memory surfaced. This was exactly what the old man had said to him in the café, marking the start of the end of it all.

***

Ellie devoured the food with an intensity that suggested a primal need as if she were reclaiming a part of herself long lost. Hunger had gnawed at her for too long, and now, with each mouthful and every sip of coffee, a renewed sense of vitality flowed into her. She moved with urgency, almost like a creature rediscovering its strength, until a spark of life returned to her eyes, pushing away the shadows that had lingered too long.

North observed quietly, a witness to the revival of a spirit forged in the furnace of deprivation. In the raw hunger reflected in her gaze, he recognized a profound depth beneath her gaunt form and haunted demeanor - an inner resilience that burned with quiet defiance.

Once she had finished, she leaned back and wiped her mouth with the back of her hand, pushing aside the remnants of the stew. A glimmer of life returned to her eyes as she turned to

North and offered a smile. "Thank you, That was delicious. It was heaven."

North smiled back. He could see that she was still weak, but she was starting to look better.

"Just something I cobbled together," he mumbled, taking a sip of coffee. "Nothing grand, but…" He trailed off, unable to finish the thought. He saw a question linger in her gaze, her fragile strength demanding answers.

"The supplies," she whispered, "this place . . . this light… how?"

"We've everything we need. Right here. But explanations can wait. Right now, what's important is that you rest."

But rest was the last thing she wanted. That could come later if it came at all. Rest was a stranger now, something she chased through the wasteland haze. Words, stories, fears - these were the embers in the ash of her exhaustion. She needed to know more about this place and this man called North. So they talked. They talked through the morning and into the early afternoon, sharing their stories, and listening to each other's fears.

"I saw them die," she said, her voice faltering. "My parents, my brother, my sister. . ." She paused, her eyes shimmering with unshed tears. ". . . my husband. They simply disappeared. One moment they were with me, and the next they were gone. I tried to tend the farm," she continued, "but then the animals disappeared as well. They vanished. I was left all alone."

He reached over, his hand finding hers. "I'm so sorry. So sorry you had to bear that burden in solitude."

She looked up, a gleam of something like gratitude gracing her face. "What about you? Your parents? Your family?"

"My father passed away many years ago and I never knew my mother. No brothers or sisters."

"You were alone?"

He offered a slight nod. "Most of my life," he added, managing a clumsy smile, "until now."

An uncomfortable silence settled between them. Then, her voice took on a gentle tone, almost soothing, "Maybe loneliness isn't a prison, but a bridge, a silent invitation to lean into the storm together, two souls adrift trying to find comfort in the shared wreckage."

His smile returned, slow and sincere. "Maybe, just maybe."

Their hands locked, rough edges finding comfort in each other's grip. Outside, the wind sighed through the decaying branches, and it sounded, for the first time in a long time, not like a lament, but a song of quiet beginnings.

"Tell me how you came to be here?" he asked.

She shared her dreams, recounting how he had appeared within them, how a brilliant light had drawn her across the desolate expanse.

"I followed the light. Day after day. So many fears, not knowing when the shadows would claw back at the edges of day." Her breath hitched. "The world blurred, everything familiar was foreign. The rhythm of my life, once a steady drumbeat, became a frantic journey towards the unknown. For days, I wandered, a ghost in a ghost town, searching for a whisper of life, anyone, anything. But all I found was emptiness. I thought I was the last one, that I would die alone. But all I could do was continue to follow the light. And here I am. It's the first I've felt any hope in a long time."

North gave a smile, a thin line that creased the corners of his mouth. "I'm glad you found your way here."

He drew in a sharp breath, gathering his thoughts, his voice tremulous as he began to recount his story. He told Ellie of his life as a professor of creative writing, just going about his morning routine, when the unimaginable happened.

"It's so very strange," he began. "The end wasn't like the movies No fireballs, no screams. Just . . . a silent unraveling. Like someone had pulled the thread on existence and watched it fray at the edges. One moment, Margie was bringing me more coffee, the next, she was dead on the floor. I was so frightened. I didn't know what was happening or why. I just stood there, frozen in place, watching as people around were dead. Even this tiny fly that was buzzing around. Dead. It was like something out of a nightmare. Then there was the old man. Standing there. Holding a dog leash." North swallowed hard, the recollection was vivid and haunting. "And here I've been, preparing for those who are yet to come."

"Old man? Others?" she asked.

"The old man told me that three women would come here, to this place. Women like yourself."

"Like myself?"

"Pregnant. You are expecting, aren't you?"

Ellie's hand moved to rest protectively on her belly, a silent affirmation. "Yes. But how did you know?"

He met her gaze, his eyes holding a depth of understanding she hadn't known was there. "The old man spoke of such things," he said gently. "He entrusted me with the task of safeguarding them, of nurturing this new beginning. You are the first to arrive. How far along are you?"

A brief silence hung between them before she whispered, "Almost three months." Another whisper followed, just the faintest brush of breath against her dry lips: "Adam and Eve."

"It's a lot to take in, I know," North replied. "What's crucial now is your trust. It's the only way forward."

A tight knot of apprehension formed in her chest.

Trust? Trust this stranger who had appeared from a dream? Trust is a fragile thing, easily swept away by the winds of doubt.

But his words were a lifeline cast over a chasm of fear. His smile held a hint of something undeniable – defiance against the shadows, a promise of a world just beyond her relentless anxiety.

She took a deep breath. "I trust you."

"Thank you. There's much left to do. Two more are on their way."

They sat in silence for a long time, the quiet between them charged with so many unvoiced questions, a melody of hopes and fears. Ellie cradled the curve of her belly, a tiny universe blossoming within. She gazed at North, his face set in concentration, his eyes intense, as if he were unraveling some dark mystery.

He's right. We're the first of a new world. But what will this new world be like? Will it be better than the old one? Or will we make the same mistakes?

She didn't have answers to those questions, but she understood they had to try.

Maybe this is an opportunity. To get it right this time.

"We'll make it," she assured North. "We'll create a better world."

"I know we will," he affirmed. "We must. It's not like we have many options, is there now?"

She nodded then asked, "What else did the old man tell you? Do you think he was God?"

"I asked him that."

"What did he say?"

"He told me he was the truth-sayer, the one who had come to make the change. He knew everything about me. Even a conversation I had with someone years ago, and something my father once told me."

"But why? Why do this?"

"He explained that the world had become broken," North replied, his tone somber. "That we had made too many bad choices. He said that he had tried to warn us, but that we didn't listen. That his words fell on deaf ears."

"But why did he have to end the world?" Ellie pressed. "Couldn't he have just found a way to fix it?"

North sighed. "I don't know. I think he felt that it was too late. There was a sense of hopelessness in his voice as if the world had crossed the point of no return."

"Why us?"

"I asked him that."

"What did he say?"

"He told me that some questions are not meant to be answered," North replied. "I even told him I was too old for this, that I wasn't ready. He just looked at me and said I would learn. Then he added something strange."

"What was that?"

"That I didn't realize the power he had given me."

"What power?"

"To shape the world."

Ellie stared at him, her brow slightly wrinkled, a half-smile teasing her lips. "Shape the world? How do you even begin to do that?"

North chuckled, a dry, dusty sound that boomed in the quiet room. "He didn't provide a manual. No how-to guide for sculpting a world. It's like releasing a child into a sandbox and telling them to create castles."

Ellie leaned in, her eyes sparkling with a blend of curiosity and amusement. "Castles, huh? Seems ambitious for an old man with a pipe wrench."

He grinned. "Maybe so. But castles are built one brick at a time, Ellie. Maybe we start small."

"Where did he go?" she inquired.

"He just faded away like everyone else."

The coffee swirled in Ellie's cup, echoing the storm brewing in her eyes. "Questions not meant to be answered." Her words cut against the chipped rim of her cup. "Some grand cosmic joke this is, North." She shook her head, tears welling—the first she had allowed to fall since leaving the farm. "It's all just . . . gone. Everything I've ever loved. All the hopes and dreams. We were to have a child and raise it together on the farm. Then, in a blink of an eye . . . everything changed. What cruelty if this?"

North pulled her close, his arms a tender shield against the vast waves of sorrow. "We're here," his voice a gentle reassurance in her ear. "That's what matters. We, and the little star you carry."

She smiled, a fragile bloom daring to unfold amid turbulent emotions. "Stars?" The word, barely a whisper, was lost amid the storm of her despair. "In this wasteland?"

North met her gaze, his eyes reflecting the embers of a fire yet to be lit. "Yes. Our stars. Seeds pushed through ash, watered by the tears we can't hold back. We'll build a world, brick by ragged brick, with grief as mortar and hope as our hammer. It's all we've got, isn't it?"

She leaned against him, her delicate frame pressed close. He squeezed his eyes shut, sensing the tremor that ran through her, a reminder of a world shattered.

He smiled. "I'm grateful you're here. I can't imagine facing all this without you. Rest now. Then, we'll dance with ghosts and try to revive life from this graveyard."

Sleep, heavy and tear-laden, claimed her in his arms. He carried her, this precious burden, to a shadowed corner, a leather sofa offering a fragile sanctuary. She curled up, the weight of the world momentarily lifted.

12 What is it

The late afternoon sun angled through the windowed slits of Browers, painting long, praying shadows across the floor, stretching with the day's decline into grotesques that would haunt Ellie's dreams. By the time night crawled out, those shadows had swallowed everything whole, leaving only a hollow stillness.

In the morning, she rose late, and after a simple breakfast, North led Ellie down the second-floor hallway. Their footsteps bounced against the bare walls until they reached a door at the end, which North pushed open.

"This used to be a classroom," North remarked, as Ellie set down the pillowcase she had brought. "It's yours now. I know it's not much, but it's all we've got."

Ellie's eyes skittered around the concrete cave he called a room. It was large, furnished only with a bed, a dresser, and a nightstand, all salvaged from the dormitories. A window slit high up on the wall offered a sliver of light.

She turned to him. "This is more than I could've imagined." Gently, she unpacked the photographs of her family and arranged them on the nightstand. "Thank you."

North shifted, almost as if speaking more to himself. "You're welcome. I've been collecting supplies for a while, so you should be alright here. And if you need anything, my room is just down the hall." He gestured toward a door a little further along.

A flicker of motion by the doorway caught her attention. It was Shadow, sleek and dark as night, slinking silently into the room. Her tail, a plume of smoke, swished with suspicion.

"Meow. Meow."

"Her name is Shadow," North informed her.

Ellie lowered herself, extending a cautious hand. "Well, hello there," she murmured softly. Shadow, cautious, studied Ellie for a long moment, before leaning in to nudge against her palm, a feather-light touch. The quiet vibration of a purr hummed with an unexpected warmth.

"She seems sweet." Ellie forced a small smile.

North gently scratched behind the cat's ears. "She is. Been my only company since all this started."

Shadow twined between their legs, forming a quiet bond in the fragile space between them.

***

North guided Ellie through the maze of hallways on Brower's second floor. He had been preparing for this moment since the end started. He had stocked up on provisions, assembled a small medical room, and even learned the building's security system with monitors that covered every corner of the compound.

Now, he was finally unveiling his masterpiece to another human. He wanted Ellie to see that he had everything they would need to survive in this new world.

He threw open a door, revealing a large room with several refrigerators and freezers, each bulging with food. To one side of the room was another door, leading to a pantry, its shelves stocked with canned goods, dehydrated meals, and bottled water.

"There are several rooms like this one. We'll eat our way out of this horror, one lukewarm bowl of soup at a time." He tried a smile, but it came out more like a grimace. "For a while, at least. Maybe longer. Who knows? Maybe we'll even grow fat on the ashes of the world."

Ellie forced a smile. This wasn't survival, not really. This was hoarding, a desperate clinging to the remnants of a life that was gone. "It's . . . impressive. You've really thought of everything."

Yet as she looked at the overflowing shelves, a quiet dread took root in her thoughts.

What will happen when the fridges and pantries are empty? Will this place become our tomb?

But she kept these fears to herself.

North led her to the medical room next, a small space outfitted with two beds, a desk and chair, and enough supplies to cover both minor injuries and more serious cases, with medications in refrigerators, and others in a freezer.

"I hope we never have to use anything in this room," he remarked.

On their way back downstairs, North described the ingenious self-sufficiency of Browers: solar panels capturing energy, batteries storing it for future use, and a water system ensuring fresh water.

"I've tried to understand the mechanics of it all, but I'm not the right person for the job," he admitted. "We need someone who knows how to keep it all running."

Then, he took her to the security room on the first floor. Shadow now followed along. He pushed the door open spilling out cold air that made Ellie shiver.

"No windows," he told her. "Sunlight doesn't play here. Not in this kingdom of hissing computers and flickering screens. But a lot of AC to keep things cool."

There were dozens of screens, like vacant eyes staring into the darkness, each one broadcasting a slice of Browers, both inside and outside. North saw a question hang in her eyes, a question about the locked closet tucked into the corner.

"Just some storage," he said, thick with finality.

But she wasn't buying it. Not one bit.

Trust is a fragile thing.

"This is how I'll keep us safe." North was firm. "No one or no thing will ever get in here without my knowledge."

Looking at the monitors, her eyes darted from one to the other. She could see the grounds of Browers, the front entrance, and inside, down several hallways and rooms. But she couldn't look at all the monitors as North quickly ushered her out and closed the door.

"There is one thing I must ask of you," North said.

"What?"

"I'd rather you didn't go out there by yourself. It's dangerous."

"Dangerous? How?"

"A group of dogs. I can't explain why they've shown up."

Shadow's back rose in a curve, her ears pressed tight against her head. The hiss she let out was sharp and full of menace, more like an omen than a typical warning.

"Dogs?" Ellie's voice held a sharp edge. "What kind of dogs are they?"

"Not the kind that comes running for a pat on the head or to fetch a bone," North replied. "These aren't friendly. Big as wolves, their eyes glow like embers in the dark, and their teeth are like razors. They just stand there, watching you, waiting. It's like they can see right through you - to whatever's hiding in the pit of your soul."

"Coyotes, maybe," she suggested, thinking back to her farm days. "They used to creep around sometimes, getting brave."

North scoffed. "Coyotes don't have eyes like fire, and their teeth won't crush bone like these things can. No, Ellie, this is something far worse. Something that doesn't belong. Just promise me, don't step outside by yourself."

Ellie met his gaze. "I understand."

A small smile crept across his face. "Thank you. But there's more I need to show you - something I've been saving for just this moment. I think you'll appreciate it."

Her brow lifted in curiosity. "A surprise?"

"That's right."

"What is it?"

"Come with me."

They made their way to the rear of Browers, to an old door covered by a sheet of plywood. North heaved it open with a groan, and what lay beyond left her breathless.

Greenhouses, lined in succession, each one leading into the next. Their vivid greenery spilled out in a lush array, like secret gardens, a hidden oasis in a world gone mad. It was a whisper of hope, life flourishing in defiance against the dust-choked wasteland that stretched beyond.

Ellies' heart, a sparrow trapped in a rib cage for weeks, fluttered back to life. This wasn't just a surprise – it was like stepping into a dream, a safe haven in a world that had disappeared. The ever-present fear - that cold, relentless presence - loosened its grip, replaced by a rush of warmth that coursed through her veins.

North laughed softly. "If only you could see your own face right now. Like you've stumbled upon a lost treasure."

"Amazing," she breathed. "How did you do this?"

"I had no hand in it," North replied. "It was already here, part of what was taught here."

They stood in the doorway of the greenhouses, both caught in the spell of the thriving life before them. The air inside was thick and warm, carrying the rich scent of soil and growth, intoxicating in its abundance.

"I've never seen anything like it," she whispered, her breath misting faintly in the humid air.

The greenhouses stretched on, each connected, brimming with life. Rows of ripe tomatoes glistened, plump and red, and seemed to pulse with a quiet insistence. Beans wove through the structure like vines, persistent and twisting, refusing to be subdued by the bleakness outside. It wasn't just the crops that tugged at her soul; flowers bloomed in bursts of color, a daring contrast to the surrounding grayness. Fruit trees - laden with apples, peaches, and pears - held onto the warmth of the low-hanging sun, their branches heavy with promise.

Ellie's wonder deepened as she took it all in. "It's... incredible. And the old man left it untouched?"

North nodded. "It's as though Eden has found its way back, thriving in spite of what surrounds it. His gift to us, perhaps."

They strolled through the greenhouses, taking in the variety of plants. Ellie's hand brushed the leaves, marveling at their perfection, almost too flawless to be real. Corn stood tall, cucumbers hung sleek and smooth, while squat orange squash punctuated the undergrowth. Sunflowers, their heads turned skyward, gave the impression of playful winks. In a tucked-away corner, Ellie discovered a hidden patch of strawberries, tiny and red, catching the dappled light like small, vibrant jewels. Potted flowers filled every gap, alongside fruit trees thriving in abundance.

North gestured toward a tangle of pipes running along the walls. "Seems they collect rainwater here, keeping everything alive. These pipes - veins, really - carrying life to every inch of this place." He pointed toward a control panel, its buttons blinking faintly, with a few books stacked nearby. "Manuals, I think. Instructions on keeping this green heart pumping."

Ellie's wonder deepened with every step. The world outside felt distant here, the memory of it fading into the background. She could almost believe none of it had ever touched them.

"But that's not all," North's voice broke the stillness, pulling her out of the dreamlike calm.

He pushed open the final greenhouse door, and Ellie's breath caught as she stepped into the space beyond. No longer just rows of plants under glass, the scene opened up into something more alive. A barn nestled within, surrounded by grazing livestock - horses and cows, strong and well-fed, pigs rooting contentedly in a nearby pen. The greenery stretched in every direction, a patchwork of life she hadn't thought possible.

Ellie's chest tightened, caught between disbelief and something else. "I can't believe it," she murmured, emotion rising in her throat.

North gave a soft smile. "Sometimes, even here, you get something good. It's a kind of promise, I guess. A chance to start again."

Stepping forward, the earthy smell of hay filled her senses, and Ellie felt something shift inside. This wasn't just a sanctuary. It could be a home.

She was excited, a new determination lighting her face. "I can do this."

"Do what?" North asked.

Her grin widened as she met his eyes. "Run it. I grew up on a farm, I know how to raise crops and livestock. I even took veterinary courses. I was going to be a vet, before . . . "

Her words trailed off as her hand drifted to her belly.

"That's good news, Ellie," North replied, visibly relieved. "I've been wondering how I'd manage it all. There's a fridge and freezer back there in the barn, powered from Browers. And an office, stocked with medications and supplies."

"Medications?" she asked.

"Yeah, quite a few. Thought you'd want to know."

Her face, long since shadowed by the end of it all, continued its bloom with a bright smile. "I'll take a look," she promised.

***

Ellie and North stepped through the straw, the wind's low hum filling the air like a restless spirit rattling the barn's ribs. In the shadows, cats slipped by, their eyes catching the faint light, soft shapes against the stacked hay.

"Shadow's friends," North commented.

He led her to the back office and opened the door. Ellie moved toward the shelves, scanning the supplies - bandages, gauze, syringes, needles, and even surgical masks. She found bottles of pills, powdered substances, and, in the refrigerator, vials of vaccines and medications. On the desk sat a stack of veterinary science books, their spines well-worn.

Ellie traced a finger along the dusty scalpel, its edge glinting in the pale light filtering through the window. A strange feeling stirred inside her. "Everything we could need."

North glanced at her. "I know." His eyes lingered on hers. "I'm glad you're here."

As they stepped out, Ellie cast one last look at the shelves of medical supplies. She knew that this was just the beginning. With this, she could help to rebuild the world. But the abundance unsettled her, a stinging sense of something too convenient lurking beneath it all.

"It's all a bit too much, don't you think?" she whispered, her words laced with doubt. "Like someone laid this out for us."

North paused, his gaze following hers. "Feels like this place was waiting," he said. "And funny how one of the women who ended up here knows farming."

"Coincidence or something more?" Ellie wondered aloud.

North shrugged. "Don't know. Maybe we're not meant to question. We've got what we need."

"But that's not a guarantee, is it?"

"No. Humanity had all it needed once, and look where that led."

Ellie knew that North was right.

A heavy silence settled between them. Ellie's spirit, though weary, refused to surrender. "We have to try," she insisted, her voice a fragile hush. "We can't give up."

North's eyes held hers. "We plant the seeds," he offered, his voice a steady rhythm in the quiet. "We tend to the garden, even as storms rage."

They stood quietly for a moment, looking out at the fields before turning back toward Browers, where Shadow waited by the door.

***

Another night came, and North found himself fumbling for the frayed edge of his bedsheet, his fingers grasping for something solid while the ceiling seemed to blur above him. He had hoped sleep would offer some escape from this strange, terrifying reality, but his eyelids refused to surrender. The old man's cryptic words - those fragments of a broken prophecy - kept circling through his thoughts: three pregnant women, bearers of a new beginning.

His mind drifted to Ellie. Her wide, luminous eyes surfaced in the darkness, her hand warm and sure in his, a presence felt even from afar. In his imagination, her face cut through the chaos, casting him as something more than he knew himself to be as if he were chosen. That unearned faith both soothed and unsettled him.

What does it mean, to hold the world in your hands, a world born of blood and breath?

Fear, cold and creeping, wound itself through him.

Am I ready? Is anyone ever ready for a destiny carved from ashes?

A small sound escaped him, quickly muffled by the set of his jaw. He pictured Ellie again, her hair catching the light like strands of silver, her chin lifted in quiet rebellion against the night. Her belief in him, fragile yet unshakable, pushed him forward.

I cannot fail her, nor those who carry the future inside them, for the promise of what is yet to be.

Turning, he sought relief in the worn indent of the mattress, but it offered no comfort. Sleep was a distant shore, and he, a ship lost in a sea of uncertainty. He closed his eyes tight, pulling in a breath that felt heavy with dust and dread. He had to find his strength.

Sleep, when it finally descended, was a treacherous journey through a landscape of shadows. The darkness wrapped around him like a suffocating cloak when a sound stirred him from his half-sleep. A subtle scuffling, reminiscent of something small and quick moving, like paws on pavement.

A sharp sound pierced through the stillness of the night, rousing North from his slumber. Slowly, he turned his head toward the source of the noise, only to find himself confronted by a snarling beast. The dog, a tangled mass of sinewy muscle, loomed against the silvery glow of the moon. Its eyes, glinting with malice, held the promise of a violence as ancient as time itself.

Without a moment's pause, North seized his trusty pipe wrench, swinging it with all the force he could muster. The impact struck the beast's skull, eliciting a pained yelp, yet it refused to yield. In an instant, the creature lunged, sinking its teeth deep into his arm. A scream tore from his lips as he fought to shake it off, but the dog's strength overwhelmed him. It brought him to the ground and began its assault.

North writhed in agony, striving to fend off the beast, but his efforts proved futile.

I'm going to die.

He shut his eyes, resigned to his fate. Yet, in a twist that defied belief, the assault suddenly halted. Cautiously, he opened his eyes, bracing for a renewed attack, but instead found the dog transforming before him. The creature twisted and convulsed as if caught in a surreal ballet. Fur fell away in clumps, littering the pavement like forgotten garments. The limbs elongated and reshaped, as familiar features emerged from the chaos. The snout morphed into a human mouth, teeth morphing into sharp, jagged edges. Ears folded back, eyes widened, shedding their canine ignorance for the unsettling clarity of a human gaze.

The metamorphosis was agonizing, each crack and snap an unholy hymn. Yelps, sharp and wild, erupted from the creature's throat, shifting into guttural growls before finally manifesting as a deep, resonant roar that echoed through the night. The transformation continued, a crescendo of sounds that fluctuated until, with a final, earth-shattering roar, the creature emerged fully formed.

Gone was the dog, replaced by a man who stretched lazily, his stringy hair resembling damp cobwebs, framing a face pale as death, with glowing red eyes.

He lifted his head, inhaling the night air, and smiled - a grin that revealed a row of sharp, pointed teeth.

"Welcome to my neck of the woods, Mr. North," he drawled, he drawled, his voice gravelly, like stones crunching underfoot.

North swallowed hard, a question burning within him, its taste bitter as ash. "What do you want?"

"A feather," the man replied, his smile fading like mist under a rising sun. "A single, delicate feather of your trust."

North blinked, reality shifting around him as if caught in a haze. The dog, the primal growl, the flash of teeth in the pale light - each terrifying moment replaced by this figure, demanding what seemed impossible. "Trust you?" he rasped, the words feeling foreign as they left his mouth. "You just tried to rip my throat out."

The man chuckled, a dry, humorless sound that felt like a sharp wind. "Ripping throats is for amateurs, Mr. North. Besides, if I wanted you dead, we wouldn't be having this little discussion, now would we?" He sighed, a sound like air escaping a tire. "Though I must admit, there are times when your value, shall we say, leaves much to be desired."

North, adrift in a sea of unease, found himself drawn to the embers in the man's eyes, seeking answers that might be lost in ashes. "Worthy?" he repeated, the word tasting bitter on his lips. "Worthy of what?"

The man's voice was a low hum. "Joining me. Becoming one of us."

"One of who?" The question spilled from North's lips.

"One of the Others," the man snarled. "Those who exist in shadows. Those who shape the night with their will."

North shook his head slowly, as though mired in thick water. "I don't want to be one of you," he insisted, his voice small against the vastness of their surroundings. "I want to be human."

"Human? That's a skin you shed the moment you stepped into this game, Mr. North." The man scoffed, his tone as frigid as a gust sweeping across a desolate field. "You can't be human anymore. You've seen too much, tasted what you should not. There's no returning to the familiarity of normalcy."

He moved closer, his eyes never leaving North's face. "The sun has set on your old life The path back is overgrown, choked with thorns."

North stumbled back, his hands trembling like windblown leaves. "I don't want to be like you," he whispered, the words torn from his throat. "I don't want to be one of those."

The man threw back his head and laughed, a sound that scraped at the edges of sanity. "But you already are, Mr. North." The words rang out in the cavernous space between them. "You already are."

North screamed and jolted awake, gasping as his eyes flew open. The room glowed with the soft gold of dawn, the remnants of the nightmare clinging to him like a lingering shadow. He hurried to the security room, where the monitors revealed a black dog, its outline stark against the muted, reddish-gray sky. It stared into the camera, its eyes glimmering like embers in the fading night.

North clenched his jaw, the image searing into his mind. He couldn't brush it aside as a mere dream, not with that burning gaze. The dog let out a low growl, a rumble reverberating through the stillness. Then, with a flick of its tail, it turned and vanished into the shadows, leaving North alone with the haunting memory of its predatory stare and the chilling certainty that the nightmare was far from over.

13 Anevay

The fluorescent lights buzzed overhead, a constant drone hat had melded into the background alongside the scent of disinfectant and lukewarm coffee. Anevay sat at the far end of the cafeteria table, her fingers wrapped around a cup that barely managed to fend off the chill.

Five years. Hard to believe. Five years of late shifts and stolen sandwiches, moments of our hands brushing in the hallway, and laughter echoing off the linoleum floors. Five years with David. Five years of promises and shared breakfasts. Five years.

Yet, here she was, now drowning in coffee and doubt. He'd been talking to Marie, her friend, far more frequently lately. Their hushed conversations in the hallways lingered longer than seemed appropriate, their bodies leaning toward one another as if drawn by an invisible force. Anevay, ever the perceptive one, couldn't ignore how his gaze rested a moment too long on Marie's smile or how his laughter flowed more freely when she was near.

She pushed the coffee aside, its bitterness mirroring the uncertainty swirling in her thoughts. Shoving back from the table, she attempted to focus on the weary faces flowing through the cafeteria doors, faces that reflected her own fatigue. Each time she sought to dismiss the image of David and Marie - hands grazing, voices mingling with unspoken implications - the knot in her stomach twisted more painfully.

The idea of confronting him crossed her mind, but the thought felt like standing on the edge of a precipice - what if the truth shattered everything? What if Marie's smile was merely the faint reminder of a kiss intended for another? Or worse, what if the love she believed they shared had already dimmed like the spirits of those who once occupied the empty chairs around her?

She drew an unsteady breath, trying to calm her racing thoughts. Making accusations without evidence was foolish. Yet the disquiet persisted, an icy grip around her heart. She drained the last of her coffee, its final sip leaving a sour taste, and gazed up at the harsh overhead lighting.

Back to the grind. Back to the routine of IV drips and sterile bandages.

As she turned to leave, her eyes found Marie - a quiet figure amid the cafeteria bustle, nursing a coffee and soup. An unexpected peace settled over her.

No accusations yet. Just a talk. A careful step towards understanding.

She approached Marie slowly like one might enter an unfamiliar space. "Marie," she said softly, "could we chat?"

Marie looked up, eyes wide and startled. "Anevay," she stammered, "Sure. What's on your mind?"

The question remained unanswered for a moment. Anevay didn't need to explain; she had already noticed the fleeting looks, the quiet conversations tucked away, the flimsy excuses for late nights.

"David," she said at last, the name itself an accusation. "You're taking him from me, aren't you?"

Marie's eyes widened, her head shaking in quick denial. "I've done nothing. David loves you, Anevay. He's never seen me that way."

"Don't lie to me. I've seen how he looks at you."

"It's not what you think. He admires you, can't you see? Look at yourself, Anevay. Those high cheekbones, the tilt of your eyes, your gentle smile, your long black hair – you're beautiful. David's captivated by you."

"Stop the bullshit," Anevay snarled. "I don't believe a single word you're saying."

Marie recoiled, her small figure tense with the effort to keep control. The spoon rattled against the bowl, betraying the lie that she struggled to shape.

"We're just friends," she said, her voice shaky, almost pleading. But the words themselves wavered, as if on the brink of breaking. "Really. Only friends. You have to believe me."

But Anevay couldn't. Trust had soured, leaving only doubt and suspicion in its wake. "You're lying," she said softly, the bitterness of unspoken hurts leaking through.

Fear washed over Marie's face, draining her expression of its usual warmth. Her eyes, once lively, now showed nothing but worry.

"What do you want me to say?" Marie's voice broke as her defenses crumbled.

Anevay wanted honesty, even if painful. "Tell me," she demanded, her voice filling the space between them. "Tell me the truth."

"Alright . . . I'll tell you . . ." Marie began, her words fragile, like something about to fracture.

But she stopped, staring at Anevay with wide, frightened eyes. Her face twisted in agony, skin paling to a sickly hue. Her skin leeched into a sickly pallor, and her eyes bulged with terror, mirroring the sudden emptiness in Anevay's stomach. Then her body folded in on itself like a wilted flower, collapsing onto the table with a sickening thud.

Anevay trembled as an icy chill enveloped her, coursing through her body. A sense of wrongness gripped her, something beyond her comprehension.

She reached out, her fingers grazing Marie's cheek. It was ice cold.

Panic rising, Anevay's gaze darted around the cafeteria. The usual bustling atmosphere had vanished, replaced by an unnatural silence. All around her, people crumpled forms - doctors, nurses, patients, visitors - slumped over their meals and drinks. Their eyes stared blankly, faces frozen in expressions of horror. Half-eaten food clung to slack mouths.

Nausea welled up inside her as the grim scene unfolded before her eyes. She struggled to maintain her composure, fighting back the urge to retch.

What just happened?

She had been sitting there only moments before, finishing her lunch, talking with Marie, and now . . . now everyone was dead.

Her throat tightened, an attempt at a cry escaping as a dry whisper, swallowed up by the heavy quiet. She rose slowly, her legs shaking beneath her. She tried to shout, to force some sound from her, but nothing came. Stuck in place, she could only stare, eyes wide and unblinking, scanning the scene of devastation around her. It felt as if she was encased in ice.

She squeezed her eyes shut, desperate to push the horror away, but the gruesome images remained vivid, seared into her mind.

Her gaze shifted back to Marie. Her heart raced as she saw Marie's form begin to dissolve, clothes collapsing onto the floor, the lanyard with its ID and shoes left behind. As she watched the other bodies begin to fade too, a deep sense of dread settled over her.

Overwhelmed and uncertain, she rushed from the cafeteria, her pulse quickening. The hallway offered no comfort. It too was scattered with the fragments of abruptly ended lives - clothes, shoes, coats, wallets, and purses - all evidence of the abrupt ending, the silent scream of a lost moment in time.

Anevay moved cautiously, her pulse quickening with each step. Questions - why, what, how - swirled through her mind, only to be drowned out by the rising tide of fear. Yet she knew fear had no place here, not now, not with the cold grip of dread curling around her spine.

Determined to keep moving, she forced her legs to obey, driven by the instinct to flee from the unseen danger pressing closer. Her lungs burned, but she kept her gaze ahead, unwavering. She hurried up the stairwell, two flights in rapid succession, and down the corridor, her steps falling with mechanical precision. She pushed through the door to an office.

The room was swallowed in darkness, an emptiness that seemed to deepen with each breath. On the floor lay the traces of what had once been - a pair of shoes, an ID lanyard, and a watch, its hands forever marking the moment when everything had changed.

She bent to reach for the lanyard and watch.

"Dr. David Marlow, Head of Pediatrics," the ID card read.

Turning the watch over, her fingers brushed against a simple engraving: *With love, Anevay.*

She turned it over again, over and over, as if the repetition might somehow will David to appear. But no one was coming. He was gone, like all the others.

Tears clung to her, reluctant to fall, until eventually, they dried, leaving only the hollow ache in her chest. She stood, wiping her face with hands that still trembled, but inside, there was a stubborn flicker of life. One final glance around the room, a silent farewell to what once had been, and she slipped the watch and lanyard into her lab coat.

She drew in a long breath and left the office, walking without direction but feeling the need to move. The hospital's exit led her into a world that had dimmed as if all its color had been drained. The sky, smeared with a bruised hue, hung overhead while trees, once lush, now stood stripped bare, their branches brittle and fragile. There was an odd taste on her tongue, metallic and unfamiliar.

Her thoughts drifted to her parents, and she pulled out her phone, trying to reach them. The device felt cold, and useless in her hand. A heavy worry took root - had they met the same fate as everyone else?

She wanted to drive to their home but the vast stretch of highways and state lines stood between them. The journey seemed an impossible feat.

Not advisable. Survival. What to do.

A woman of quiet resolve, she told herself not to succumb to the paralysis of grief, to keep going.

Don't stop.

The parking garage filled with the sound of her keys clinking, a graveyard of forgotten vehicles, and stale air. The engine coughed to life, a reluctant chug breaking the pervasive silence. As she drove, the road stretched ahead like an endless ribbon, scattered with abandoned cars. She didn't know where she was going, but the urge to leave - to find some other place - was undeniable.

Maybe somewhere where the sky is blue and the trees green. If there is such a place.

She drove for what felt like an eternity, every bump, every scrape against an abandoned car, was a thread she clung to. When she finally pulled into a gas station and tried the pump, it didn't work.

Dread was beginning to consume her. She knew she was in trouble. She was all alone and started to think about how she would survive.

Is whatever wiped out everyone coming for me too?

She didn't have the answer. But moving forward seemed to be her only option. Her eyes scanned the horizon, searching for anything - a sign, a flash of something beyond the gray.

Nothing.

She got back into the car, the engine roaring to life once more. The hours bled into each other, the road unspooling before her. The radio remained a silent companion, leaving only the steady hum of the engine and the soft push of the wind against the windows. More abandoned cars littered the streets, and her mind spun with unanswered questions, worry pressing deeper into her every thought.

Still, she clung to one certainty.

Keep moving.

Then, out of the corner of her eye, something caught her attention. A light, dim at first, began to grow brighter with each mile. It pulsed gently, drawing her attention. She pulled the car over and stepped out, feeling its pull, though she didn't understand why. As she approached, the light revealed a figure - an old man's face, marked by wisdom and sorrow, eyes that bore the weight of the world yet offered a sense of comfort.

Follow the light.

Without a second thought, she climbed back into the car. The engine stirred to life, humming as if sharing her resolve. The warmth of the steering wheel grounded her, guiding her toward that light, toward the unknown. Fear lingered, uncertainty shadowed her thoughts, but now there was something more - something close to hope. She pressed on, the road stretching ahead like a quiet assurance, every mile pulling her farther from what she'd left behind and closer to something she couldn't yet name, but trusted all the same. The horizon stretched ahead, carrying with it the promise of renewal.

What will I find?

Then she wondered.

What was it that Marie wanted to tell me?

***

Anevay had been driving for days, the odd light in the distance her guide. It hovered just out of reach, always in the same spot, drawing her deeper into the unknown. No matter how far she traveled, it remained, neither gaining nor losing ground, as if waiting with silent patience, holding a secret she wasn't yet meant to know.

Nights fell heavy, turning the world outside her car into an impenetrable void. She'd lock the doors and try to sleep, but it evaded her, dancing just out of reach, chased away by the memories of what had transpired. The old man's face, so full of secrets, seemed to float in the darkness, his voice softly shattering the silence: "The light will guide you."

One sleepless night, she jolted awake, certain she'd heard something. A scratching noise, faint but undeniable, skimming across the metal of the car. Her pulse quickened, and then she heard it again - closer. She looked around but the night gave nothing away, only the unsettling sense that something was there.

She rolled down the window cautiously. The damp air hit her skin, bringing with it the musky smell of the wild. She took a deep breath, trying to steady the erratic pounding of her heart. The light still pulsed in the distance, steady, almost mesmerizing. It pulled at her, urging her to come closer.

Stepping out of the car, her feet crunched against the gravel. The surrounding sleeping forest seemed to hold its breath, and only the strange sound off in the distance broke the silence. She took a tentative step forward, then another, her attention fixed on that far-off glow. As she drew nearer, the light brightened until it became a wall of whiteness, banishing the darkness.

She shut her eyes, bracing herself. The old man's face materialized once more, his features old and wise, his smile soft but knowing. "Welcome home," he said.

A scream ripped through the air, tearing apart the stillness. It was a raw, feral cry, cutting through the night with vicious force, the sound of the wilderness, a guttural challenge from something ancient and untamed. She felt like she was plummeting. She felt herself falling. Her eyes flew open.

Her forehead hit the steering wheel, jerking her awake. She blinked, disoriented.

A d*ream.*

Her breath staggered.

It was a dream. Just a dream.

But the memory of that scream clung to her, leaving her breathless. She sat there, frozen, waiting for the dawn to chase away the shadows.

Another howl broke through the silence, sharp and real this time. Her eyes darted to the dark woods, straining to make sense of the shadows. Though she couldn't see anything, a disturbing certainty told her she wasn't alone.

She started the car. Just as she moved to drive, the howl came once more, closer than before. Branches cracked, something moved. She hit the gas, tires spinning on the gravel, pushing her away from whatever followed. She didn't dare look back, unsure what stalked her, but certain she didn't want to meet it.

More days dragged by as Anevay traveled through one abandoned town after another, each one a shadow of its former self. She scavenged for supplies, gas cans placed in the trunk, and food tossed into the backseat as she kept moving. That distant light always stayed ahead, a stubborn companion leading her forward, no closer but never farther away, beckoning her toward an end she couldn't yet see.

It took time for her to realize that it wasn't a place she was fleeing from anymore. It was a truth, something buried deep, a truth she wasn't ready to confront. And the road? It became her way of running from it all, a silent, desperate plea for salvation, or maybe escape - whichever came first.

One afternoon, a shape caught her eye in the rearview mirror, a flash of white, a fleeting vision. A woman, barely visible against the barren landscape. Her hair, dark as a raven's wing, tumbled down her back, her eyes deep pools of nothingness. Anevay slammed on the brakes, dust swirling around the car, but when she looked again, the woman had vanished.

Was she real? Or just a hallucination, brought on by exhaustion and the endless miles?

She continued driving, following the light once more. The steering wheel now felt icy against her damp palms. The glow that had once seemed like hope now felt more like a taunt.

What choice do I have?

The road stretched before her, winding like a serpent through the twilight sky. Unwelcomed images flared through her mind - visions she wished would stay buried. They faded quickly, leaving confusion in its wake, and with it, the feeling that she was teetering on the edge of madness.

There came a tremor, then a word, fragile and unrefined, stormed its way into her mind.

End.

It had all come to an end. Not with a burst of flames or a violent roar, but quietly, softly, like the final sigh before sleep overtakes you. No dramatic finale. No final curtain. No dramatic flourish. Only a dimming of the light, a slow drift into the shadows, leaving everything in the cold dark.

She could see it now, not in flashes of destruction, but in the world's slow fading. The hope she once held retreated, like the tide pulling back to reveal a barren shore. And she, now, was merely a passenger on a relentless journey watching, as the world crumbled around her, carried onward by a chariot of fear and gleaming metal.

14 The second

North's mornings followed an unyielding routine. At dawn, he hovered in the kitchen, the burnt toast's char mixing with the sharp scent of coffee. The buttered bread disappeared with each quiet bite, marking time's slow passage. Then came his habitual journey to the security room, a sterile place bathed in the dim blue glow of monitors.

He'd ease into the familiar, worn chair, scanning the endless grid of screens. Rewind. Replay. Study. The campus unfolded pixel by pixel, each building quietly resting beneath the pre-dawn shadows. Students, once a chattering stream, were now mere traces of memory, their voices nothing more than faint whispers. The scene before him, captured in still frames, seemed to tense with a quiet anticipation. Every image felt suspended, as though waiting for the moment when ordinary calm might fracture.

And yet, nothing disturbed the silence. The quad remained empty, the library still, the buildings just standing there. North would rub his forehead, feeling the lines deepen with each day. He'd push himself out of the chair, joints creaking, and shuffle toward the door. Outside, the sky stretched out in muted colors, bruised and worn, offering no consolation. His eyes found the horizon, where the sun was hidden, slowly rising behind thick clouds, the promise of another day one he had come to dread.

It wasn't darkness that unnerved him anymore. No, the night itself no longer troubled him. What haunted him now were the things it could bring into existence - the figures it might cast from the wreckage of their shattered world. As the first glimmers of daylight fought to break through, North sensed that today's real challenge lay ahead, an invisible battle not waged with weapons, but within himself. These shadows, quiet and persistent, threatened to pull him under, to awaken every doubt he harbored. But he would confront them. He had to. In that delicate space between fear and resolve, North understood the path forward, however narrow, was the only way through.

"There's always something watching," he'd mutter to himself.

He could feel it, a presence, elusive yet constant, just beyond reach. He couldn't stop the feeling, but he could try to ignore it, by keeping his mind active.

So, each day he immersed himself in a routine, a sequence that had become ritualistic. After checking the screens, he would step outside, boots pressing into the damp grass as his eyes combed the tree line for any sign of movement. Then it was back inside, descending to the cool basement, where he'd inspect the supplies - batteries, sensors, anything that might stave off the looming unknown. His fingers would trace along the shelves, checking, cataloging, attuned to the smallest changes.

The day continued like this, ceremonial, predictable. When his morning tasks were done, he'd head to the second floor, where the quiet remnants of what life used to be were kept in neat rows - canned goods, and medical supplies, all carefully counted, his pen always scratching on the ledger. If the stores dipped too low, there would be no choice but to venture out into the unpredictable world beyond the compound. But for now, there was work. In the greenhouses, Ellie was already at her post, tending to the plants that defied the gray landscape outside. North would join her later, their silent partnership forged in the steady rhythm of the earth beneath their hands.

Ellie's mornings mirrored his in her own way. She rose after him, ate her breakfast, and disappeared into the greenhouses, inspecting the plants for pests or diseases. She would then prepare for the day's tasks, gathering tools or loading equipment. She was always careful to lift only what she could manage, mindful of her condition. By midday, she'd work the back fields, tending to crops, harvesting, or planting, caring for the livestock, milking the cows, feeding the pigs, or tending to the chickens.

North always found his way to her, first navigating the maze of tables and pipes of the greenhouses, then out back to the fields and the barn. He'd join her, hands in the rich soil, planting seeds of tomorrow amidst the remnants of the past, or mucking out the barn stalls. In these shared moments, amidst the sound of shovels and the sigh of a breeze, they found a fragile relief. For within these simple tasks, their new ritual, there was a promise, not quite breathed, but quietly conveyed through their actions: We will endure.

"Day sixty-one," he would remark, as though keeping time with the seasons.

Ellie, propped against her hoe, would smile, the effort a reminder of the burden they both carried. "You never forget, do you?"

"Time," he would reply, his voice reflective, "is one of the few things we still have."

"And tomatoes," she would tease, though her voice carried a weariness that hinted at something deeper.

"How's everything?"

"Okay. A bit concerned with mildew on the cucumbers. Hopefully, that baking soda trick holds out."

North let out a sigh. "I meant you, not the cucumbers."

His concern, a gift more precious than rain, brought a lump to her throat. "I'm fine. Really. Just hoping for some rain."

"Only rained twice since the end," he said, echoing her silent pleas. "We could use a whole monsoon, couldn't we?"

Their work continued, each motion grounding them in the present. Until, inevitably, the silence broke. A low rumble, almost imperceptible, cut through the still air. They froze, exchanging a look. The sound didn't belong here. North stiffened.

"Get inside," he ordered her. "Now!"

Ellie didn't argue. She dropped her tools and ran, North close behind. Inside, the security alarms pulsed, their shrill rhythm heightening the tension. They rushed to the screens, eyes glued to the image of a car rolling to a stop in front of Browers. The driver's door opened, revealing a figure that moved slowly, deliberately.

"It's her," Ellie whispered, watching as the woman stepped into view.

The woman stood lanky and lean, her raven tresses cascading down her back. A lab coat hung loose around her frame, tattered and torn. Her complexion glowed with the color of burnished copper, and her features were strong and angular.

She spoke, her voice crackling through the speakers. "Hello. Is anyone there?"

"I'll handle this," North told Ellie, grabbing the pipe wrench.

"Professor, no," Ellie protested. "Maybe she's the second."

"Or maybe she's not. Stay here and lock the door until I call for you."

North left the security room and made his way to the front door, the throbbing of the security amplifying his anxiety. He took a deep breath, holding it as his muscles tightened. She was just beyond the entrance, waiting for him.

"Hello?" she called again. "Is anyone there? My name is Anevay. Is anyone there?"

He remained silent, resisting the urge to respond. Every instinct urged him to retreat, convinced that whatever lost soul had come to their threshold would soon depart. Yet something in the tremor of her voice, an open fragility that pierced his defenses, compelled him to reach for the door and pull it slowly open.

Anevay stood before him, her gaze fixed on him with an intensity that suspended time.

"It's you," she gasped, covering her mouth with her hand. "The old man in the light."

As their eyes locked, a spark ignited in the shadows, an unspoken bond forged in their shared loneliness. In that instant, he understood with complete clarity that she was the second.

"Welcome home," he offered, his voice a steady reassurance. "You're in a safe place now."

Her exhaustion was unmistakable, reflected in her pallor and bloodshot eyes, suggesting she hadn't rested in days.

"Rest," he urged. "Food and water await."

Tears brimmed in her eyes. "I don't understand." Her voice trembled. "What's happening?"

Then, inexplicably, her gaze shifted past him, as if she were looking at something beyond. North turned to see Ellie approaching.

He cursed under his breath.

She didn't listen to me.

As he turned back, Anevay spotted the pipe wrench in his grip. Panic seized her. "What's that? You were going to kill me!"

"No! No!" he exclaimed, reaching out toward her.

But it was too late. Anevay bolted for the car.

He had to bring her back. He began to chase after her, but Ellie was already there. She intercepted Anevay at the car door, grasping her arm. Anevay spun around, eyes wide with terror.

"We're not so different, you and I," Ellie said, her gaze warm and inviting, as if confiding a secret meant only for them. "We both carry a future, fragile as eggshells, hidden away inside."

Anevay stumbled back. "You know?" Her eyes darted to North, then back to Ellie. "How?"

Ellie smiled, a bittersweet curl of her lips. "Sometimes there are no answers. Sometimes we bear burdens together. We are the builders of our own destinies. With each knot, each twist of the thread, we can create something far more remarkable than what we were given."

Anevay opened her mouth, but no words emerged. She stared at Ellie, her face pale, before finally speaking. "To begin anew."

"The world is lost," Ellie's voice was heavy with sorrow. "Everyone we knew. Everything we had. All gone. Yet we remain. We're the only ones left. Yes - to begin anew."

"Why us?" Anevay asked. "Why us?"

"I think there are many reasons."

Anevay fell silent for a moment. "The world . . . it's so turned upside down. I don't know what to believe anymore. I'm not sure I believe you."

"That's all right," Ellie said. "You don't have to believe me. You only need to trust me."

Anevay studied Ellie, her gaze lingering, a slow, thoughtful appraisal tracing the lines in her face, a record of weathered days and enduring despair. The world's ruin was mirrored in her eyes, a desolate landscape where hope had once flourished. Yet, amidst this bleak terrain, Ellie stood resolute, a resilient seedling pushing through the cracks of a fractured world, her eyes reflecting a challenge to the shadows. There was a flicker of hope within her, a spark Anevay had nearly forgotten.

"I trust you," she declared softly.

Ellie smiled. "Thank you. We're going to need each other."

"What about him?" Anevay tilted her head toward North. "Why did I see him in the light?"

Ellie's reply was measured. "As I said, sometimes there are no answers," she began. "Only questions that linger. By the way, my name is Ellie." She extended her hand.

Anevay took the gesture. "I'm Anevay."

"A pleasure," Ellie replied, a simple statement bearing the weight of mutual understanding. "You're the second."

***

Ellie and North welcomed Anevay into Brower's with a quiet warmth. She felt an odd sense of calm in their company as if they were the steady hands guiding her through the chaos that surrounded them. In the common area, the large windows filtered in a dim, pale light from outside.

"So," Ellie began. "I suppose you're wondering why we brought you here."

Anevay swallowed, her throat tight. She glanced at North, then back at Ellie. "I followed him through the wasteland. He showed me the way here, but I don't understand why."

North's voice was calm as he spoke. "We believe you're meant to be here. That you're one of the chosen, one of the three who will bring life into this world again."

Anevay placed her hand on her stomach, her fingers brushing lightly over her skin. The life inside her was both wondrous and frightening.

David's child.

Everything since the end had been surreal, a whirlwind of survival and revelation. North and Ellie's words stirred a mix of terror and awe. She had known a world teeming with life, but now death reigned, and it was hard to believe that anything could grow again.

"But why me?" she asked.

North's expression softened, his eyes filled with something like understanding. "Because you have the strength, Anevay. The strength to bear this and bring something good into a world that's forgotten what that feels like."

Anevay's gaze drifted to Ellie, who watched her with a silent empathy, as though the unspoken burden they carried was shared between them. In that moment, Anevay felt a connection, a sense of belonging, however fragile.

Together.

As they sat in that common area, Ellie and North spoke of their plans for what lay ahead, Anevay felt something stir within her, small and delicate. Hope, faint but present. She hadn't known it for so long, but now it was there, a frail thing, flickering in the darkness.

Maybe, just maybe, there's a chance for life to begin again.

"The road ahead won't be easy, but you won't be walking it alone," North added, his voice solid, a reminder that they weren't defeated yet.

Anevay breathed deeply, letting the words settle within her.

My new family.

North and Ellie guided her up the stairs, through a narrow hallway where her boots tapped quietly on the floor. The air had a crispness to it, a sense of renewal. When they reached a door, it opened with a creak, revealing a haven carved from shadow and sunlight.

There was a bed at the center of the room, its linen clean and smelling faintly of lavender. Two small tables flanked it as if waiting for moments of stillness, for a cup of tea or a book to be placed upon them.

Ellie's voice, gentle and close, drifted to Anevay. "This is your room," she said. "Where our children will be born. Where it all begins."

Anevay had brought little with her - a few maps, a coffee mug, and some well-worn paperbacks, the bits and pieces of a life always in motion. She didn't even have spare clothes, just what she wore, but North had thought of everything. In the corner stood a small dresser, filled with garments he'd scavenged and carefully cleaned for her.

They continued to show her around, North explaining how they sustained themselves, walking her through the back of the building where the greenhouses and barns stood.

Ellie smiled as she spoke of their work. "Fresh vegetables, eggs, milk from the cows. With the greenhouses, we can sustain ourselves through every season."

North looked at Anevay then, his eyes settling on the lab coat she still wore like a forgotten skin. "You worked in the medical field?"

Anevay paused, caught off guard by the question. "Yes," she answered quietly. "I am . . . I mean . . . I was a nurse."

North smiled, something genuine lighting his face. "Then I think you'll want to see this."

Ellie's smile mirrored his. She knew what was going to happen. North led Anevay back into Browers, up the stairs, and down the hallway, not too far from her room.

He stopped at a door and opened it, revealing a large room lit by the harsh glow of fluorescent lights. "I thought you might want to take a look," he said, stepping aside so she could see.

Anevay stepped inside, a small gasp escaping her lips.

"An infirmary," she breathed. "I don't believe it."

Anevay entered, her breath catching as she took it in. It was more than she had hoped for - clean beds, well-stocked shelves of medical supplies, and at the back, refrigerators, and freezers, stainless steel giants, humming quietly, keeping things preserved.

"Not sure what's inside them," North admitted. "But everything seems labeled."

"How did you pull this together?"

North shrugged with modest pride. "I've been gathering what I could since I came here, knowing we'd need it someday."

Anevay felt a swell of gratitude, her eyes stinging with unshed tears. This wasn't just survival; it was something more. It was a place to heal, a place where life could begin again. "Thank you," she managed, knowing the words fell short of what she felt. "This means everything."

North's gaze shifted to a slit of a window high on a wall. "There's still one more," he said, almost to himself. "Another like you and Ellie. I don't know who she is or where she's coming from, but she's out there."

Anevay looked between them, at the quiet strength in North and the patient resilience in Ellie. They had built this together, out of the ashes, and now they waited - waited for the future they believed in. They were three now, but they were waiting for the storm to break, waiting for the world to bloom anew, waiting for the other to arrive.

***

The evening settled over the kitchen like a worn, threadbare shawl, casting its shadows across the mismatched plates and bowls that crowded the table. Three figures sat together, their meal simple - soup made from leftover vegetables and meat, beans, rice, and a salad. The room was thick with the scent of food, the only noise was the quiet clink of utensils on dishes.

Ellie recounted her story first, her voice steady. When she finished, it was Anevay's turn.

Her eyes, catching what little light remained, held a distant reflection as she spoke. "It felt like a nightmare - people vanishing in an instant, the halls suddenly empty. I couldn't make sense of it." She placed an ID badge and David's watch on the table for North and Ellie to see. "I don't even know why I kept these."

North, his own gaze haunted by unspoken memories, offered a faint smile. "We hold on to what we can. Little odds and ends of a world that's slipped away."

Tears gathered at the corners of Anevay's eyes. "Maybe when this child of mine is grown, I'll tell them about their father. Show them these things, letting them know he's more than just a fading memory."

"Ellie reached across the table, her hand gentle. "A promise meant to last."

"I'm sorry," North murmured softly. "Didn't mean to stir up painful thoughts."

Anevay's voice was fragile. "Not your fault. Just ... "

"We're in this together," North cut in, his voice firmer now. "Caught in the same storm, drifting along with it."

"There's something else I need to say," Anevay began, her voice faltering as the words stuck in her throat.

North leaned in, his eyes intent. "What is it?"

"As I drove here," she began with a voice a thread in the darkness, "I saw a woman. She had on a white dress, wrapped in it like a thing waiting to be covered up. Her hair, it was dark, spilling down her back, drowning in the dusk. But her eyes. There was nothing in them. Just black hollows looking back at me."

Ellie's face was lined with concern. "What happened?"

"She vanished," Anevay replied, shaking her head, the movement unsteady. "One second she was there, then gone, like smoke. Just a trick of this madness we're all caught up in. Do you think I'm losing my mind?"

North thought of his own nights, those uneasy dreams full of whispers from the edges of waking. "No, Anevay. I believe you. This ... all this ... it's warped us all. We've all been warped by this place. We've seen things that don't make sense, things that don't belong."

Anevay's voice trembled. "What kind of things have you seen?"

North took a deep breath, the memories settling uneasily in his chest. He told her of the old man he had spoken with, the cryptic words, the ominous walk through town, the strange dogs, and his dreams that seemed to carry the weight of something dark. Anevay listened, dread building in her expression, the thread of her fear unmistakable.

"I don't know what's happening," North confessed, his voice shaking. "But I know this - whatever it is, we're not alone. I can feel that much."

Ellie spoke quietly. "I know. I feel it too."

The quiet returned, but it had changed, transformed like a caterpillar emerging from its chrysalis. It carried a new meaning, a silent understanding between them, heavy with unspoken truths and shared fears. The world outside had shifted, its familiar edges worn away by an invisible hand, leaving them stranded in a strange and shifting landscape, with no map to guide them and no stars to light their way. They stood together, yet alone, in this new reality, their breaths synchronizing in the stillness of their altered existence.

15 The other

Anevay's arrival was like sunlight pushing past drawn curtains – warming, unexpected, and profoundly necessary. Not only was her medical expertise invaluable, but it was the way she fit into the fabric of their days that made her indispensable. Each day followed a familiar, reliable tune, with Anevay, in her calm way, helping to hold it all together.

Every morning, Anevay shared breakfast with Ellie, the warmth between them growing without the need for words. Steam rose lazily from their mugs, swirling in the pale dawn light, a silent comfort between them. Afterward, Anevay would walk among the greenhouses and fields, her steps unhurried as she breathed in the crisp morning air, savoring the simplicity of the moment. The plants, full of life, greeted her with the familiar scent of soil and greenery, grounding her in the present.

From the fields, she'd return to the infirmary, her haven of quiet efficiency. Every day unfolded like a well-practiced routine: restocking supplies, taking inventory, organizing bandages and medicines. Each item was perfectly in its place, ready for whatever the day might bring. North often stood by, his quiet presence a steadying force. He'd listen as she reported on their supplies or Ellie's condition, his usual tension easing with her calm updates.

Anevay's hands, which had nurtured life and provided comfort in death, were always busy. She worked with an ease that spoke of deep care, her fingers just as comfortable digging in the earth as they were tending to wounds. Whether planting fragile seedlings or caring for animals, she gave the same attention to every task. Her strength and resilience were a constant, an anchor in a world that threatened to pull them under.

In Ellie's words, Anevay was a "steady light," and North had never argued with that. She was more than a helping hand; she was a stabilizing force, a presence that brought calm amidst the disorder that had overtaken their world.

Anevay attended to North and Ellie's minor scratches and bruises. Thankfully their injuries never extended beyond that and she was always relieved with this. She diligently monitored Ellie's pregnancy, making sure that Ellie was eating right, taking her prenatal vitamins, getting enough sleep, and staying active. Ellie was grateful for Anevay's care and tried to do the same for her.

Days spun into weeks, weeks into months, the same predictable waltz of routines and responsibilities - until one morning when everything changed. It was a gray, early hour, and Anevay was in the greenhouse, moving between the rows of plants. Out of the corner of her eye, she caught a glimpse of something white. She turned, her heart skipping, and there, standing amidst the green, was a woman. Thin, pale, her gown the color of bone, the woman's hair a tangle of midnight tumbled down her back, framing eyes that seemed endless.

Anevay froze, silence wrapping around her. She knew the woman, had seen her before. There was something terrifyingly real about her presence, and as she tilted her head at an unnatural angle with a horrid crack of bones, a shiver ran through Anevay. Her smile was cold, filled with hatred. Anevay knew - somehow, deeply

- that this apparition signaled a shift. Their steady routine, the life they had built, was about to be upended.

How did she get in? What does she want from me?

Instinctively, she moved, her feet propelling her toward the exit. The greenhouse walls seemed to close in around her, the plants blurring as she rushed past. The woman followed, swift and silent, her hand reaching out with fingers that felt like icy vines wrapping around Anevay's arm. A cry ripped from her throat, but it was swallowed by the silence. Alone, she could taste the metallic fear on her tongue.

Then, as suddenly as it had started, the vision broke. Anevay woke with a start, sweat beading on her forehead, Ellie's concerned face inches away. She had been dreaming - only a nightmare, but it lingered like a shadow, refusing to leave her. The woman in white wasn't just a figment of her imagination. Anevay was certain of that now.

"Are you okay?" Ellie asked. "You were thrashing about, screaming . . ."

Anevay managed a shaky nod. "I must've fallen asleep and had a nightmare. I'm fine," she said, but the words felt empty.

She didn't feel fine. The woman in her nightmare was real, and the memory of her eyes, black holes devouring light, was too real.

She's coming for me.

For Anevay, the following days felt different, bringing a change she couldn't place, something in the way the world sat heavy on her. The greenhouse, her once-cherished refuge, now held an uneasy stillness, as though the pale figure still lingered there, unseen but never gone. Even the sunlight, which used to spill warmly through the windows, seemed colder, and harsher, as though it too had been touched by her fear.

She moved among the plants, her fingertips grazing leaves that felt strangely distant, as though part of another time. The familiar creaks and sighs of the place, once steady and reassuring, now hinted at concealed threats, as if she were never truly alone. Sunlight streamed through the tall windows, casting a pale glow that seemed to leech color and life from everything it touched.

Even the dust motes, which used to twirl so happily in the light, now felt strange - like they carried some unknown weight, performing an unsettling dance just out of reach. Anevay caught herself holding her breath as if even the smallest disturbance could shatter the fragile calm and expose the truth behind the illusion.

Sleep evaded her, leaving her eyes bruised with exhaustion, nerves stretched tight. The room she knew so well transformed in the dark; shadows stretched into reaching shapes, and the faintest breeze carried what felt like a whisper of her name. Each time she startled awake, her pulse wild, she was convinced the woman from the rearview mirror had found a way in, her gaze devouring the last trace of light and hope.

The toll it took on her became impossible to hide. Ellie and North noticed the subtle changes - the tremble in her hands, the way her gaze drifted, haunted by something she couldn't name. Ellie, ever kind, tried to coax her back with quiet jokes and gentle words, while North kept a watchful eye, his concern masked by his usual silence.

Yet Anevay was caught in a spiral, trapped by her own mind. Every moment felt distorted, as though she was walking through a distorted mirror, her reality no longer what it seemed.

Even as she carried out her duties, the woman in white lingered, a silent threat hovering just out of sight, her presence a constant weight on Anevay's heart.

Day ninety came and went, and Anevay knew, without a doubt, that something was coming. Something was about to change.

***

The greenhouse was a sanctuary, a place where the troubles outside seemed to recede behind its walls of glass. Inside, Anevay spotted Ellie, her hands deep in the dark soil, coaxing seedlings to life with a tenderness that revealed the tremor in her fingers. Morning light streamed through the panes, dappling Ellie's face and casting a soft glow over her, as though smoothing the edges of their harsh reality.

"Mind if I join you?" Anevay asked, her voice gentle.

Ellie glanced up, a fleeting smile crossing her face. She motioned toward a nearby chair. "Of course."

Anevay eased herself down, her rounded belly making the movement slower than usual. She picked up a trowel and looked at Ellie. "Can I help?"

Ellie smiled again and nodded. "Please."

They worked together in easy quiet, hands moving in sync to create small spaces for new growth. The only sound around them was the gentle whir of the fans circulating air through the greenhouse. After a time, Ellie broke the silence.

"Isn't it strange," she said, patting the soil around a fragile sprout, "how nightmares still find us when we're already living one?

Like our minds are trying to make sense of the chaos, even when we sleep." Her smile turned slightly wry as she glanced at Anevay.

Anevay's hands paused, her gaze resting on the plants before her. "Can I tell you about mine?"

Ellie stopped her work and looked over. "Of course. We're in this together."

Anevay's eyes met Ellie's, something fragile and hopeful breaking through the fear. "There's always a woman in white," she began, her voice faltering, "hovering at the edge of my sight. She's always there, in the corner of my eye. I can feel her watching, waiting."

Ellie reached over, resting her hand on Anevay's. "Tell me more."

Anevay sat quietly for a moment, her eyes fixed on the dirt under her nails as she gathered her thoughts. Then, with a slow exhale, she began.

"She's always there, you know? The woman in white," Anevay said softly. "At first, she's just a blur - like something you catch out of the corner of your eye. But then she. . . she's clearer. Always watching."

Ellie, still working the soil, looked over at her but said nothing, giving Anevay space to continue.

"It started in the car, after everything - after we lost so much." Anevay paused, her hand trembling as she dug the trowel into the earth. "I saw her in the rearview mirror, and there she was until she wasn't there any longer. At first, I thought I was just tired, imagining things. But no matter how far I drove, no matter how many roads I took - she was there, always behind me, in my mind."

Anevay's breath hitched. "And she's in my nightmares, in the greenhouse. The shadows – but they aren't just shadows. They move. Whisper. And there she is again, just standing there, watching me work. I - I can hear her breathing, Ellie. Like she's right there, right next to me. It's like she's waiting for something, like she's always just out of reach, but still too close." A tear slipped down her cheek, and she wiped it away hastily. "I'm so tired."

Ellie squeezed her hand, her voice low and steady. "You're just - carrying too much alone."

Anevay shook her head, biting back the tears. "What if she's real? What if - what if it's not just in my head?" She looked down at their joined hands, feeling the warmth and steadiness of Ellie's grip. "I just - I don't want to be afraid anymore."

Ellie held her hand firmly, offering warmth and grounding. When Anevay finally fell quiet, drained from sharing her burden, Ellie squeezed her hand, a wordless assurance of understanding. The world beyond their shared space felt distant as they focused on each other.

"You're not alone," Ellie said quietly. "Whatever this is, whatever she represents, we'll face it together."

Anevay studied Ellie, really seeing her in a way she hadn't for days. "Together?"

Ellie smiled - a true smile, one that reached her eyes. "Together. Because that's what we do here. We take care of each other."

Standing, Ellie brushed off her clothes and extended a hand to Anevay. "Come with me. I have something for you."

They left the greenhouse and walked into Browers. Ellie led Anevay to her room, rummaging through a drawer before pulling out a small, smooth stone.

"Here," she said, placing the stone in Anevay's hand. "It's a worry stone. My mother gave it to me when I was a child. Whenever I felt scared or alone, I'd rub it, and it reminded me of her, that I was loved, that I wasn't alone."

Anevay turned the stone over in her palm, feeling its cool surface. "Ellie, I can't take this."

Ellie shook her head gently. "You're not taking it. You're borrowing it, until you don't need it anymore."

Anevay closed her fingers around the stone. "Thank you," she whispered.

That night, Anevay held the stone close as she lay in bed. When the shadows stirred and the whispers began, she rubbed the stone, thinking of Ellie's words - "We take care of each other." For the first time in weeks, she slept peacefully.

The following morning, she found Ellie in the kitchen, making breakfast. Without a word, she wrapped her arms around her friend in a tight hug.

"Thank you," Anevay murmured, her voice muffled against Ellie's shoulder, the gratitude spilling out in a rush of emotion that spoke louder than any words could convey.

Ellie returned the hug. "Always."

As they ate together, sunlight pouring through the windows, Anevay felt a sense of calm she hadn't known in ages. The woman in white remained at the edge of her thoughts, but Anevay knew she wasn't alone in facing her. She had Ellie, North, and this strange new life they'd pieced together.

And for now, that was more than enough.

16 Myra

"Professor!"

The scream rang through the greenhouse, a piercing sound that cut through the humid air, sharp and desperate. North and Anevay froze mid-action, their hands still gripping the watering cans.

"Professor! Come quickly!" the voice cried, strained with panic.

Anevay's hand found North's, her fingers cold and shaking. "Did you hear that?" Her voice barely rose above the pounding in her chest.

North's eyes met hers, eyes wide and filled with dread. "Ellie," he breathed, the name catching in his throat. "It's Ellie!"

He tossed the watering can aside and ran to the greenhouse door that led outside. Anevay was right behind him, her breaths shallow and rapid. They burst through the greenhouse into the open, where Ellie crouched, her body folded over something on the ground.

"What's wrong?" North called as he closed the distance.

When they reached her, they saw what she knelt beside - twisted limbs, a mess of blood and ruin.

"What is it?" North asked.

Ellie didn't look up. Her voice was thick, trembling. "A calf. What's left of one."

The mangled body lay sprawled, torn open, the flesh peeled back in jagged strips. Where eyes once were, now there were empty hollows, and the head hung to the side, its tongue slack. The legs were bent in ways they shouldn't be, hooves sunk deep into the mud, and the once-soft fur was matted with thick blood. Flies, drawn by the ghastly feast, buzzed around the carcass.

The stench hit them all at once - a thick, sickening mix of death, decay, and something far worse. North gagged, covering his mouth and nose with his hand. "What happened?"

Ellie shook her head, her face ashen. "I don't know. I've never seen anything like it. This wasn't an attack – this was torture."

Anevay's voice was barely a whisper. "What could've done this?"

Ellie's eyes stayed fixed on the carcass. "Not a dog, not a wolf. This - this is something else. It's like it was done out of cruelty, not hunger."

The woods surrounding them seemed to fall into an unnatural stillness, the quiet growing thicker by the second. Then, from deep within the trees, came a low, guttural growl. It reverberated through the air, crawling under their skin and setting off a visceral terror.

North's voice broke through the tension. "We need to get inside. Now. Stay together. No heroics."

They moved quickly, almost running, their footsteps pounding the ground in time with their fear. The shadows seemed to stretch and twist around them as if the forest itself had turned hostile. The growls behind them were closer now, persistent and unrelenting.

At last, they reached the greenhouses, the glass walls offering a flimsy barrier against whatever was out there. They slammed the door behind them, leaning against it as they tried to catch their breath, hearts thudding wildly in their chests.

"What was that?" Anevay's voice shook, disbelief tinged with fear. " "I thought - I thought everything was gone except for us."

Ellie's face was grim. "We were never alone."

"No," North said. "We were never alone. Whatever it is, it knows us. And I don't think it's finished with us yet."

***

Inside Browers, North rushed to the security room, Ellie and Anevay trailing behind. He flung open the closet and pulled out a rifle tucked behind dusty file boxes.

"What . . .?" Ellie choked, struggling to find her words.

North, already fumbling with a magazine clinking with bullets, offered a strained shrug. "What does it look like?" He tried for a grin, but it crumbled into frustration as the magazine slipped, scattering bullets across the floor. "Dammit!"

A heavy silence settled, broken only by the soft scuff of shoes and the sound of North's frustrated curse. Ellie and Anevay stood stunned in disbelief and a sense of betrayal. North felt the cold trickle of sweat slide down his neck as heat crept into his face. He'd miscalculated, badly.

"Look," he began, "it's not what you think. I just . . ." But the words faltered, the explanation dying in his throat. What explanation could smooth over this?

Ellie's voice sharpened. "Just what, North? Just kept a rifle stashed away like some shameful secret?"

He fumbled for a response. "I didn't want to alarm you." The excuse sounded flimsy even to him.

Anevay, usually measured, let out a bitter laugh. "Alarm us? This isn't about fear. This is about trust - about not shutting us out."

North knew they were right. His misguided need for control and routine had built a wall between them.

"I'm sorry," he said, his voice low. "I was scared. Okay? I didn't know what we might be up against, and I thought - " He swallowed hard. "I thought we'd need it."

Ellie stepped closer, her gaze intense as she searched his face. "You don't even know what you're doing," she said, her voice like ice. "Give it to me."

North bristled, anger flaring briefly before being extinguished by the logic of her words. He didn't know how to use the gun, and his clumsy attempts could likely only endanger them further.

Anger flared in him, but only briefly. She was right. He hadn't thought this through. Reluctantly, he handed her the rifle. With skillful precision that caught him off guard, Ellie slid a fresh magazine into the chamber, the sound of it clicking into place and breaking the tense silence.

"I grew up on a farm. Remember?"

North's face tightened.

Control.

"We need to secure the animals," he commanded abruptly. "From now on, no one goes into the fields without someone on watch with a rifle. Anevay, stay inside. We'll handle it."

Ellie led them out, the rifle in her hands, her focus sharp. North followed, uneasy, glancing behind them as they moved through the greenhouses and toward the fields. He couldn't shake the feeling that they weren't alone.

Ellie pushed open the barn door, its hinges groaning. "Get the animals inside."

North did as he was told, herding the skittish creatures into the dim shelter. Once inside, the animals were restless, huddled into the corner, tense and wide-eyed, sensing the same approaching darkness.

With the barn secured, they retraced their steps, the silence broken only by a sound in the woods beyond.

North stopped. "Did you hear that?"

Ellie's jaw tightened. "I don't like it."

They stood there, the sky growing darker above them, straining to listen to the murmurs of the wind, the air growing thick with the promise of something unknown.

"I think it's gone," Ellie whispered.

North didn't answer. He didn't believe it. He was convinced that a predator was still out there, hidden in the shadows, waiting for the perfect moment to strike.

A howl pierced the quiet, long and mournful. It was a sound from the wild and raw, that spoke of ancient hungers. Without speaking, they hurried back inside Browers. In the security room, Ellie stowed the rifle. North, eyes glued to the monitors, urgently scanned for movement while Anevay watched from his side.

"See anything?" she asked.

Ellie's expression remained hard. "No, but it's out there."

Anevay didn't flinch. "Whatever it is, it's coming."

The silence grew heavy, only the ticking clock marking time.

"What do we do now?" Anevay asked quietly.

North looked at her, his voice betraying the worry he couldn't hide. "We wait."

They wouldn't have to wait long.

***

The three were finishing their dinner, their conversation winding through the mundane events of the day, when a piercing alarm shattered the air in Browers. It was relentless, a sound that rose and fell in waves, throwing off their composure. In an instant, the meal became irrelevant as their expressions shifted to unease, exchanging glances heavy with meaning. Something was out there, pressing closer to their fragile sanctuary.

No words were needed. They moved in unison, urgency propelling them toward the security room. The alarm grew louder, reverberating through the narrow hallways, heightening their sense of dread. It wasn't just the noise that gripped them - it was the knowledge that something, or someone, had breached the boundary.

Inside the security room, their worst fears were confirmed. The monitors, designed to keep watch over Browers, displayed an unsettling image - a solitary figure moving toward the entrance. North narrowed his eyes, trying to make sense of what was barely visible on the screen. It looked like a person, though the details were lost in the poor light and shadow.

"Do you see that?" His voice was low, tinged with a quiet tension. "What is it?"

Ellie leaned closer. "I can't tell," she admitted, squinting at the grainy display.

Anevay stood beside her, eyes glued to the shifting image. The room felt smaller, the dim glow of the monitors the only thing grounding them to the moment. The form on the screen began to emerge more clearly - a woman, though something about her seemed off. Her outline wavered, the pixels struggling to keep her in focus. A familiarity lingered, but it was wrong somehow as if the woman didn't quite belong.

Anevay's hand flew to her mouth, stifling a gasp that nearly drowned out the droning alarm. Her eyes, wide and unblinking, were fixed on the woman who now occupied the screen with an eerie stillness.

"It's her," she whispered. "The woman from the rearview mirror."

The figure stepped out of the fading light, a spectral silhouette. Her frame was gaunt, draped in a torn dress that clung to her frail body, while a wild tangle of black hair hung down her back. Her face, smeared with dirt, appeared hollow, and her eyes—dark, empty pits - seemed to pull at them. But it was her belly that caught their attention. Swollen to a grotesque size, it jutted out unnaturally, a harsh contradiction to her thin frame.

Anevay took a step back, her fear rising like a tide. "She's here."

The woman moved with a strange calmness, unaware of their scrutiny. Her footsteps were light, almost graceful, until suddenly, she stopped and looked directly into one of the cameras. Her gaze was sharp as if she could see right through the lens. Slowly, deliberately, she raised a hand, long fingers extending toward them like claws catching the last traces of sunlight.

As she drew closer, the truth hit them with a strange clarity. This was no woman in her prime. She was a girl, barely out of adolescence, though her appearance had fooled them at first. The burden she carried aged her in a way that felt impossible to comprehend.

"Help me," the voice on the monitor pleaded, thick with desperation, the words neither soft nor faint, nor lost in the static. They were the kind that scraped against the very core of one's being. "I won't hurt you. Please, let me in."

Anevay spun toward North and Ellie, panic rising in her voice. "We can't let her come near us," she choked out.

"What's wrong?" Ellie asked, stepping forward.

Anevay's gaze darted back to the screen, haunted. "She's the one. The one I saw on the drive. And the one from my nightmares."

Ellie's eyes widened, an understanding passing through them. "The ones we've talked about?"

Anevay squeezed her eyelids tight, a tremor rippling through her body. The face that had haunted her rearview mirror, the specter that had plagued her dreams - they merged now, etched into her mind's eye with a sharpness that mocked logic. Those nighttime terrors, once a jumble of disconnected shards, had crystallized into a harsh truth. The woman, her words, her desperate appeal - they were here, real, tugging Anevay towards a shadowy realm she dared not turn away from.

"I don't want her here," Anevay told them, her eyes filled with horror. "We can't let her in. We can't!"

Ellie gave a gentle touch to Anevay's arm. "It's okay. They were just nightmares"

North frowned, a look of troubled understanding passing over him. "We've all had nightmares since the world went quiet. Some of them worse than others," he said, his voice steady. "But nightmares aren't real. They don't control what happens here. You know what they used to say, right?" North asked Anevay. "Nightmares are just dreams. Darker dreams. They don't mean anything. They're simply a way for our subconscious to process our fears and anxieties."

Anevay barely registered his words. Her eyes were locked on the girl's face, twisted with something beyond fear, beyond exhaustion. The girl's nails scraped against the screen, a plea hanging in every breath, her eyes screaming for mercy. Anevay's heart pounded, the pull to run nearly overwhelming.

"I'm pregnant," the woman's voice broke through the static. "I need help. Please."

North turned off the alarm, plunging the room into an uneasy silence. All that remained was the girl's voice, her words trailing into the night as she pressed her face closer to the camera. Her wild eyes, sunken and pleading, told a story too horrible to imagine. Strands of matted hair clung to her gaunt face, and her thin arms cradled the burden she carried - a burden that had clearly taken everything from her.

"We have to let her in," North said, his tone resolute. "There's no other choice."

Ellie and Anevay exchanged a glance, their fear unspoken but shared. The woman on the screen was a mirror of their own nightmares brought to life, but North's words weighed heavy. The woman needed help, but what would happen if they opened the door?

***

"Please," the woman begged, her voice like a siren's song that pulled at their resolve. "I know someone's there. I need help. I'm alone, and I'm carrying a child."

Anevay, no stranger to the hollow ache of isolation and the desperate search for something to fill the emptiness, felt a sting of sympathy. She remembered scrounging for food, huddling under threadbare blankets, praying for daylight. But a warning stirred within her. Something was unsettling about this woman - a presence she couldn't shake. "Something's off," she muttered to herself. "She's not safe."

"She's pregnant," North said, a quiet plea in his voice. "And she's young, barely more than a child herself . . . but she's the third . . . just like the old man with the leash told me."

He took Anevay's hand, squeezing gently, his eyes searching hers for any sign of hesitation. Her gaze, however, remained fixed on the figure outside. Anevay's instincts screamed that danger was near.

"There's something wrong with her," she said firmly, turning toward Ellie seeking reassurance. "What do you think?"

Ellie's shoulders sagged. "I don't know what to think anymore," she admitted. "Ever since the sky turned red, nothing feels solid. But North's right. She's the third - whether we like it or not. We don't have many choices left."

Anevay sighed, her frustration barely contained. "I know we don't have a choice. But I still don't trust her. Let her in if you have to, but I'll be keeping an eye on her."

North nodded. "Fine. But you're the one who'll be responsible for her care. You're the healer."

Anevay's lips pressed into a thin line, but she gave a reluctant nod. "I won't like it."

North smiled, the kind of smile that held little joy but plenty of understanding. "We don't always like what we have to do."

They left the security room and made their way to the entrance. North cracked the door open, just enough for a slice of the gray light to cut through the gloom. He leaned toward the narrow gap and asked softly, "Who are you?"

"Myra," the woman answered, her voice shaky. "I followed a face in the light. It sounds mad, but I saw it weeks ago - an old man's face, ancient and wise, floating there like nothing I've ever seen."

North didn't reply. His eyes scanned her face, searching for something he couldn't name. Slowly, he pushed the door open a little more and stepped outside.

Myra's breath hitched. "It's you," she whispered, tears brimming in her eyes as her hand lifted, trembling, to touch his face. "You're the one I saw."

But Anevay, quick and sharp, slapped Myra's hand away. "Where are you from?" she demanded.

North's expression darkened. "Anevay!"

Myra recoiled, like a wounded animal. "Nowhere. I've been walking for days, following that face. I knew it had to mean something."

Anevay crossed her arms, glaring at the stranger. "This isn't a place for wanderers. Turn back."

North cut in, his voice low. "We've talked about this. She's one of us. Chosen."

Anevay scoffed. "There's something about her that's - that's - not right."

Myra, startled by the suspicion, stammered, "No. No, there's nothing wrong. He said it – I'm chosen. Here to help."

Anevay glanced between Myra and North, her distrust deepening. But North wouldn't meet her eyes. Instead, he spoke calmly, "Let's get her inside. We'll deal with this later."

Ellie stepped forward, offering a soft smile. "Come with me. We'll find you a room, and get you cleaned up."

Myra hesitated, then followed Ellie inside, passing by the common area where Shadow, the cat, was curled up. As Myra drew near, Shadow bolted upright, her fur bristling, a low growl rising from her chest. She stood, eyes fixed on Myra, back arched in hostility. Myra paused, staring at the animal with an unnerving calmness, something wild flashing in her gaze.

North noticed the exchange, troubled by the intensity of Shadow's reaction. She had never behaved like that before. There was something strange about Myra, something that seemed to agitate the cat in a way he couldn't understand.

Anevay's fingers dug into North's arm like claws. She pulled him close to her. "You saw that. Didn't you?"

North cleared his throat, trying to dismiss her fears. "It's just a cat reacting to someone new. Nothing more."

Anevay shook her head. "It's more than that. Even the cat knows something's wrong."

North wanted to brush it aside, but a gnawing doubt had lodged itself in his chest. He longed to calm Anevay, to pull her back from the edge she seemed to be hurtling toward.

"We have bigger things to deal with," he said. "This is more important than a cat's behavior."

Anevay's eyes narrowed. "And what's so important?"

"We had an understanding, you and me."

Anevay's expression hardened. "We did. But I'm not so sure anymore."

She walked away, leaving North standing there, her words hanging between them. For the first time, he wasn't sure he could keep it all together. Doubt clawed at him. He had never seen Anevay like this before. She seemed like someone entirely different, someone he no longer recognized. But there was something in him that told him she could be right.

What if Myra is dangerous?

He shook his head, pushing the thought away. Whatever was happening, he had to stay focused.

Keep them all safe, no matter what the cost.

***

North sat with Myra at the table in the common area. His words flowed easily at first, as he painted a picture of Browers - a place that thrived on its own rhythm - and spoke of Ellie and Anevay, whose steadfastness kept him anchored. But as he recounted the events of that day, the one that marked the end of what had been, his voice began to tremble. His routine, once his fragile armor against loneliness, shattered as he spoke of the café, its familiar corner booth offering solace before his morning classes. Then his tale darkened. The old man appeared, his eyes deep and unfathomable, and the leash in his hand, empty but significant, a reminder of something precious, irreplaceable. His dreams, too, took on a chilling tone - a world where silence clung to everything, and faces were frozen in expressions of startled disbelief.

Cradling the mug, Myra let the warmth seep into her skin, thawing the edges of a chill that had seeped deeper than a winter's wind. She took a cautious sip, feeling the burn as it made its way down her throat. When she looked up, North's gaze was steady, ready to break through whatever walls she had raised. She sipped again, the quiet between them growing longer, more intense, waiting for her to speak.

"Where do I even start?" she hesitated.

"Wherever you feel you need to," North said softly.

"It was all so simple, really," she began. "Seventeen, foolish, in love, and pregnant. Everything I did was against what my parents believed. Their faith, their principles. They could never understand, not about Mark, not about the baby."

North stayed silent, his eyes filled with empathy, though he already knew the outline of the story. Small-town whispers, the sharp condemnation, the fury of her religious parents.

"They were pillars of the community," Myra went on, her voice bitter. "Deacon and deaconess of the church. But when I told them about the baby, everything they stood for crumbled."

North let the silence absorb her pain, a gentle acknowledgment.

"They called me a Jezebel," she said, her voice rising. "My own parents. Can you imagine that? I was barely an adult, pregnant with their grandchild, and they called me that." Her fingers tightened around the mug, knuckles turning pale. "They didn't care. Just told me to leave."

Her voice shook, a tremor swallowed by the vast emptiness of Browers. Her eyes, clouded with hurt, stared past the table. She pushed the coffee away, its steam rising like a silent plea. "Kicked out, pregnant, with nowhere to go. I still get so angry."

Silence filled the space between them again. After a moment, Myra exhaled sharply, her bitterness raw. "They said I was a disgrace. That I was ruining their good name. As if this baby growing inside me was something to be ashamed of." A brittle laugh escaped her, sharp and hollow. "I told them – 'I'm the one carrying your grandchild.' But that was it. They were done. Told me to go and never come back. So I left. Left them and school."

"Where did you go?" North asked quietly.

"A friend let me stay with her for a while," Myra said. "She had a place and said I could split the rent if I got a job. And I did, for a while."

"And Mark?"

"Mark? His parents wouldn't have me either," she said, bitterness creeping into her tone. "His father acted just like mine - full of fire and damnation. After that, I never saw him again."

"Did you find a job?"

She nodded. "Nights at the Quick-Shop. Until the manager started making comments about how I wore the uniform. Said it was too revealing. I told him where he could shove his minimum wage job and his leering looks. The next morning, my name was crossed off the schedule in red ink. No more job. I couldn't find anything else for days. And my roommate was starting to give me shit about not having a job. Then it happened."

"What?"

"Everything just - stopped. People, sounds, movement. It all disappeared. And you know what? I was kinda glad. Shit. I'd been alone the whole time anyway. But now I felt free." She leaned in, her voice dropping further. "And then I saw you. Your face, in the light. Didn't have anything else to do. I just started walking towards it, following you."

North shifted uncomfortably. "Anevay - she's wary of you. Do you know why?"

Myra's expression flickered briefly, something hidden stirring behind her eyes. "No idea. Never met her before this. Maybe she can sense the mistakes I carry, the ones I can't hide." She looked at him, reaching across the table, a hand over his. "Or maybe it's because she sees something in you that draws me in, something she thinks is only hers."

North pulled his hand from the table, retreating to the warmth of his pocket.

"Don't play games with me," he growled. "We're all but souls shipwrecked on the same shore, clinging to whatever wreckage is left behind, waiting for the tide."

Myra's smile was a crooked thing, not warm, but sharp, something that seemed to enjoy the tension. "I get it," she purred with a soft chuckle. "But when the time comes, will you stand on your own, or will you let someone like me share your raft?"

His gut knotted. Her words felt like a challenge, daring him to respond. He stood abruptly, ready to leave, to escape her unsettling smile. But something stopped him, and he turned back, his anger simmering beneath the surface.

"Ellie works in the greenhouses. Anevay is a nurse," he said, his voice hard. "What do you contribute, Myra? What do you offer Browers?"

She smiled again, slower this time as if she held some secret only for him. "Nothing."

North's jaw clenched. "You'll clean this place. Every day. There will be a list, and you'll follow it. And if I ask you to help Ellie or Anevay, you'll do it without giving me any - shit. Do we understand each other?"

Her smile widened, full of mischief. "Of course. Now, how about showing me around this place you want so spotless?"

North scowled, his patience worn thin, and walked away without another word.

***

North climbed the stairs, each step a reminder of the uneasy silence Myra had left behind. Her voice, laced with anguish, stayed with him, a burden that seemed to grow heavier with each thought. Once in his room, he sat at his desk and switched on the lamp. The faint light cast shapes that reminded him of Myra's smile, ghostly and haunting on the walls.

He opened a drawer, took out a pad of paper, and began drafting a cleaning checklist, one that Myra would need to follow. As he wrote, her story crept back into his mind, raising a flood of uncertainty. The image of her - isolated, cast away by both family and society - stirred something in him. He had seen that same emptiness in others, the kind that came from wandering too long through life's cruelties, searching for something they might never find.

He considered what their relationship might become.

Surely, it will be fraught with complexity, built on a foundation of hardship and a mutual understanding of survival in this harsh world. There's something in her, though, a glimpse of strength that won't quite die. Still, she hesitates, unwilling to face her demons. If nothing else, she thrives in the disorder she leaves behind.

Despite this, North didn't trust her. He didn't care for her playful provocations or the spark of something unspoken between them.

Was it all a game to her, a strategy to unsettle Ellie and Anevay?

His gaze fell to the list before him, an attempt to impose order and control. But he had another purpose.

These menial tasks will keep her at arm's length.

After copying the list multiple times, he went to bed. Closing his eyes, he tried to push away the memory of her touch, her laughter. Yet the quiet darkness magnified it all, twisting it into something grotesque, far from any human connection. When sleep finally came, it was fitful, full of disturbing visions. He wandered through endless corridors lined with faces - students, frozen in agony, accusing him with eyes full of questions for which he had no answers. And then, from the depths, Myra emerged, her smile twisted, pulling him further into the shadows of his own mind.

He awoke suddenly, gasping for breath, his skin damp with sweat. The pale morning light began to creep through the high window, exposing the room with an unforgiving brightness. Glancing at the clock on his bedside table, he saw it was only 4 a.m.

He turned on the lamp by his bed, letting its warmth dispel the shadows that clung to the room's corners. With a practiced motion, he reached for the bookshelf. His hand hovered over Hemingway before settling on the familiar leather spine of a Keats collection.

Pulling it from the shelf, the book's weight and feel provided a strange comfort. As he flipped through the pages, he stopped at "Ode to a Nightingale," lingering over the lines before pausing at *But, to the world, is blind and deaf.* He remembered his old lectures, how he used to talk about the beauty that lay beyond human understanding, a vastness that made the world seem both inviting and unknowable.

He remembered his lecture notes. *Beauty exists outside of human comprehension, suggesting a vast unknown universe beyond our senses. The speaker might fear this vastness and his limited understanding of it.*

North snapped the book shut, the sound cutting through the early morning stillness.

"Professor, is everything okay?"

It was Ellie.

"What are you doing up so early?' he asked, surprised.

"I saw the light under your door. Thought I'd check on you."

He sighed. "I'm fine."

Her eyes caught the book on the desk. "Keats again. Why do you read him so often?"

North hesitated, searching for the right words. The old certainty he once had about such things felt far away now. He looked at Ellie, noticing the freckles scattered across her nose in the first light of dawn. Keats seemed almost out of place here, in a world so drained of beauty.

"He reminds me of something we've lost," North said, slowly. "Of a world that once held beauty, even in its chaos. Maybe it's what we're trying to reclaim, even now."

Ellie smiled gently. "I'll make us some breakfast." She rested her hand on his shoulder briefly before heading to the kitchen.

Alone again, North glanced at the checklist in front of him, once a symbol of control and routine. Now, it felt like something else - a small step toward surrender.

17 *The eleven tables*

Anevay walked over to the sink and scrubbed her hands with an intensity that mirrored the unease settling deep within her. Myra's presence lingered on her, not physically, but in a way that was hard to explain - something about her didn't sit right. Anevay couldn't point to a single cause, yet the disquiet gnawed at her. There was an unfamiliar wrongness, like a faint distortion in something that should have been straightforward.

She dried her hands briskly, turning her attention back to the task at hand. The exam room felt oddly changed, as though the space had absorbed the intimacy of what had occurred. The gown, discarded and forgotten, draped from a hook in the corner, its folds still bearing the imprint of Myra's fragile form. Anevay wiped down the exam table, the antiseptic scent clashing with the lingering phantom sweetness of new life in the air.

"Another exam already?" North's voice startled her. "How many has it been now?" He stood in the doorway, his face lined with concern, the perpetual worry evident in his eyes.

Anevay glanced at her notes. "This was the thirtieth."

"How is she?"

"She's - " Anevay paused, her professional veneer faltering. "She's managing, but tired, as you'd expect."

"And the baby?"

"Thriving." Anevay nodded, but her smile wavered. "Everything's right on track."

North exhaled heavily, though the relief was tempered by something deeper, a worry that ran beneath the surface. "That's good news."

"There are things to watch, though," Anevay added carefully.

His eyes narrowed. "Medical?"

"Always medical," she replied, managing a humorless smirk. "She needs more rest, more food. Her blood pressure is creeping higher, and her heart's skipping beats. She's healthy for now - but that could change."

"How so?" His voice grew tight.

"She's at risk. Preeclampsia. It's serious."

North leaned forward. "What does that mean?"

"The high blood pressure, the irregular heartbeat - it could lead to seizures. Worse. Death."

The starkness of the word clung to them.

"Is there anything you can do?" His question came on the heels of worry.

"I've started her on medication. But it's not a cure. She needs rest, and less stress. That's the key."

North's gaze hardened. "Did you explain that to her?"

"I did," Anevay nodded. "Though I'm worried about her cleaning routine. I don't like her using all those chemicals."

"She's careful," North replied, irritation creeping into his voice. "She takes precautions, wearing a mask and gloves."

"It's still not ideal." Anevay shook her head, the concern persistent. "Especially with the baby."

North dismissed the comment. "Where is she now?"

"Resting, then back to work. I'll check on her later."

"Thank you." He sat down heavily. "We need to talk. There's something I've been putting off."

Anevay's heart sank. His tone was serious, the weight of it heavy in the room. "What is it?"

"When it all ended, I was with the old man," North began, his voice quiet. "I was terrified. Everything I knew, every routine, every shred of normalcy - gone. I'm sure you felt it too. But he asked me a question, one I can't forget. He asked me what I'd say to God if I was told I'd have to start everything over again."

Anevay blinked, unsure of how to respond. "What did you say?"

"I told him I wasn't ready." North smiled faintly, a hollow expression. "But he didn't like that. He said God doesn't wait for us to be ready. Then he told me to face my fear, to step into the unknown. Said that's the only way forward."

North's gaze locked onto hers. "I asked him one last thing."

"What was it?"

"I asked, 'What if I fail?'"

Anevay swallowed, feeling the tension between them.

"And he said, 'Then you fail. That's all anyone can do.'"

His voice cracked on the last word. "We have to try, Anevay. Myra - she's part of this, whether we trust her or not."

Anevay didn't speak for a long moment, then finally whispered, "I don't like her, North. Something about her - it's not right. When I examine her, her skin feels off - too cold, almost translucent."

North searched her face. "You've never seen that before?"

She shook her head. "No. The changes brought by pregnancy are unpredictable. Perhaps it's nothing." She hesitated and North felt there was something more. "It's just - there's something - off -. I can't explain it. It's a feeling I have. Something's different about her. Maybe it's just me."

He took her hand, his grip firm. "It's not just you. I feel it too."

"Then why did we let her in?" Anevay asked, her voice strained.

"We've been through all this before. You know the reason - because we had no other choice. The old man said there would be three. Now there are. And for the sake of the babies -all of them - have to work together if we're to survive what we're living in - this divine reset."

Divine reset.

The phrase struck Anevay as both oddly amusing and profoundly disturbing. Her heart pounded in her chest, the reality of their situation pressing down on her. She wasn't ready for this, for the uncertainty that had crept into every corner of their lives.

She swallowed hard and looked down at her belly, the tiny life growing inside of her a reminder of the choices she had made. She had never wanted to be a mother, but now that she soon would be, she would do anything to protect her child.

Anevay took a deep breath. "I'll try."

"That's all I ask," North said.

"Have you told all this to Ellie?"

"I did when she first arrived."

"Myra?"

"She knows about the old man," North admitted, his gaze drifting. "But not - not in such detail."

"Why haven't you told her everything?"

He shrugged, the motion more a reflex than a casual gesture. "What difference would it make? I doubt she would grasp the deeper, more spiritual aspects of it all."

North stood, leaving Anevay alone with her thoughts. The silence of the room was deafening, filled with a tension that had no resolution. Her fingers drifted to her own belly, tracing the slight curve there. She wasn't prepared for motherhood, for the weight of responsibility it carried, but she had no choice now.

Later, in the cold grasp of her bed, sleep remained distant. Behind her eyelids, Myra's face emerged, distorted in a way that gnawed at Anevay's sense of safety, dragging her deeper into the murk of fear.

Myra - what is she? What does she seek?

Anevay had no answers, only the certainty that Myra posed a threat. Not a serpent lying in wait, but a gathering storm on the horizon, promising an inevitable downpour. Anevay needed to be prepared.

She shut her eyes again, not with any hope of rest, but as an act of defiance. Dawn would come, and with it, the decision to face that storm directly. Myra was waiting.

***

That night, North sat with his pen poised above the paper, not writing but hovering, as if uncertain of how to begin. What had once been a tool for recording lectures now felt foreign in his hand, and the blank page stared back at him, vast and unforgiving.

So many days had passed. Mornings swallowed by smoke, nights overcome by shadows that never seemed to lift.

Civilization had crumbled, leaving behind a husk of faded colors and fragments of a life long gone. He had watched it all dissolve into dust and silence. There was no going back - no return to what once was - but there remained a duty to carry forward, to create something from the wreckage. Life had to go on. He envisioned a set of instructions, a guide for survival, something to leave behind for those who would come after.

But how to capture the unraveling of everything? How to describe the hollow, eerie laughter that echoes through empty streets, the wind tugging through skeletal remains of buildings that once held so much life?

Memories of the past assaulted him, the scenes of devastation replaying in his mind. He shut his eyes tightly, willing them away, but they lingered, vivid and unshakable. The lifeless bodies that had littered the streets, the metallic taste in the air - he could almost feel it now, biting and acrid. Oddly, there had been little blood, no pools marking the end. People had simply vanished, erased from existence, leaving behind nothing but emptiness.

The world had shifted, changed in ways he couldn't have imagined. In the immediate aftermath, grief had consumed him, his thoughts scattered, unable to process the magnitude of it all. He'd wanted to cry, to scream, to fight against the cruel suddenness of it, but numbness had set in. There was no energy left for feeling.

And then, the howling. It had started softly, a distant, sorrowful sound that seemed to grow with every second. Soon it became a force, a wall of noise so powerful that it made the ground tremble. The sound still haunted his dreams, though they had grown fewer. The glowing eyes, the sharp teeth - they had appeared without warning, leaving him shivering as the memory of them returned.

He tried, but there was no forgetting. Every moment was too sharp, too real as if the past refused to let go. It clung to him, relentless.

His eyes flicked around the room, taking in the surroundings that offered some measure of peace. Order, control - this was his sanctuary, untouched by the chaos outside. Everything had its place: books, papers, tools. All aligned perfectly, providing a sense of stability.

Not like it was before.

The walls were bare, except for a few carefully chosen pictures, each one hung with exactness. And in the silence, the rhythmic ticking of the clock was the only reminder that time still moved forward.

Yet, even now, after all that had happened, a flicker of hope stirred in him. They had come - the three. Just as the old man had promised. They were here to plant the seeds of what might grow. Perhaps, against all odds, there was still a chance. A new beginning. A place where the mistakes of the past would not be repeated, where they could forge something better, kinder.

Maybe. Just maybe. There's still a chance to build a new and better world. A world without war, without poverty, without hatred. A world where everyone can live in peace and harmony.

Enough. It was time. He put the pen to paper. The scratching sound was grating, but he forced himself to focus, his hand steady. There was no room for error. This was important -

what he needed to pass on, what those who remained needed to hear.

He wrote:

To whoever finds this,

You don't know me. I am a time traveler of sorts. A voice of someone who remembers a time when the world was beautiful. When the forests were green, the rivers were clear, and the air was clean. There were animals and plants of all kinds. And there were people, billions of them.

But that all changed. In a single moment, in a blink of an eye, the world was gone. Cities were empty, the forests dead, and the air stale.

I was one of the chosen ones, along with three others, the mothers of all the living. We were the only ones spared from the destruction, and we were tasked with rebuilding the world.

I'm writing this to you, whoever you are, in the hope that you will find it, you will read it, and you will understand that there was a time before yours. A time when the world was full of life and hope. I want you to believe that it's possible to rebuild that world, to create a better future for yourselves and for your children.

It won't be easy. It will take hard work, determination, and cooperation. But I believe that you can do it. I believe in you. Why? Because I know the mothers of all the living. I helped to protect them, to save them from the emptiness, so that you may have life.

The road ahead will always be long and hard. You must always be determined to see it through, and you have to believe that a better future is always possible, even if it seems impossible.

I know that you may be scared. I know that you may have seen things that no one should ever have to see. But you're not alone. Everyone is in this together. And you will get through this.

As I write this I know I must not dwell on the past, what the world once was. It serves no purpose. All that is necessary for you to know is that everything has changed. But even though things have changed, know that the rules of life still apply, rules set down over ages upon ages, by many civilizations that came before this. I now give you these rules, eleven of them, what I call tables. I use this word because there was an ancient time, well before the end of it all, when rules were inscribed onto bronze tablets and displayed in a public area where they could be read by all people.

It is important that you live by these rules. Doing so will help you to rebuild the world, to create a better future for yourselves and for your children.

1. Cherish life. Life is a precious gift, and it must be valued.
2. Protect the innocent. The innocent must be protected from harm, no matter what the cost.
3. Do no harm. Even in the most difficult of times, we must always strive to do no harm to others and be kind to one another.
4. Respect the natural world. We are stewards of the Earth, and we must care for it.
5. Be strong. In the face of adversity, we must be strong. We must never give up hope.
6. Be wary of the unknown. The world has changed in ways that we do not understand. There are new dangers lurking in the shadows. Be careful and trust your instincts.

7. Never give up hope. The future may seem bleak, but there's still hope. If you work together, you can rebuild the world, and create a better future for yourselves and your children.

8. Honor your elders. The experience and wisdom of the old can guide the young.

9. Never forget the old ways. The knowledge and wisdom of the past is essential for rebuilding a better future.

10. There will always be dogs. But where there is darkness, shine a light. In the darkest of times, it's easy to give in to despair. We must never forget that there's always light, even in the darkest of places. Find the strength to shine that light, even when it seems impossible.

11. Never ever forget the mothers of all the living, and never forget that they sacrificed for you.

He folded the paper carefully, his fingers tracing the worn crease, before slipping it into the drawer. Each word, penned with care, was a spark, warm against the memory of fear. He hoped that one day, those who came after would read these lines, take them to heart, and shape a world better than the one left in ruins.

Hope. A flame that is difficult to extinguish.

His knees stiffened as he rose from the chair, making his way to the window. It rose high on the wall, offering no view, yet he could picture the world outside enveloped in the dusky hues of twilight, so unlike the life he had once embraced. Still, even in the face of this altered reality, he held onto the belief that the world could still be a place of hope.

He drew a breath, a small smile tugging at the corner of his mouth, tentative at first before growing with quiet confidence. He'd endure. They'd endure.

At least, he hoped so.

18 Sunflowers

The next several weeks tested them all.

Ellie tended to the greenhouses and fields while North, rifle in hand, kept a vigilant eye on the horizon. His mind remained fixed on threats beyond their walls, though this took him from the repairs and checks he normally managed to keep everything running smoothly. Anevay did what she could, helping when her time allowed, though her focus stayed on her daily physical checkups of Ellie and Myra. Meanwhile, the weather was beginning to change.

Days shortened, and the nights took on a sharper chill. The wind, once gentle, had gained an unsettling edge, tugging relentlessly at the periphery of their world, its voice growing harsher with each gust. Every stir of air seemed to carry an unspoken warning, the promise of winter tightening its grip, with its own bitter challenges lurking at the edges of their already strained lives.

North's presence never strayed far from Ellie as she worked. His eyes, once fixated on the detailed work of managing supplies and overseeing the building's equipment, had shifted outward, surveying the horizon for any sign of danger. Vigilance was necessary, but it stole from him the hours he needed to tend to his other tasks.

"We've got enough stores to last for a while," he said to Ellie. "But what if the winter stretches longer than usual? What happens when we're snowed in with no way to resupply?"

Ellie's eyes met his, calm yet unyielding. "We'll manage," she replied. "We always do."

But North couldn't shake the growing fear within him. It burrowed deep, transforming from a simple concern to a deepening sense of dread. It felt like a cold stone lodged in the pit of his stomach. Shadows seemed to creep in at the corners of his vision, vanishing the moment he tried to focus. And at night, new sounds began to punctuate the dark - strange, dissonant notes that disturbed what little rest he managed.

One evening, a crash from outside jolted him awake. Grabbing his rifle, North rushed out to find Ellie already near the barn, her face pale and stricken.

"What are you doing out here?" he demanded, his words lost in the wind's roar. "You know the rules."

A choked response escaped her lips. "I saw something - near the woods. In the clearing. Listen."

He held his breath, the world narrowing to the sound of her fear and the rustle of hidden things. Waiting.

The wind tore through the night, a wild, relentless force. North squinted, straining to catch anything beyond its roar. Then it came - low and feral, a growl that seemed to thrum beneath the skin, seeping into the very marrow. Something prowled in the dark, advancing with silent precision toward their fragile shelter. A creeping dread settled over him, heavy and undeniable - their sanctuary wouldn't protect them for much longer.

"Get inside the barn," he barked.

But Ellie stood motionless, gripped by a terror that mirrored his own.

"Now!" His voice broke, raw with fear. "Do as I say!"

At last, she stirred, her body jolting back into action. She fled into the barn, vanishing into the dark as North followed, slamming the door shut behind them with a force that rattled the structure. Inside, Ellie shrank against the far corner, her eyes wide, reflecting the dim light filtering in through the small window.

"I'm scared," she whispered.

North pulled her close, his own fear cloaked in the gruffness of someone used to hiding it. "You're safe," he said, though the quiver in his voice betrayed him. "I'm here."

But even as he held her, North knew the truth. He was afraid, too.

When the noises outside finally faded, replaced by the steady howl of the wind, North eased the barn door open, peering out into the gloom. Nothing stirred. With a swift motion, he brought Ellie to his side, and together they moved quickly through the cold, their breath sharp in the air as they bolted toward the safety of the greenhouses.

***

The days dragged on, each one more burdensome than the last, with fear trailing behind like a shadow that refused to leave. Ellie's laughter had begun to fade, replaced by startled cries in the middle of the night and nervous glances cast over her shoulder. Anevay moved through the hours with a fragile stillness, her smile stretched thin and her eyes unfocused, as though she saw something just out of reach. North knew that her unease wasn't merely due to the hidden dangers in the woods; Myra too weighed heavily on her mind, drifting through Browers like a wisp, leaving behind an air of unease wherever she passed.

North was starting to lose hope. The air thickened with unspoken thoughts, shadows seeming to stretch and creep toward the edges of their fragile world. He had always believed that careful preparation would be enough to face any threat. Yet now, this lurking dread, this intangible menace, was unsettling his confidence. He feared for himself, for Ellie, for Anevay, and for Myra. How much longer could they endure like this?

One night, as fear clung to the room like a bitter scent, North sat in the common area, a book of Keats' poetry idly resting in his hands. His mind churned with sounds from earlier - a rustling in the woods, something like branches breaking underfoot, or perhaps something far more sinister moving unseen.

Ellie was asleep in her room, and Anevay was making tea, the sharp whistle cutting through the silence like a plea. Yet even the familiar rhythm of the household couldn't soothe the tightness in his chest. His dreams, those feverish landscapes of whispers and menacing shadows that took on terrifying shapes, replayed behind his closed eyes. The sense of being watched never left him.

Then, a sound from outside. North tensed, rising from his chair. He crossed the room and glanced through the window, eyes narrowing against the darkness. Something large and fluid moved among the trees, its form both graceful and disturbing.

Fear, cold and sharp, surged within him. He grabbed the rifle, the metal slick against his trembling grip, and stepped out into the night. The creature, a vague, shifting presence, glided silently between the trees, its movements too swift and smooth to be human. North gave chase, his breaths ragged, uneven bursts in the stillness, trying to keep pace with its unnatural glide.

At last, the figure paused, turning to face him. In the faint moonlight, its form solidified - tall and impossibly thin, its limbs like twisted branches, and its eyes glowing with a malicious light. The creature roared and North fired, the rifle bucking against his shoulder. The shot hit, but the creature barely flinched. A low, guttural growl filled the air before it sprang forward.

North raised the rifle again, but it was too late. The creature was upon him, claws slicing through the space between them. He felt the world go cold, the night closing in.

Ellie's voice pulled him back from the abyss. "Just a dream," she said softly, her hands steady against his trembling ones. "It was only a nightmare."

He exhaled shakily, and managed a tired, defeated nod. "Another one."

But this one felt different. The dream was too vivid, too sharp. The creature was out there, somewhere, and its shadow threatened ever closer. Sleep, when it returned, offered little peace. North lay in the dark, alert to every sound, every movement, unwilling to let his guard down again.

***

Dawn arrived, a dim wash of gray smeared across the clouds, and North quietly stepped outside, his rifle resting in the crook of his arm, eyes scanning the stillness. The woods offered no hint, holding their secrets tightly. Silence was all he found.

Inside, breakfast was subdued. Anevay stirred her oatmeal absently, her face drawn, a shadow of herself in the pale morning light. North knew she was plagued by the same troubled dreams, the ones where Myra's laughter lingered, and the eerie sensation of being watched followed her like a ghost. He'd thought of sharing his own dreams with her, but the risk of stirring something dangerous held him back. Ellie, meanwhile, focused on her toast, only bothered by the cold that seeped through the walls and the cows waiting to be milked.

"Heard you get up early," Ellie remarked, taking a sip of coffee. "How are you feeling?"

He offered her a thin smile and gave a slight nod.

"Did you find anything outside?"

North shook his head. "Same as always. Just the wind."

Ellie glanced at the window. "Looks like it's going to be a nasty one. Clouds look bruised, and the wind's got a mean bite."

North's voice roughened with unspoken worry. "Matches how I'm feeling, I suppose."

Anevay finally spoke, her voice a soft murmur. "It's more than just the weather. More than the dreams."

North turned to her. "You feel it too?"

"I'm sure of it," Anevay replied, eyes sincere. "The same images, the same unease. It's a warning, isn't it? Something's out there, watching."

North caught a brief glance from Ellie, her eyes betraying her concern.

"Then we keep watching," he said firmly. "And make sure whatever it is knows we're not backing down." His gaze swept the room. "Where's Myra?"

Anevay's lips curled into a small, knowing smile. "Where she always is, somewhere in the shadows."

Ellie shrugged in agreement.

Later, as the pale sun struggled through the dense clouds, Ellie found Myra in the greenhouse among the sunflowers. Her laughter filled the space, bright against the yellow blooms. Yet beneath it was a sharpness, a cold edge Ellie couldn't quite ignore. It was a sound that seemed to belong to a world only Myra knew, a tune woven for the gathering dark.

Sensing Ellie's gaze, Myra turned, a teasing smile on her lips. "Sunflowers," she said lightly, "always face the light, even when it's barely there."

Ellie didn't respond, her eyes lingering. "You don't have to keep up the act," she said gently. "Not with me."

Myra's smile faltered. "Act?" she shot back, a touch defensive.

Ellie stepped closer. "Even sunflowers get tired of chasing the sun."

19   The illness

"Sunflowers," Myra cracked, a sound that could have been a laugh or a sigh. "Always reaching for a light they can barely feel. Stubborn little things, aren't they?"

Ellie watched Myra as she idly toyed with the sunflower in her hand, fingers deftly plucking its petals. She watched, unsure whether she was looking at the troubled girl she'd known or something far more elusive.

Is she a troubled seventeen-year-old, or something else?

A sharp unease settled in Ellie's chest. It was a feeling she couldn't quite name, a tension between Myra's playful cruelty and the quiet suffering she sensed in the flower being pulled apart. It was the ache of witnessing beauty being dismantled, petal by petal.

"I wish you wouldn't do that," Ellie's voice came out more strained than intended.

"Do what?"

"Just - leave the flowers alone."

Myra's expression softened, almost as though she was surprised by the request. She held the sunflower with a surprising tenderness now. "You and your flowers," she mused. "Always wanting the world to be kind, even to things that struggle against it."

Ellie's patience snapped, her voice rising. "Stop it already."

"Stop what?"

"You don't have to pretend with me. Not anymore."

Myra's lips curled, a faint trace of amusement. "Pretend? I'm not pretending anything."

Ellie stood firm. "You don't have to be what you think we expect. The fragile thing, the girl lost in the world. Maybe there's something else beneath all that - maybe you're protecting yourself with thorns."

Myra's smile faltered. "I'm not playing any part," she replied coolly, turning back to the sunflower. "I'm just here to learn a bit more about the plants you fuss over."

Ellie refused to back down. "I see more than you think. We all care about what happens here. We work hard, and we survive."

"Surviving doesn't mean playing by the rules, Ellie," Myra said lightly. "Sometimes, the most important work happens when no one is looking."

Ellie took a step closer, her tone steady. "Hiding in the shadows can twist things, Myra. It can turn something good into something dangerous."

Myra's gaze shifted to the flowers around them, bright and full of life. "Intentions are just stories we tell ourselves," she remarked quietly. "They don't matter. What matters is the end result."

"And what's the end result here? What are you after? What secrets are you hiding?"

Myra's eyes narrowed with a sudden sharpness. "Secrets," she said, her voice low, "are like weeds. They grow anywhere, whether you want them or not."

Ellie felt something fragile in Myra's demeanor as if the lightness of her words no longer matched the gravity of what lay beneath.

"But even weeds seek warmth," Ellie replied, her own voice steady despite the uncertainty inside.

Myra's face changed, a fleeting shift, something raw showing through the layers she had built. "True," she said. "But the sun burns. Sometimes the only mercy's in the shade."

Ellie saw it then. Myra wasn't some broken thing, not a soul lost to the tide. She moved through her own pain, carrying it in ways no one else could. The hard lines she showed weren't rebellion. They were how she stayed alive. It was clear now.

"We all live in shadows sometimes," Ellie said, her words carrying a weight of understanding. "But we can't grow without light. Together, we can find our way through."

Myra reached out, her fingers brushing Ellie's hand. "Together," she echoed, her smile faint but genuine. "Thank you, Ellie. You've shown me something today. But I've been wondering... there's a plant I noticed that doesn't seem like it belongs here."

"What do you mean?"

Myra led her to two tall shrubs with deep green leaves and stems that gleamed a reddish-purple, weighed down by clusters of dark berries.

"What are these?" she asked.

Ellie's voice tightened. "Pokeweed. It's toxic."

Myra's hand hovered near the berries. "Toxic?"

Ellie's tone grew sharper. "Yes, don't touch them. They're poisonous."

Myra pulled her hand back, a puzzled look on her face. "I was right then. It doesn't belong here. So why would they keep such a thing in a place like this?"

"Danger has its place too," Ellie acknowledged. "They often blend in with their surroundings. Even things that can hurt have a purpose. The berries can be used for a vivid crimson dye, and the leaves and roots, when prepared properly, can help with inflammation and infection." She lightly touched a pokeweed leaf, her gesture both cautious and respectful. "But it must be boiled twice. Even then, there's always some risk."

"So boiling it twice . . ." Myra started.

"Doesn't always remove the danger," Ellie finished.

Myra stepped closer, and without warning, she embraced Ellie. Her voice was soft, almost wistful. "These moments we share - they matter. Promise me we'll have more."

Caught off guard, Ellie found herself nodding before she could speak.

Myra clapped her hands, light and giddy. "Good. I won't forget this. Together."

With a smile that seemed to say more than words, Myra turned and walked away, leaving Ellie standing there, the warmth of the hug fading faster than she liked. A biting sense of doubt crept in, a question forming in her mind.

Was it real, that closeness, or was she just another flower Myra planned to pull apart?

***

That evening, they gathered for a simple supper: roasted vegetables and scrambled eggs, fresh from the hens. The conversation came in starts and stops, awkward and fleeting. Myra, trying to keep the mood light, recounted her morning stroll through the greenhouses, her eyes gleaming with an uncharacteristic excitement.

"I swear," she said softly, "those tomatoes, Ellie, are nothing short of magic. Maybe I could lend a hand in the greenhouses. Help you out."

North raised an eyebrow, clearly taken aback. Myra wasn't one to volunteer for chores, let alone follow through on her daily tasks. Still, there was something almost innocent in the way she offered.

"That would be - nice," he replied, his own surprise softened by the warmth of his smile. "Ellie could use the help, especially with harvest approaching."

Ellie nodded slowly, though her tone carried a note of caution. "As long as your own work doesn't fall behind."

Anevay remained quiet, her gaze distant as she sipped her tea. The silence stretched between them, until Myra, sensing the shift, stood with a faint rustle of her dress.

"Anevay, more tea?" she offered, her voice light. "I'll heat some water."

Anevay hesitate. She wasn't sure how to respond. "Oh - sure. Thank you," she managed.

North noticed the flicker of tension in Anevay's posture. "Myra, I can - "

But Myra was already moving, taking Anevay's cup with brisk purpose. "Nonsense. After all the care you've given, let me spoil you for once."

Though wary, Anevay held the cup out. Myra took it with a flourish, her movements deliberate, almost theatrical, as she turned her back to them, busying herself with the teapot.

"It's a blend I came up with," Myra called over her shoulder, her tone cheerful. "Fresh herbs from the greenhouses."

Ellie blinked in surprise. "I didn't know you'd been experimenting with the herbs."

Myra handed the steaming cup back to Anevay. "Be careful, it's hot."

Anevay accepted it cautiously. "Thank you. It does smell wonderful."

North observed as Myra smiled - a brief, sharp expression, gone in an instant. He thought he saw something flicker in her eyes, but dismissed it as a trick of the dim light.

Taking more sips of her tea, Anevay joined in the talk of harvest plans and schedules. But soon, the easy flow of words broke. Anevay gasped, her hand shooting to her stomach, her face blanching as pain overtook her. The cup fell from her hand, its contents splashing across the table in a vivid crimson.

Anevay collapsed, her breath coming in gasps, her body trembling uncontrollably. Ellie and North jumped to their feet, the earlier comfort in the room replaced with panic. North cleared the space around Anevay, shoving aside chairs and pulling a cushion to place under her head.

"What's happening?" Ellie cried, her voice shaking. "Anevay, what's wrong?"

Anevay's body continued to convulse until she vomited, a flood of bile spilling onto the floor. She clutched her abdomen, her words strained through clenched teeth. "Pain . . . nausea . . . cramps . . ."

North's heart raced, a deep fear sinking in as he watched Anevay, someone he cared for like family, writhing in agony.

Ellie knelt beside her, tears glistening in her eyes. "We'll get you to bed. You're going to be alright."

As Ellie and North helped Anevay to her feet, Ellie's eyes flicked toward the teacup. The reddish stain on the table seemed more pronounced now, a dark hint of something troubling. A thought struck her, sudden and cutting. She remembered Myra's interest in the pokeweed plants.

North sensing Ellie's focus, followed her gaze. "What is it?" he asked, his face, now showing deepening dread. He turned sharply to Myra, his expression hardening. "You! What have you done?"

20 *The cage*

North gripped Myra's arm, dragging her up the stairs with an intensity that could hardly be contained. Her cries of protest vanished under the relentless pounding of his heart, each beat driving him forward with an unrelenting force. He didn't release her until they reached her room, where the tight corridor magnified every sound - their footsteps, their breathing, their anger.

"Let go of me!" Myra twisted in his grasp, but North's fingers only dug deeper, pinching her skin with exacting cruelty. "You can't treat me like this!"

His voice was dark and brimming with menace. "Keep your mouth shut," he hissed, every word a deliberate strike. "After what you did – I'll do whatever I damn well please!"

With a final, brutal shove, he sent her stumbling into the cold, empty room, the door slamming shut with a detonating clang. He stood there for a moment, chest heaving, nerves frayed. "I'll deal with you later."

The key in the lock turned slowly as if resisting the finality of the action, the grind of the metal matching the churn in his gut. From behind the door, Myra's laughter drifted through, distorted and eerie, needling him with every note. The sound ripped at his core, stoking the fire of his anger. He had let this happen. Let her get to him.

Leaving Myra's chaos behind, North made his way to the infirmary. Ellie sat beside Anevay's bed, her body stiff with tension, her gaze distant. The only movement came from the muscles in her jaw, clenching and unclenching in a steady rhythm.

"Did you take care of her?" Ellie asked, the words struggled to escape her throat, coming out soft and brittle. Her eyes, shadowed by something North couldn't quite place, were locked on his.

North gave a brief nod. "For now." His voice sounded hollow, even to himself. Looking at Anevay's pale, unmoving form and Ellie's silent vigil beside her, he felt an urge to fix things, to make it all right. But what could he offer beyond empty gestures and futile promises? "What've you done to help her?"

"I've given her plenty of water," Ellie's voice wavering with a fragile hope. "I think it should help."

North moved closer, resting a hand on Ellie's shoulder, feeling the tension that coiled there, the silent fears she kept tucked away.

"You're doing everything you can," he offered quietly, though the words felt thin, as much for his own comfort as hers.

Ellie gave the faintest of nods, her eyes still fixed on Anevay. "I hope so," her voice breaking slightly. "I just … I need her to be okay."

North squeezed her shoulder gently, the only reassurance he could offer. "We'll get her through this, " he promised.

Anevay stirred, her head shifting on the pillow as she blinked up at them. Her skin was pale, her expression faint, but she managed a small, fleeting smile. It was a brave attempt, though it quickly faltered, her head sinking back with a soft sigh.

Her voice snagged on the question. "What happened to me?"

"We're not sure," North admitted, his frustration simmering beneath the surface. "But Myra ... we think she did something to the tea."

"She was asking strange questions earlier about the plants, especially the pokeweed," Ellie's voice trembling as she approached a truth they all feared. "It's a pretty plant to look at, but dangerous if you don't know what you're doing."

Anevay's eyes widened slightly as she absorbed the information, her breathing shallow. "Well, whatever it was, the worst seems to be passing." She paused, gathering what little strength she had left. "The fever's breaking. But the trick's in the mending."

"What can we do now?" North asked.

Anevay offered a tired smile. "More water, some ice to keep me cool. And ... one more thing."

His voice was barely controlled, full of desperation. "Anything. Just tell me."

"Myra..." Anevay's voice faltered, her lips barely moving.

North leaned over. "Yes?"

Anevay gave a shallow sigh. "She needs to go away."

Ellie was quick to agree, her voice firm despite her exhaustion. "I'll second that."

North stood tall, his resolve hardening. "I'll handle her. You just focus on getting better."

The hallway felt narrower as North left, Anevay's request lingering in his mind. Myra wasn't just a nuisance—she was a threat to the fragile peace they had worked so hard to maintain. Something was shifting, and he couldn't afford to let it unravel. He clenched his jaw, frustration simmering inside him.

His jaw clenched tight. *What game is she playing? If she did this, then . . .*

The stillness inside Brower's wasn't comforting. It was heavy and oppressive. And then, breaking through the silence, came the sound of laughter. Not joyous laughter, but something twisted and cruel, like a wail from some wicked creature keening at the moon. It was Myra, somewhere behind those closed doors, and her laughter crawled over his skin, cold and relentless.

North stood frozen, every nerve on edge. Something had to be done - before it was too late.

***

North hesitated before taking another step forward. The hallway seemed to groan beneath him, each sound amplifying the tension in the air. He hadn't come this far without purpose before, yet now he stood at Myra's door, uncertain. The sound of her laughter and giggles twisted inside him, something strange and wrong in the way it came. He fumbled for the key, trembling, fingers stiff, unsure whether to turn or retreat. The handle was cold beneath his grip, waiting for him to decide.

The laughter stopped, replaced by a faint whisper that barely reached his ears. "North?"

His hand shook over the cold handle, lingering before sliding the key into place. The door opened slowly, revealing Myra crumpled on the floor, her face hidden in her hands. The laughter that had filled the space moments before was gone, replaced by the harsh sobs of someone breaking apart.

He stood there, frozen in place. Words failed him as if the enormity of her despair could swallow his own anger whole. Yet the questions in his mind were relentless. He took a step closer, his movements quiet, and lowered himself to the floor beside her. He didn't try to speak or interrupt her grief. He simply sat there, a silent observer, unsure of what to do with the anger still coiled inside him.

"Myra," he began, his voice stretched, raw with the tension he could no longer hide. "We have to talk."

Her body tensed at his words, her face turning away as if avoiding a blow. "North, I . . . I didn't . . . I didn't mean to . . ."

She choked on the words, her voice collapsing beneath the weight of their situation. The lighthearted façade she had carried for so long had vanished. Her tears flowed freely now, and with each drop, her defenses fell further away.

He moved a little closer, torn between the anger that simmered just beneath the surface and the fragility of the moment. There was no room for tenderness, yet the fire in him demanded a release. He clenched his fists, holding himself back, trying to find a way through the storm. He spoke again, his voice low, almost pleading.

"Myra, you have to tell me the truth."

Her breath hitched, her gaze flickering toward him briefly before she surrendered. "It's not what you think," her voice shook in the stillness. "I didn't mean to . . . to hurt her."

North watched her, searching for something genuine in her words. She flinched under his scrutiny, the truth written in her trembling hands and tear-streaked face. He could see it all - the cracks in her story, the lies she had tried to bury under layers of guilt.

"Tell me everything," he urged, his voice a cracked vase holding the dregs of his anger. "I need the truth."

Myra's shoulders slumped. She looked at him, her eyes red-rimmed and raw. A single, stubborn sniffle escaped her nose. She knew the futility of resistance, the way he'd pick apart her lies, sift through the sand until he found the truth, hard and glittering like a buried gem.

"I put the berries in her tea," the ugly truth spilled. "I didn't mean . . . I thought it would be harmless. Just for a little color."

Fury flared in North's chest, rising to the surface in an uncontrollable wave. "You poisoned her for the sake of color?"

Her face paled as she stammered to explain, her words disintegrating under his fury. "I didn't know. I didn't. Ellie said –"

North cut her off, his voice harsher now. "Ellie told you what? That the berries were safe?"

Myra's voice shrank, reduced to a desperate whisper. "She said they were used for dye."

North's anger boiled over. "And you thought that meant they were harmless? You thought that was all there was to it?"

She recoiled from his words, guilt pressing her further into herself. The room felt smaller, the air thicker, and the silence that followed was unbearable.

North's anger burned fiercely, but beneath it was something darker - a realization that they had all reached a point of no return. But there was a smoldering, deeper ache, the rotted fruit of their shattered trust. He could see it in the way she looked at him now, her eyes hollow with the knowledge of what she had done.

He stood, his eyes falling on her swollen belly. The life she carried would alter their world irreversibly. He exhaled slowly, making a decision he had been avoiding.

"This room will be your prison," he said, his voice cold, detached. "I'll lock the door, and I will hold the key. You'll eat here, sleep here, live here. Once daily, Ellie and I will bring you to the bathroom to bathe. And I will stand guard as Anevay does her daily checkup. This is how it will be."

Myra's eyes grew distant, her spirit worn down by the storm they had both endured. She gave a small, resigned nod, knowing there was no other way. The trust between them was gone, and now only the rules remained.

"Shadow was right. She's always right," he told her.

"I hate that fucking cat," Myra shot back.

He paused, shaking his head, stunned by her words. As he turned to leave, his eyes fell on her rounded belly.

The child.

He took a deep breath. "This room will be your cage," he declared.

Myra, her tears dried up, gave a slow nod of resigned acceptance. The storm had passed, leaving everything behind fractured, but silent.

He opened the door. "This place is our home. But you've broken it."

"I am not a shadow," her voice trembling.

His eyes met hers with quiet understanding. "Remember, Myra, shadows only exist where there's light."

He closed the door behind him, locking it with a click that resonated in the now-empty hallway. Inside, Myra sat alone, resting her hand on her stomach. She knew the life growing inside her was the only tether she had left to the outside world.

***

Ellie stirred the pot, the steam curling upward like quiet secrets. "And Myra? How's she handling all of this?"

North took a long swallow from his cup, worry on his face. "She's like a bird in a cage. Trying to sing, trying to keep calm, but knowing full well the door remains locked."

Ellie's mouth set in a hard line. "So, she's a prisoner now?"

He nodded, the muscles in his jaw corded under his skin. "No choice in the matter."

"North, she can't stay." Her voice was firm.

He shook his head, frustration clear in his eyes. "What would you have me do? There's an unborn child to think about. You know what's at stake here."

Ellie bit her lip. She couldn't argue with that.

"We have to decide if she's dangerous," she said slowly. The words felt strange on her tongue. "Or if she's just lost. Lost to the things that happened before."

"Don't start down that road, Ellie."

"What road?"

"Don't make excuses for her, for what she's done."

But Ellie could see the way North's hand trembled slightly as he pushed his plate aside. Myra was more than just a threat to him. She was a threat, a painful reminder of the world they had left behind.

"Maybe there's a way to keep Anevay safe while still finding a place for Myra," Ellie said softly. "She has skills, North. She could help in the greenhouses, or even learn from you. We're going to need all the hands we can get with everything that's coming."

"Do we? Do we really need her?" His voice was heavy. "After what she did to Anevay?"

Ellie's gaze didn't waver. "We can't forget," she said, calm but firm. "But perhaps we can remember it differently."

North stood abruptly, the scrape of his plate against the sink breaking the quiet. "I don't know what the hell that means," he muttered, turning away. "And frankly, I'm not sure I want to. There are consequences to the choices we make."

He walked down the hall to check on Anevay. Ellie watched him go, her heart heavy. "Let me know when you're ready," she called after him, "and we'll take dinner to our caged bird."

***

Sunlight filtered through the willow branches outside, casting shifting patches of light across Anevay's face as she propped up on the pillows. Her eyes, though still marked by traces of pain, held a spark of resilience that North had come to expect.

"Seems you're doing well," North said, his tone lighter with relief. Then a grin broke through. "But what does the doctor say?"

Anevay smiled. "She says another day or two and I'll be back to my annoyingly lively self."

North chuckled. "Good. Just don't forget, once the doctor gives the all-clear, there'll be someone keeping you on your toes. Any idea who that might be?"

"You of course, with those damned checklists."

They laughed together.

He beamed, though it was a fragile gesture. He brushed a loose strand of hair from her forehead. "Take your time. Rest as long as you need." His eyes shimmered, a tear forming at the corner.

Anevay's hand instinctively moved to her belly. Her expression softened, a touch of maternal wonder dispelling the shadows. "The baby," she whispered, the word carrying a new reverence. "I can still feel the baby kicking about in there."

"That's wonderful," North replied softly. "But about Myra . . . I need to tell you. She won't be a threat to you again. I've made sure of it. She's locked in her room now, with no way to harm anyone."

Anevay's fingers dug into the mattress. "Good riddance. I hope she rots in there. But she shouldn't be here."

"I understand, " North placed a reassuring hand on hers. "But listen to me - this isn't over. We have to be smart. We need to think about the child that's coming. There's a future we need to build. Myra... well, she's part of that future, whether we like it or not."

Anevay's fingers gripped the edge of the mattress. "Good. Let her rot in there. She doesn't belong here."

"I know," North placed his hand over hers, trying to offer comfort. "But this isn't finished. We have to be careful. We need to think about the child, about what's ahead. Myra . . . she's still part of that, whether we like it or not."

Anevay turned to him, disbelief clouding her face. "North, are you out of your mind? She tried to kill me!"

"And we stopped her," he replied, his voice calm and steady. "She can't hurt anyone anymore. But we have to keep our eyes on the future. The three children, they're all we have left."

Anevay shifted her gaze, following the slant of sunlight as it moved across the wall. The silence stretched, filled with unspoken emotions. After a while, she sighed a long, weary breath.

"I won't trust her," she said quietly. "Ever. But I understand. For the child. For the future."

He squeezed her hand gently. "Don't worry. Right now, you just need to rest. Myra's locked away, and Ellie and I will be with you whenever you check on her."

Anevay glanced back at him, a hint of trust returning to her expression. "Thank you, North. For everything."

He managed a smile. "That's what family does. And this little one . . ." he gestured toward her belly, "this is family. We'll keep it safe, no matter what, even if it means dealing with a snake in our midst."

21 Mortimer

Mortimer settled deeper into his armchair, its arms worn and cushion flattened from years of use. Across from him, Edna lay on the couch, knitting needles resting in her hands. She had started a scarf for him, the dark brown wool a complement to his winter coat. Yet now, her fingers were still, and Edna too seemed at rest.

A tightening in Mortimer's chest quickened his heartbeat. "Edna," he called, his voice wavering. He reached for her hand, expecting its warmth. Instead, her skin felt cool under his touch.

In a fumbling motion, he grabbed the phone from the side table, but the line was dead, as quiet as the still room. His eyes flickered to the lamp. Its glow had dimmed and finally faded away. A strange discomfort filled him as he clicked the switch repeatedly, though darkness remained in the house, and outside the window, the familiar world had vanished into a consuming night.

I need to get help for Edna.

Neighbors were far off, and the nearest hospital was even farther. He pictured the journey he'd have to make, lifting Edna into the truck, driving the empty roads, hoping against hope that some distant town still held life.

Maybe I can get her to the hospital.

But as he approached her, something changed. Edna's form, once so solid, now shimmered at the edges, like a memory losing focus. "Edna?" His voice dropped to a whisper, his hand reaching out, but she was slipping from him. Slowly, impossibly, she faded, her body dissolving into nothingness, leaving behind only a faint trace of where she had been - her clothes, the unfinished scarf, knitting needles, wedding ring, and necklace.

Mortimer's chest heaved with a sorrow too deep to name. He bent down, clutching her wedding ring and the necklace he had given her on their fiftieth anniversary. He pressed them to his heart, tears falling silently, his world shrinking into the unbearable absence left behind.

What happened? Where did she go?

He sank back into his chair, his mind reeling. The world, as he knew it, had vanished in an instant, leaving him adrift, clinging to the fading memories of a life that had slipped through his fingers. He called for their dog, who came running, a loyal companion in the face of chaos. The dog looked at him, a silent question in its eyes, and gave a soft yelp before dissolving into nothingness. Whatever was happening was swift, merciful perhaps, but for Mortimer, it was a cruelty beyond measure.

The silence, a heavy blanket, enveloped him, drawing the breath from his lungs. No birdsong, no distant traffic, no human voices - the world had become a vast, empty stage, and he, in his sorrow, its unwilling actor. Clutching the small tokens of a life shared and now lost, he felt the crushing weight of his solitude, a burden so immense it threatened to consume him.

In the weeks that followed, Mortimer moved through a blur of routines, each day bleaker than the last. He didn't know what to do and stopped trying to make sense of what had happened eventually focusing solely on staying alive. He spent his time scouring stores for canned goods and dry supplies, always keeping his handgun close for protection against the eerie silence that now ruled the world. As he traveled from place to place, he never encountered another person - not a single soul – only the pieces of lives once lived, seen in scattered clothing and belongings. Occasionally, he caught sight of wild dogs, prowling the land, their eyes filled with a relentless hunger, but people - living, breathing people - had become a memory, like Edna, fading from his grasp.

Months passed, a relentless march of time that seemed to mock his solitude. Loneliness, a gnawing beast, consumed him. Memories of Edna, a haunting melody, that refused to fade. Her laughter, like the tinkling of delicate chimes, filled his thoughts, a bittersweet reminder of the joy they had once shared. Her touch, a gentle caress, lingered on his skin, a phantom warmth that offered fleeting solace. She had fussed over him with a love as steady as the rhythm of the tides, her presence a constant in his life. Without her, the emptiness was a vast chasm, a void that threatened to engulf him. In his darkest moments, when silence was a suffocating weight, he contemplated the unthinkable, a desperate yearning for release from the relentless ache of her absence.

One morning, as he settled into the familiar creak of the kitchen chair, the dim sunlight filtered through the half-drawn curtains, casting a soft glow over the table. He cradled the handgun in his hands, an odd comfort amidst the harsh silence that surrounded him. Each breath he took seemed to sting in the stillness, amplifying the sense of isolation that was his constant companion.

I've lived too many years. What does it anymore?

As he stared at the handgun, his mind drifted, contemplating the sensation of its chill against his lips. Suddenly, a brilliant light pierced through the murk of his mind, bright and strange. It shimmered, distant yet drawing him in. Squinting, his rheumy eyes strained against the radiance that seemed to pulse and shift, a living thing that sought to confound his senses. It was as if a match had been struck in a vast cavern, a pinprick of light blooming in the distance. The light grew clearer, resolving into the form of an old man, one who looked eerily familiar - like himself, but somehow different. Mortimer's breath faltered.

The figure before him was a reflection of his weathered flesh and bone. Every wrinkle, every age spot, every wisp of thinning white hair was achingly familiar. Yet, this other self, radiated a luminescence, a glow that seemed to emanate from within, like his very soul were alight.

As Mortimer stood transfixed, a voice whispered in his ear, so close he could feel the warmth of breath against his skin. It was a voice similar to his own, yet stripped of the gruffness of age, imbued instead with a soft, insistent urgency that made his heart quicken.

"Follow me," the voice whispered, soft but insistent, as though it knew him intimately, "for I am the light."

The phrase sank into the chambers of his consciousness, each repetition a pull that tugged at the very fabric of his being.

Mortimer moved with purpose, loading his truck as he had done countless times before. Tools, a coil of rope, a thermos of coffee, some dried foods, an old suitcase with clothes, and Edna's unfinished scarf were packed away carefully, as if preparing for a journey he couldn't yet understand. The truck creaked under the load, but Mortimer paid no mind. He opened the passenger door, speaking softly to the empty seat.

"Ready when you are, love," his voice soft as a prayer.

In his mind's eye, he saw Edna there with him, her silver hair catching the dim morning light, her smile as warm and familiar as ever. He settled into the driver's seat, the familiar leather yielding beneath his weight with a soft sigh. His hand moved instinctively to his coat pocket, fingers brushing against the cold, hard outline of the handgun. It was a gesture of reassurance, a new habit born of caution and uncertainty.

As Mortimer drove the car down the driveway and onto the main road, he found himself talking out loud to the empty space beside him. "Lovely day for a drive, isn't it, Edna?" he mused. But the words just hung there, unheard and unanswered. His gaze drifted toward the horizon where the sun, low and heavy, seemed to hang like a ripe peach on a tree.

With the open road ahead and the memory of Edna filling the seat beside him, a strange blend of loneliness and comfort settled in. The miles passed beneath the tires, marked only by the steady rhythm of his voice. He talked about the changing leaves, their garden plans, and how the trim on the house needed repainting again. The air in the car seemed to shift, bringing with it a warmth from the passenger seat. A fleeting movement caught his eye, but he didn't turn to look. He knew better than to chase what might vanish. But there she was, Edna, though silent, filled the space beside him as she had for over fifty years.

Her presence filled the space with a relief so overwhelming it brought a sting to his eyes. Tears threatened to spill over, but he blinked them back, focusing on the road ahead. He drove on, an old man and the ghost of his beloved, chasing a light towards a destination known only to the heart's compass.

Then, as if part of some natural rhythm, her voice broke through: "Don't forget to get your retirement check from the power plant." The words were as clear as if she were there.

He chuckled, half-surprised, half-saddened. "Everything's online now, Edna," he shook his head with a gentle smile. "Your memory is playing tricks on you, love."

"Tricks, is it?" her voice sharp as ever shot back. He could almost picture the familiar raise of her eyebrow, how it sometimes arched unmistakably. "My mind's as clear as ever, thank you kindly. It's you who's in need of a good shake. Make sure you get your due, you hear? All those years with grease under your nails and aches in your back - don't let them shortchange you now."

"Alright, alright," he chuckled.

"And that thermos, you brought. Coffee, no doubt. Mind the doctor's words now. One cup, that's your lot. You need to be careful with your blood pressure."

"Yes, yes," Mortimer sighed, the words escaping like steam from a kettle. "One cup. I remember."

They slipped into an old conversation, one they'd shared many times over the years. Life had changed so much, yet they often wondered if all those so-called advances had been worth the price. Talking with her, even like this, was a comfort. It was like a familiar dance, a shared contemplation that had become a comforting ritual.

When the truck finally sputtered and stalled, its engine giving one last, mournful cough, Mortimer didn't hesitate. He rolled up his sleeves, hands moving with the skill of a man who had spent a lifetime fixing things. He scavenged from abandoned trucks and cars, each part a small triumph. The work was a welcome distraction, a way to channel his restless energy. And Edna was there, as always, by his side, her presence steady offering solace to his aching heart.

Once the truck was back in motion, the landscape slipped past until something unusual caught his attention by the roadside. He stopped, eyes narrowing at a patch of unexpected color against the muted backdrop.

"Stay here," he muttered to Edna, half out of habit.

Mortimer's boots scraped the parched earth as he inched forward, each step measured and wary. The scene before him sent a wave of nausea through his gut. A woman's corpse lay contorted, her limbs askew in unnatural angles. Near her, a blade glinted in the harsh light, its edge stained red.

The stench of putrefaction hung heavy around her. Mortimer's gaze traced the woman's form, absorbing the grim details. Her flesh, once likely supple and vibrant, now bore the mottled hues of death. Tangled locks framed features frozen in an expression of terror.

What pained Mortimer most, constricting his chest, was the rounded swell of her belly. She had been with child, nurturing new life even as her own was brutally extinguished. The savagery inflicted upon both mother and unborn child left him reeling with revulsion.

A thought whispered at the edges of his mind.

Who would do such a thing?

Then, another.

There are others. Those who haven't faded.

He scanned the surroundings, but nothing moved. The world remained still. He got back in the truck, his face pale.

"What was it?" Edna's voice held a trace of worry.

He forced a small laugh. "Nothing for you to worry about."

They drove for miles more through the desolate landscape, drawn by the mysterious glow ahead. The silence in the truck was dense, filled with unspoken fears and a delicate optimism. Mortimer's fingers clenched the wheel, his gaze unwavering from the road ahead.

As they crested a hill, a sprawling university campus came into view, its buildings looming like quiet watchers in the gathering dusk. The guiding light intensified, revealing more clearly the face that had been a silent presence throughout their journey.

Mortimer brought the truck to a stop, the engine's growl fading into the uncanny stillness. "I think we're here," he told Edna.

Beside him, Edna's form shifted slightly, barely more than a shadow now. Her voice, fragile as a breath, followed the faint wind through the deserted streets. "Finally. I'm tired, Mortimer. And hungry."

He almost laughed at the absurdity of it all.

Ghosts don't get hungry?

The thought amused him, unexpected and absurd.

He reached toward her in an attempt to offer comfort, his hand moving through hers as though it encountered nothing more than a cold, weightless mist. "Wait here, love. I'll check things out."

Edna's gaze, a blend of weariness and trust, met his for a moment. She gave the slightest motion of agreement, barely there, like a thought that slips away before you can hold it.

With his handgun tucked away in his coat pocket, Mortimer stepped out of the truck. The crunch of gravel beneath his boots was loud in the heavy silence. Before him stood Browers Hall, its imposing concrete façade staring back at him. The narrow windows seemed to watch him, holding secrets he wasn't sure he wanted to know.

Thunder rolled across the sky, while lightning flared on the horizon. The smell of rain thickened, the wind stirring with a restless energy. He drew in a long breath, taking his first step towards the building, each footfall landing with a crunch as if he were stepping on the bones of a world long gone.

22 The fourth

Ellie's clothes carried the earthy scent of damp soil and the faint green of sprouting seedlings. Moving through the greenhouse, her fingers grazed the jagged leaves of the tomato plants, scanning for signs of pests or drooping stems. The sun, tentative behind the gray clouds, cast elongated shadows against the glass, painting the room in soft hues.

As she rounded a corner, a cluster of tomato plants came into view, their fruits ripening in clusters. The tomatoes hung heavy from the vines, their skins a deep red, glowing faintly in the diffused light. She paused to admire them - their perfect roundness, the way they weighed the vines down with their fullness.

She reached out and cradled one in her palm. The warmth of the fruit surprised her as if it had absorbed every bit of sunlight that had touched it. She imagined the sweetness of it, the burst of flavor it would offer if she plucked it right then.

But she let it be. Harvest would come soon enough.

She tried to recall the number of days since the tomatoes had taken root, but the passage of time had slipped into a haze. In truth, it hardly mattered. If she were inclined to track it, she could always ask North.

"Winter's on its way," came his voice, cutting through her thoughts.

She flinched slightly, startled by his presence. He stood at the greenhouse door, cradling his rifle. "Didn't mean to surprise you," he added, his tone gentler. "We'll need to get ready. How are the tomatoes?"

She looked up at him.

"They're almost ready," Ellie answered, her eyes catching on the rifle. "You know, you only need to have that thing with you when we're outside."

North held her gaze for a moment before answering, "I know. Just being careful."

Ellie understood his caution. The tension had been rising ever since they'd found the calf torn apart, and with what happened between Myra and Anevay, no one felt truly at ease anymore.

"There's something out there, beyond the safety of Browers," North muttered, more to himself than to Ellie. "It's not safe anymore. Not like the world used to be."

Ellie brushed the soil from her hands and moved to stand beside him, resting her hand lightly on his arm. "It's never been that safe, really."

North's face softened slightly as he looked down at her, worry and determination marking his features. "I just wish we knew what we're facing."

"We may never know," she replied quietly.

North walked to the edge of the greenhouse and laid his hand against the cool glass. Outside, the world seemed to be shifting. The once-placid gray clouds had darkened, and a gusty wind whipped through the trees. A low rumble in the distance vibrated through the panes, stirring something restless inside him.

He glanced back at Ellie, surrounded by the orderly rows of tomato plants. Beyond the campus, the world was unstable and full of threats, but here, amidst the steady work and familiar faces, there was still a measure of calm.

"I suppose you're right," he said.

Ellie gave a small smile, her expression calm, as if they both understood what had to be done without the need for words. They had faced hardships before, and this was no different. Whatever was coming, they would handle it, as they always had, with resolve and unity, protecting what little peace they had managed to preserve.

She returned to her task, her fingers moving swiftly among the plants. The greenhouse felt like a world unto itself, a fragile shelter in an increasingly hostile landscape. In the repetition of her work, she found a kind of solace, a small but steady act of defiance against the uncertainty that pressed at their doors.

North watched her for a while, the quiet precision of her hands. For a moment, he could almost forget the rifle in his arms, the ceaseless watchfulness that had become second nature. Almost.

Outside, the smell of rain thickened in the air, the thunder growing nearer. Ellie paused and lifted her head, listening. Something strange lingered in the distance, a sound she hadn't noticed before, and it made her uneasy.

"North. Do you hear that?"

He did. His grip on the rifle tightened, though not noticeably. A low hum seemed to vibrate through the greenhouse, just at the edge of perception.

They stood still, ears straining to separate the sound from the mounting wind. The plants around them swayed slightly as if they too sensed the shift in the air.

Then, as the wind fell away, a sharp sound broke through the quiet, startling them both. It was the alarm. Something - or someone - -was at the front entrance.

***

Mortimer moved slowly across the campus, each step heavy with sorrow and doubt. The guiding light that had once brought him here seemed to wane and falter as the storm gathered strength. As he neared the entrance to Brower's, a thin mist of rain started to fall, adding a sense of cold unease to the air.

The rain, at first soft and barely noticeable, soon became stronger, driven by a wind that gained intensity with every gust. Mortimer, lost in thought, barely noticed the chill creeping through him, his mind fixed on the image of the face that had appeared in the light. It was only when he felt the wetness on his cheeks that he realized he was crying, his tears blending with the rain.

He stopped in front of the building, its high windows bleak and closed off. Before the imposing doors, Mortimer paused, uncertain.

What's inside? Answers? More questions? Or just another empty space filled with memories and loss?

"Edna," he whispered, his voice shaking. "I hope you're with me now."

As if in response, the image of the old man, which had been his guide, brightened for a brief moment before disappearing entirely. With it gone, a strange and unexpected resolve settled within him.

His eyes were drawn to a small security camera above the door, its red light blinking in a steady rhythm. Before he could decide whether to knock or push forward, a voice crackled through an unseen speaker.

"Who's there?"

Mortimer flinched, startled by the sound. It was a person - someone real. He stepped closer, rain now streaming down, soaking his clothes.

"My name is Mortimer," he called out clearly. "Mortimer Finch. I've come a long way. I … I'm looking for … I guess I really don't know what I'm looking for … answers maybe … hope …."

There was a pause before the voice spoke again, now more cautious. "How did you find this place?"

Mortimer closed his eyes, trying to order his thoughts, searching for the words to explain the unexplainable. The journey here felt impossibly long, yet at the same time, fleeting like something half-remembered from a dream. He thought of Edna and how she'd always believed the simplest truths were often the hardest to believe.

"I followed a light," he answered, the words slow. "There was a face in it, an old man's. Not clear, but full of life somehow. It led me here." His voice caught as he swallowed against the emotion rising in his chest. "Please," he continued, hating the desperation but unable to conceal it, "I've been alone for so long. Is there anyone here? Anything left?"

The speaker crackled with static before the voice returned, a bit softer now, tinged with curiosity. "This is a secure facility. Are you alone?"

Mortimer hesitated, looking back at his truck parked not far behind. For a fleeting moment, he saw Edna sitting in the passenger seat. Her silver hair framed her face, and her smile—so familiar, so steady - seemed to hold him up, as it had for all those years together. His heart lifted, a fleeting sense of peace he hadn't experienced in months.

But just as quickly as she had appeared, Edna faded. Her outline blurred, then vanished, leaving only the worn fabric of the empty seat behind. The truck now seemed far too big for one person.

Mortimer blinked, willing her to reappear, but she didn't. She was truly gone.

"Yes," he replied, his voice barely holding steady. "I'm alone. Very alone."

He stood in the rain, waiting for any response, but the silence stretched out. The downpour worsened, each drop a harsh reminder of his solitude He shivered, pulling his coat tighter, though it did little to ward off the growing chill.

Inside the security room, tension hummed low. The blue glow from the monitors illuminated Ellie and North's faces, casting sharp shadows. Ellie's gaze stayed fixed on the screen showing the man outside, her chest tightening as she watched his hunched figure standing in the increasing storm.

"We can't just leave him out there," she urged, her voice edged with concern. "He found us. The same way we all found this place. Maybe he can help."

North glanced at the monitor, narrowing his eyes as he studied Mortimer's soaked form, shivering in the rain. "Ellie, you know what I was told, by the old man. There are supposed to be three pregnant women left. He said nothing about a fourth person. This could be a trap."

"A trap? From who?" Ellie snapped, her voice rising. "Everyone else is gone, and if he's telling the truth, he's alone and desperate. We need all the help we can get."

North pressed his fingers to his temples, tracing small circles as if trying to ease the weight of his decision. His brow tightened in frustration. "And what if he's not who he claims to be? What if he's a danger to us?"

Ellie took a step closer, her tone softening. "Look at him, North. He's exhausted, soaked through. We can't just leave him out there. We need to know how he can help us."

North sighed, the strain clear in his eyes. "Fine. But we take no chances."

Relief spread across Ellie's face. She moved to the control panel and activated the intercom. "Mr. Finch, we're going to let you in. Walk slowly to the main door, hands where we can see them. We'll meet you there."

They headed to the entrance, North with his rifle at the ready, Ellie carrying an oversized bath towel, its worn fabric a small offering of warmth and decency.

From the edges of the doors, they could see Mortimer approaching, his figure a shadow against the swirling storm outside. His arms were raised high above his head in a gesture of surrender, his steps deliberate and slow.

North keyed in the access code, and the door released with a heavy click.

Mortimer was startled by the sound, his eyes locking on the opening door. Two figures stood at the threshold: North, tall and aged, and Ellie, her form gently rounded by pregnancy. For just a moment, a spark of hope lit his face.

"You're him . . . the man from the light," he breathed.

But when his gaze fell on the rifle, that glimmer darkened into something else. North's weapon was fixed on him, its barrel pointed squarely at his chest.

Ellie stepped closer, holding out the towel. Water was dripping from his tattered coat, and he was shivering. "Here, take this."

Before Mortimer could reach for it, North's voice cut through. "Hold it right there! Keep your hands up." He began searching Mortimer, and his hand froze as it pulled a gun from the man's coat. "And what's this? Stand back!"

Mortimer's eyes widened in panic. "Wait," he stammered, arms still raised. "I'm not here to hurt anyone. I swear, I just need . . . I just need help."

Ellie moved between them, her voice calm yet firm. "North, let Mr. Finch speak." She offered Mortimer a reassuring smile. "Tell us about yourself and why you're here."

North's grip on the rifle tightened momentarily, but he glanced at Ellie, then back at Mortimer. After a long pause, he lowered the weapon slightly. "Fine. Talk."

Mortimer swallowed hard and took a deep breath. "You can call me Mortimer. I used to be a mechanic at the power plant. Retired. It was just me and my wife Edna. Then it happened. She fussing over me, knitting that scratchy scarf . . . next minute she was gone. All I've got left of her is this ring and the necklace she used to wear. Been on my own ever since."

He reached into his pocket with a measured hesitation, his movements betraying a reluctance that seemed to spring from something much deeper than mere fear. But North's sharp movement made him flinch back, his hand suspended mid-air as if caught between impulse and restraint.

"Slowly. Very slowly," North commanded, his voice steady, but sharp.

Mortimer obeyed, his gaze never leaving North as his hand ventured once more into his pocket. When it emerged, it wasn't clutching a weapon or anything menacing, but rather a modest ring and a delicate silver chain. As the dim light reflected off them, tears, gathered in his eyes and rolled silently down his cheeks.

"I'm lost without her ..." he sobbed.

North's response came clipped, with a roughness that was beginning to soften. "And the gun?" His tone hinted at an understanding, though still wrapped in caution.

Mortimer met North's gaze, his eyes rimmed with fatigue, but his voice had steadied. "Same reason you've got that rifle aimed at me," he replied. "There are dogs out there. Strange things. Not like anything I've ever seen."

Ellie's eyes lingered on Mortimer, her gaze not just a cursory glance, but a careful, thorough assessment. She could see the grief woven into the lines of his face, the sag in his shoulders that spoke of weariness, but also the sharp glint of intelligence in his expression. It was a look she recognized all too well - one she had worn herself when she first arrived at Browers.

"And the light?" Ellie asked.

"It was there all of a sudden," Mortimer replied, turning to North. "Your face in it. You told me to follow it."

Ellie rested a hand lightly on North's arm. "Just like us. We followed the light too. We need him. If he's a mechanic from the power plant, do you know what this means? Think about it. He could help us with the systems here - everything."

Mortimer stood in silence, water dripping from his coat and pooling at his feet. In the lull that followed Ellie's words, the steady patter of rain against the roof became the only sound, nature's way of marking the passage of time in this strange new world.

North studied Mortimer, his expression unreadable, before giving a small, reluctant nod. His grip on the rifle loosened slightly. "Fine. But he's not leaving our sight." Turning to Mortimer, he added, "Mr. Finch ... I mean, Mortimer . . . we'll give you a chance. But know this - if you try anything, anything at all, you're out. Understood?"

Mortimer nodded, his shoulders sagging with relief. "Understood. Thank you." He gratefully accepted a towel to dry his hands and face. "I've got a bag, tools, and a suitcase in the back of the truck."

North handed the rifle to Ellie. "Keep watch. Use it if necessary." He put Mortimer's handgun in his pocket. "I'll grab his things."

The door clicked shut behind him, and the security system engaged.

Stepping into the storm, North was instantly soaked. The wind screamed through the trees, carrying with it the unmistakable scent of damp soil and something unfamiliar - something feral. He made his way to Mortimer's truck, wiping the rain from his eyes as he reached for the toolbox and suitcase.

Just as he lifted the bag, placing it under his arm, North saw them - creatures lurking in the shadows, their eyes glowing a deep, unnatural red. Massive dogs, their fur thick and wet, moved closer.

Dammit!

He quickly grabbed the toolbox and suitcase and turned back towards the entrance.

North's pulse quickened, but he forced himself to stay calm, every step a careful balance between speed and caution. The dogs watched, muscles coiled, ready to pounce. Even through the storm's fury, he could hear their low growls.

The door felt miles away. North focused intently on the keypad, acutely aware of the precious moments it would take to enter the code. He imagined Ellie inside, rifle at the ready, her eyes trained on the entrance.

Would she be fast enough if something went wrong?

Suddenly, one of the dogs lunged. North dropped everything and instinctively reached for the handgun in his pocket, but his hands flew up to shield himself as the dog came at him, teeth bared, the world narrowing to that singular moment of survival.

A gunshot rang out, impossibly loud in the storm. The dog collapsed at his feet, its body twitching once before going still. The other animals howled in confusion and then scattered into the darkness.

North turned, his ears ringing, to see Mortimer standing in the rain, the rifle steady in his hands, his face set with grim determination. What stood before him wasn't just a man overcome by grief, but a survivor - someone who had confronted the dangers of this world and emerged, capable.

"Figured you might need some help." Mortimer's voice was a gruff caress against the storm's roar.

North couldn't find the words. He bent down, gathered the bag, toolbox, and suitcase, and made his way back to the entrance. Something had shifted in him.

This man just saved my life.

He looked down at the fading body of the dog.

As North stepped inside, leaving the storm and the image of the dead dog behind, he knew that everything had changed. The world outside was more dangerous than they had imagined, but now at least, there was one more person, a fourth, to help.

***

Rain hammered against Browers with a ceaseless force, as though reflecting the turmoil of the world beyond. Inside, however, a calm had settled. North stood in the entrance, his gaze lingering on Mortimer. The man had just pulled him back from the edge of something dangerous, something that had changed North's understanding of everything. It was as if a veil had been lifted, revealing a new and unforgiving reality.

"Thank you," North smiled faintly, his voice low. "That was … that was close."

Mortimer acknowledged with a nod, his hands still gripping the rifle tightly. "These aren't just ordinary dogs," his voice carried a quiet tremor. "I've seen them before. Since things turned. They're ferocious, vicious things, almost like something out of a nightmare."

Mortimer nodded, his hands still gripping the rifle. "Those aren't ordinary dogs," his voice shaded with a hint of fear. "I've seen them before. Since everything changed. Ferocious and vicious things. Like hell dogs."

Ellie approached, her concern evident. "Are you both alright?" Her eyes darted between the two.

North gave a quick nod before addressing Mortimer again. "It's time we properly welcome you," he said, his voice now softer, extending his hand for the rifle, which Mortimer surrendered without hesitation.

"And the handgun too," North added., "I'll store it in the security room with the other firearms. We'll need to go into town to get more ammunition for it. Does that work for you?"

A wave of relief passed over Mortimer's face. "Of course. I'm just grateful to be here, to be … safe."

The word felt unfamiliar as if its meaning had been stretched thin in this new existence. Safety was relative and fleeting, but within these walls, it felt almost real.

Ellie's gentle voice interrupted. "Are you hungry? Let's get you something to eat."

"That would be very nice, thank you," Mortimer said.

As they made their way to the kitchen, Mortimer's eyes darted around, taking in every detail of his new surroundings. The halls of Browers, clean, orderly, and calm, were a sharp departure from the dead world outside.

Shadow padded over to Mortimer, her sleek fur blending into the shadows of the room. She meowed softly, rubbing against his legs, and Mortimer knelt to stroke her fur, a rare smile breaking across his face. Ellie chuckled from across the room. "Looks like you've made a friend. That's Shadow."

Mortimer ran his hand over the cat's soft coat. "Shadow," he echoed. "Fits you well, doesn't it? " We had a dog but lost him when it all ended." He paused, his gaze drifting up at Ellie's rounded form with a bit of surprise. "You're expecting."

Ellie placed her hand over her stomach in a protective gesture, a faint smile touching her lips. "Yes. Not long now. Though I must admit, the novelty has worn off a bit."

Mortimer's expression softened, a wistfulness in his eyes. "Children . . . they're such a blessing. Edna and I . . . we never had any. Always thought there'd be time, you know. We just worked so many hours, the both of us. Turns out we ran out of time."

Ellie looked at him, sensing she had touched on something delicate, but Mortimer continued, his voice steady despite the sadness behind his words.

"Maybe it's for the best now," he said, his fingers moving absently through Shadow's fur. "Losing Edna was hard enough. Losing a child . . . I can't imagine." His voice trailed off.

The room fell into a quiet that was only broken by the cat's purring and the unspoken grief that hung between them that connected them in this strange broken world.

North cleared his throat, his presence bringing them back to the moment. "Let's get something to eat."

In the kitchen, Ellie stirred a pot on the stove while North and Mortimer sat at the table. The room was filled with the comforting smell of soup and freshly baked bread. For Mortimer, it was a scent that belonged to a different time, a different world, and yet here it was, a small miracle amid his new reality.

Ellie placed bowls in front of them. "It's not much, but it's hot and filling."

Mortimer's hands trembled slightly as he picked up his spoon. "It smells wonderful," he murmured, the smell conjuring memories half-buried in the dusty corners of his mind. "I can't even remember the last hot meal I had."

Conversation began to flow more naturally after that, with Ellie explaining the greenhouses behind Browers, where they grew their own food. "Even the tea," she said, pouring him a cup, "comes from our herbs. It's not exactly Earl Grey, but it does the job."

Mortimer sipped, a contented sigh escaping him. "It's perfect."

When the meal ended, North stood. "We have a room for you. You must be tired."

Upstairs, the sleek, modern building was silent except for the gentle whirr of the climate control system. A hallway stretched before them, with several rooms on either side, their doors ajar, except for one.

"There's something inside that room," Edna's voice whispered in his mind.

He glanced at the closed door as they passed. "What's in there?" he asked North, nodding towards the door.

North's face hardened. "That's not something to worry about tonight. Tomorrow, I'll explain everything."

Sensing the finality in North's tone, Mortimer didn't push further. They arrived at a small, clean room where North gestured toward the bed. "This will be your room. Facilities are down the hall. You'll find towels there and almost everything else you may need."

The room was small but comfortable, with a bed, end table, a dresser, and a chair in the corner. A small slit of a window high up the wall looked out over the grounds of Browers.

"Get some rest," North said. "We'll talk more in the morning."

As North closed the door, Mortimer was left alone for the first time since his arrival. The silence was almost overwhelming after the constant noise of the storm and the tense initial encounter. The walls were a neutral gray, and the furniture was streamlined and functional, without any of the comforting clutter of a lived-in space he was used to.

Mortimer placed his suitcase on the bed and began to unpack slowly, each movement deliberate and considered. As he removed each item, it felt like unearthing fragments of a life that had been irrevocably altered. He carefully arranged his clothes in the dresser, the drawers gliding smoothly on their tracks. He laid out his few personal belongings on the small end table: Edna's ring, her bracelet, and an old photograph of them both on their wedding day. He tenderly placed the unfinished scarf atop the dresser.

And then he felt it - a presence. Turning slowly, his breath caught. There she was, sitting quietly in the corner chair, her silver hair neatly pinned back, her hands resting gently in her lap. She appeared as real as she had ever been.

"Edna," he whispered, barely believing his eyes.

Her warm smile was just as he remembered. "Hello, love. This place isn't so bad, is it?"

He struggled to find his voice, and when he finally spoke, his words were choked with emotion. "I've missed you so much."

"I know, love," she said softly. "But you're not alone anymore. These people seem nice, don't they."

"They do," he admitted, his eyes never leaving hers. "But I didn't know where to go without you."

"You always find your way," she reassured him. "Even when the path isn't clear. But, love," she whispered, her eyes darting to his room door. "There's something behind that locked door down the hallway. I can feel it."

His gaze followed Edna's. "What do you mean, love? It's probably just a storage room."

"No, no," Edna insisted, her voice taking on an urgent edge. "It's more than that. I hear . . . things. Whispers. Scratching. Please, Mortimer, you must look into it. For me."

He sighed. "Edna, love, there's nothing sinister here."

"But the noises, love! There are shadows that move when they shouldn't!" Edna's eyes widened. "You believe me, don't you?"

"Of course, I believe you're hearing something, love. Maybe a few mice have found their way in." He smiled.

Edna shook her head vehemently. "It's not mice, Mortimer. You always think whenever I hear things it's mice. Don't make fun of me. It's something . . . else. Something that doesn't belong here. Won't you at least check? For my peace of mind?"

He hesitated, torn between his desire to comfort Edna and his reluctance to indulge what he feared might be her growing confusion.

"Alright," he finally conceded. "I'll have a look. But I'm sure it's nothing to worry about."

They continued to talk, for what felt like hours, about everything and nothing. He shared stories of the journey, the inexplicable light that had drawn him to Browers. Edna's eyes were filled with love and understanding.

As the night stretched on, Mortimer felt his eyelids growing heavy. He lay back on the bed, his body finally finding ease after so many days of tension and fear.

"I think we're going to like it here, Edna," his voice drowsy. "It feels … it feels like we're home."

Edna's smile was the last thing he saw as his eyes drifted closed. "We're home, dear. Wherever you are, that's home for me."

Mortimer drifted into sleep, untouched by dreams, as the storm beyond the walls began to ease. The wind, once fierce, softened, and the rain fell lightly now a gentle patter. Browers stood quietly, every corner hushed, as though waiting.

North had been quietly standing in the dimly lit hallway outside Mortimer's room, his back pressed against the cool wall. From within, Mortimer's voice drifted out in a low, mournful cadence - a one-sided dialogue with his dead wife. North sighed heavily, running a hand through his hair. He turned and went down the staircase and to the kitchen where Ellie sat with a cup of tea in hand.

"Has he settled in?" she asked, her eyes soft with concern.

"He was speaking to his wife," North said, his gaze distant.

Ellie frowned in sympathy, setting her cup down. "That's heartbreaking. But maybe it helps him, in some way. We've all lost so much. If it gives him comfort, does it really matter?"

North was quiet, considering her words. "I don't know. But it worries me. We have to be clear-headed, especially if those dogs show up again."

Ellie's voice held a quiet strength. "We'll deal with it when the time comes. Let him rest for now. Tomorrow's soon enough to face reality."

Outside, as the storm was clearing a faint glow touched the horizon. Dawn was coming, promising a new day fraught with uncertainties and possibilities. But for now, as the night lingered a little longer, those of Browers slept, finding brief refuge in dreams of a world that had been lost, and drawing comfort from their memories and hopes. That is, all but one. In her room, behind the locked door, Myra sat quietly on her bed, her laughter breaking the silence as she kept herself company in the stillness.

23 The door

The scent of breakfast - bacon, eggs, coffee - wafted through the halls of Browers. Mortimer stirred, his eyes blinking open to unfamiliar surroundings slowly taking shape around him. Panic clutched at him briefly.

Where am I?

Then, the flood of memory rushed back, bringing with it a mixture of relief and sadness.

He rose cautiously, his joints protesting. The bed had been soft, but his body, weathered by time, was no longer quick to adjust. His feet found the cool floor, and the aroma of breakfast grew stronger, stirring his hunger. His stomach growled.

When was the last time I had a real breakfast? Days, weeks, maybe even months?

He couldn't remember.

Everything had blurred together in his solitary journey.

He stood, stretching carefully, and made his way down the hall to the bathroom. The sight of the shower made him pause. Running water, hot water – it seemed like an unimaginable luxury. He turned the shower handle, half-expecting nothing to happen. But the water flowed, steady and warm.

He stepped under the spray, letting out a small gasp as the warm water hit his skin. He stood there for a long moment, eyes closed, feeling the grime and weariness of his journey being washed away. He used the soap sparingly, aware that such comforts might be rationed, yet he couldn't help but enjoy the indulgence of being clean.

As he dried off, Mortimer caught his reflection in the mirror. The face staring back at him was tired, weathered by age and hardship. But in his eyes, there was something new - hope, or at least the absence of the overwhelming despair that had been his shadow for so long.

Dressing in the clean clothes he had brought, Mortimer felt something in the room. He turned, knowing who he would see. Edna sat in the corner chair, just as she had the night before. Her silver hair was pinned back, and her hands rested quietly in her lap. She looked at him with both love and concern.

"Don't eat too much, dear," she cautioned. "And just one cup of coffee, love. Remember what the doctor said about your blood pressure."

A smile tugged at his lips. "I know, love. I'll be careful."

"Oh, and remember the locked door. We must see what's inside."

"I won't."

He finished dressing and, with one last look at Edna, stepped out into the hallway. The smell of breakfast was stronger here, drawing him towards the kitchen. But something else caught his attention – that locked door, just a few steps away from his room. Remembering what Edna told him, curiosity tugged at him, and he leaned closer, his ear almost touching the metal as he strained to hear any sound from within. But before he could make out anything, a voice startled him.

"Good morning, Mortimer."

He jumped a little, turning to see North standing there, a knowing smile on his face. Mortimer flushed, embarrassed at being caught snooping.

"I . . . I was just . . ." he stammered, but North waved him off.

"No need to explain," North said. "I imagine you have plenty of questions. But first, let's get you fed. The others are waiting."

Mortimer followed, his mind racing.

Others? How many people are here?

The kitchen was bright and welcoming, filled with the comforting smells of breakfast. Ellie, already setting plates on the table, looked up with a warm smile. As they walked in, she looked up, her face lighting up with a welcoming smile.

"Good morning, Mortimer," she greeted him. "I hope you slept well."

Mortimer feeling a bit shy among new faces replied, "I did, thank you. It's been a long time since I've had the comfort of a real bed."

Across the table, another woman looked up - her dark hair neatly braided, her expression calm but attentive. There was an undeniable aura about her, a subtle yet formidable strength that lingered just beneath the surface.

"Mortimer," North's voice carrying a note of formality. "I'd like you to meet Anevay. She's a nurse."

Mortimer felt the significance of the introduction. A nurse - someone with the power to heal, to help in ways that mattered more now than ever.

"That's good," he replied, the words feeling insufficient even as they left his mouth. "And important, I imagine, in times like these."

As he took his seat, Mortimer's eyes wandered, taking in the scene. Ellie moved with gentle ease, her hand occasionally resting on the curve of her abdomen. And there - Anevay, too, revealed a similar shape to her figure.

Pregnant.

The realization unfolded within Mortimer, slow and deliberate like a flower unfurling its petals, each layer revealing a new depth of understanding. Both women were carrying new life. This revelation settled over him like a gentle but persistent rain, bringing with it an undeniable reminder of hope, of survival. So many emotions surged through him - concern, awe, and a fierce protectiveness that took him by surprise with its intensity.

Ellie laughed lightly, breaking his thoughts. "And me, I'm no nurse. Just a mere farm girl," she teased, a hint of pride in her voice. "Tending to the greenhouses, the animals. It's what keeps us going."

Mortimer's eyes widened in surprise. "Greenhouses? Animals? You mean . . . you're telling me you're . . . "

North gestured for Mortimer to take a seat. ". . . self-sufficient? More or less. We've had to be. But let's talk about that after breakfast. For now, eat."

Mortimer sat down, his mouth watering at the sight of the food before him. Eggs, bacon, toast – simple fare, but to him, it looked like a feast fit for kings. He picked up his fork, then hesitated, over the steaming cup of coffee, remembering Edna's warning.

Ellie notices. "Something wrong?" she asked.

He smiled sheepishly. "Just reminded this morning that I should only have one cup of coffee. High blood pressure, you see."

Anevay chimed in. "I can give you some medication for that."

"That's very kind, but I have some. Enough to last for another month."

Anevay gave a smile. "No need to worry. We've gathered a good amount of medicine here. We'll make sure you're taken care of."

Reassured, Mortimer nodded and joined in the meal, the warmth of conversation flowing easily around him. It was a scene of ordinary life - weather, crops, repairs. But beneath it, Mortimer sensed there was more, a tension under the surface. There were meaningful glances exchanged, topics that seemed to be carefully avoided. And always, at the back of his mind, was the question of the locked door.

As the meal drew to a close, North set down his coffee cup and met Mortimer's gaze. "When you're ready, we'll talk about this place. How you can be a part of it."

Mortimer set down his cup. "I'd like that. I have so many questions."

North's expression grew serious. "I'm sure you do. And I'll answer what we can. But there's something you need to understand, Mortimer. Being here means accepting certain responsibilities."

The mood at the table shifted, the lighthearted breakfast conversation giving way to something more serious. Mortimer studies their faces, these people who had taken him in – North's steady gaze, Ellie's kind eyes, Anevay's professional demeanor. He thought of Edna, waiting for him in his room, a ghost of a life he could never return to.

"I understand," Mortimer said, his voice sure. "I'll do whatever I can."

A look of approval crossed North's face. "Good. That's what I hoped you'd say. Finish your coffee, and we'll talk."

Before they could rise, North's expression darkened slightly, turning to Ellie and Anevay. "About the morning meal . . . don't take it to her without me there."

Ellie and Anevay exchanged a glance, understanding his meaning immediately.

As they began to clear the table, Mortimer sipped the last of his coffee, savoring the rich flavor, his mind wandering to the locked door and what Edna told him. Something was hidden away, something unsaid, hovering on the edge of understanding.

The sun outside bathed the room in light, a new day rising, painting the sky in dim shades of pink and gold. It was the kind of morning that once had been a blank canvas waiting to be filled, a promise of endless possibilities. But here, in this messed-up world, a different kind of promise was held – one of survival, of small joys, of connections, the strength of bonds forged through shared hardship.

This place, these people – they offer something I had thought was lost. A chance for life, purpose, maybe even hope. But that locked door . . .

Mortimer stood, ready to follow North and learn more. He glimpsed movement from the corner of his eye - Edna, watching with a quiet smile. Then she was gone, leaving him with an ache that he carried deep inside.

He squared his shoulders. "I'm ready."

North led Mortimer down to the basement.

***

The basement of Browers Hall stretched out ahead of them, long rows of metal racks holding batteries that stood still, almost watchful, under the harsh, buzzing lights. North led Mortimer through the narrow paths between the machinery, their footsteps resonating in the stillness. The steady hum of electricity filled the space, a low vibration that seemed to pulse along with their movements. Mortimer found himself oddly comforted by the sound, a subtle reminder of the world he'd once known. It stirred something inside him, something long forgotten - a sense of purpose.

"This is where we store the solar power," North explained. "I've read the manuals, tried to figure it all out. But honestly . . ." He paused, shaking his head. "I've done the best I could."

Mortimer's eyes roved over the room, interest growing with each step. He moved deliberately, scanning the rows of equipment until something caught his attention. He headed toward it, North close behind.

"What is it?" North asked, curiosity piqued by Mortimer's sudden focus.

Mortimer pointed to an old label, yellowed with age and curling at the corners. "Look at this," he said, excitement creeping into his voice. "These are the original installation records."

North leaned in, squinting at the faded writing. Mortimer ran his finger down the list, stopping at a few entries marked with familiar initials - MF.

"I remember now," Mortimer said quietly, a smile spreading across his face. He touched the batteries gently. "This system, it's mine. I helped set it up years ago. The power company worked with the university, and I was on the team. I'd forgotten all about it, but now . . . it's coming back to me. I know how to keep this thing running. I just need a few parts, easily found." His smile grew wider. "Feels like I'm stepping back into an old life."

North placed a hand on Mortimer's shoulder, clearly relieved. "You've no idea how much this means to us."

As they returned upstairs, to the common area of Browers, the morning sunlight streamed through the high windows, casting soft shadows across the room. North gestured to a pair of worn armchairs, their cushions once plush and inviting, bearing the signs of years gone by. Mortimer sank into one, the springs creaking slightly under his weight, while North took the other, facing him. The chairs faced each other like old friends, separated by a low table.

"I suppose you're curious how I ended up here," North began, his voice quieter now.

Mortimer leaned back, settling into the chair. "I have wondered."

North's eyes drifted, lost in memories. "It was the day the world changed. When everyone . . . faded." He paused, swallowing hard. "I was in the café, like any other morning. Routine, you know. Before my classes." He paused like he was searching for the right place to start again. "I used to teach here . . . And there was this old man, worn out, trench coat hanging off his shoulders. He had a leash in his hand but there was nothing at its end. He looked … it's hard to describe … angry, distraught, all at once … just strange. He told me he'd lost something important."

Mortimer shifted forward, giving North his full attention.

"And then it happened. People around me started to fade, to just . . . disappear. A waitress I saw every day, students—one minute they were there, and the next, gone. The old man told me to follow him outside, and all around me, it was happening - people vanishing, like the world was unraveling before my eyes. He said I was to help start things over. He said three pregnant women would come to me."

"Do you think he was . . . God?" Mortimer asked cautiously.

North shrugged, a slight smile tugging at his lips. "I don't know. But what could I do? I followed him here, to Browers. He told me this place could be a sanctuary, a place to survive."

"How did all that make you feel?" Mortimer's voice was gentle.

North's eyes clouded as he considered the question. "Overwhelmed. Burdened. Scared, mostly. Sometimes I wake up and can't believe this is real. Other times, it feels like I've been here forever, carrying this burden." He glanced at Mortimer. "But what choice do I have? If I don't do it, who will?"

Mortimer took in North's words, his expression thoughtful. Then, a sudden realization lit up his face. "The old man said there'd be three pregnant women. But I've only met Ellie and Anevay."

North's face darkened. He sighed heavily. "There is a third. Myra."

"Where is she?" Mortimer asked, surprised.

North's eyes shifted upward. "She's . . . confined. In the room you asked about."

Mortimer's eyebrows lifted in surprise. "Confined? Why?"

"She came to Browers like the others, weary and disoriented," North explained. "But she didn't have any skills to offer or anything to contribute. And Anevay . . . well . . . she had concerns."

"What kind of concerns?"

North lowered his voice slightly. "Anevay mentioned she had seen Myra before, as she traveled here. She was frightened of her. Always seeing her in her dreams. There's also something unusual about Myra - a peculiar skin condition that Anevay has never encountered before. She says it might be connected to the pregnancy, but she's not certain."

North took a deep breath and continued. "We tried to make it work. Truly, we did. I gave Myra plenty of work to do around Browers. Cleaning and keeping things orderly using checklists I devised for her. Anevay, bless her, she walked on eggshells, her smile a bit too bright, her laughter a touch too quick. And Ellie, well, she was more forgiving and tried to make Myra feel welcome. But then . . ." North trailed off, his face grim.

"What happened?" Mortimer prompted.

"Myra poisoned Anevay," North stated decisively. "We caught it time, thank God. But it was close. She used something from the greenhouse, something she learned about from Ellie. She admitted it but claimed innocence. I couldn't trust her after that. So, I decided to lock her away. It's necessary for everyone's safety."

Mortimer sat back, stunned. "My God," he muttered under his breath.

"We've strict rules for her now," North went on. "Rules for how we provide her food, how we allow her to clean herself and to use the bathroom, and how we check her health and the baby's every day. But it's not ideal. Nothing about this is ideal."

Silence settled between them, thick and heavy. Mortimer's mind churned, processing the revelation. Then, after a pause, he said, "North, there's something I need to tell you. I saw something terrible on the way here. A woman, killed by the roadside. And she was pregnant."

North's head snapped up, his eyes wide with shock. "What? Someone who didn't disappear?"

"No. The poor thing was right there. Her body carved up . . . well, like nothing I've ever seen before. Knife beside her." Mortimer shifted nervously. "It's got me thinking. The old man told you there would be three pregnant women. But what if . . . what if there were four?"

North pushed himself up abruptly, restlessly moving around the room as he grappled with the implications. "Four?" he murmured. "But he said three. He told me."

Mortimer watched him, troubled. "I don't know what it means, but it can't be a coincidence."

North stopped pacing, his eyes locking onto Mortimer's. "No," he agreed, voice tight with tension. "It can't be. But what does it mean for us?"

Mortimer stood. "I don't know."

The room grew quiet again, a quiet that felt on the edge of something. Mortimer glanced at the high windows, where the daylight reflected dimly as if the world outside had shrunk away, leaving only the two of them to reckon with these new uncertainties.

Mortimer's mind drifted, Edna's essence swirling through his thoughts like wisps of smoke from a snuffed candle. Her insistence about the locked door rang in his ears, a persistent whisper he couldn't quite shake. Edna had always possessed a gift, a keen eye that peered past facades and into the very marrow of a person's being.

He found himself yearning for her insight now, particularly regarding Myra. Edna would have seen through the layers, discerning truths that eluded Mortimer's less perceptive gaze. In matters of the heart and soul, he'd always deferred to Edna's wisdom, trusting her instincts over the fumbling machinations of his own mind.

"North, I want to see Myra," he announced.

Mortimer's words were heavy as lead and sharp as broken glass. The silence that followed was a living thing, breathing and pulsing between them. North's face twisted, a stream of emotions flaming across his features - concern, hesitation, a trace of something darker.

"Mortimer," North began, his voice low and gravelly, "you don't know what you're asking. Myra's . . . she's different."

Mortimer's chin lifted, a stubborn set to his jaw. "I'm not a child, North. I've seen my share of horrors."

"Not like this," North countered, his eyes haunted. "This isn't just about seeing, it's about . . . feeling. The weight of it. The smell of it."

Mortimer's hands trembled slightly, but his voice remained steady. "I need to see her. To understand. Edna would've wanted me to face this head-on."

North's shoulders sagged, defeat drawn in every line of his body. "Alright," he conceded, his voice barely above a whisper. "But don't say I didn't warn you. And Mortimer . . . remember, whatever you see, that's not really Myra anymore. Not in the ways that matter."

Mortimer nodded, a lump forming in his throat. "I understand. Thank you, North."

They went to the security room where North retrieved Mortimer's handgun before heading upstairs. Ellie and Anevay were still in the kitchen, their eyes narrowing at the sight of the weapon.

"Where are you going?" Ellie asked, worry lining her voice.

"Stay here," North replied firmly. "Mortimer wants to see . . . her."

They walked down the long hallway toward the locked room. The atmosphere seemed to shift. Mortimer's heartbeat quickened, a strange anticipation building. When North finally unlocked the door, Mortimer braced himself, not knowing what awaited him inside. The hallway seemed to stretch endlessly before them, the locked door looming larger with each step. North's hand hesitated on the key, his eyes meeting Mortimer who gave a firm nod, bracing himself for whatever lay beyond.

The lock clicked, the sound ricocheting off the bare walls like a gunshot. The door creaked open, unleashing a foul stench that assaulted his senses, smelling of decay and forgotten things. There, in the far corner, huddled Myra, her eyes darting about like trapped fireflies, unfocused and feral. Mortimer's gaze caught on her skin, a canvas of shifting, opalescent patches that seemed to breathe in the dim light. She was a creature suspended between worlds, neither fully human nor entirely other. As he stood transfixed, Mortimer felt a relentless tug in his chest, as if an invisible thread connected them across the threshold. This moment, he realized with a start, was both a beginning and an end, written in the stars long before either of them drew breath.

She fixed her gaze on him, a twisted smile creeping across her face. "You saw her, didn't you?" she whispered, her voice carrying an eerie calm but only in his mind. "The woman on the road. My handiwork, old man. Did you like it?"

The breath caught in Mortimer's throat as the truth settled, clear and unavoidable. The puzzle pieces, once scattered, now fell into place, painting a picture both horrific and inescapable.

A voice, soft and familiar, brushed past him like a warm sigh. For just a fleeting second, Mortimer let himself believe it could be real. "She's wicked, my love," the voice whispered, gentle but urgent. "She's not natural."

His heart raced as he turned, caught between disbelief and the aching hope that surged through him. And there she was - Edna, his Edna, standing at his side just as she had so many times before. Her gaze held his, piercing and filled with a truth that made him tremble.

"She's wicked, my dear. She's not natural," she repeated.

A sharp laugh broke into his mind. Myra, grinning as though she had heard every word, jeered, "The old bitch is senile. Don't listen to her."

Mortimer felt his hands begin to shake, the cold fear spreading through him like a chill that reached his bones. Without a word, he turned and left, his steps uneven and heavy.

North, caught in the undertow of this unspoken exchange, fell into step behind him, though his eyes remained locked on Myra, as though fearing she might vanish if he looked away. The lock clicked as he secured the door behind them, a sound that carried a sense of finality beyond just closing off a physical space.

24 A hallway of endless walls

The hallway seemed to stretch endlessly, walls tightening around Mortimer as he at them for support. His pulse hammered in his throat, each breath a struggle. North stood close, his face lined with concern.

"Edna," Mortimer gasped in a trembling voice. "She was there, North. In the room."

North's expression tightened, his gaze flicked between Mortimer and the locked door behind them. "What do you mean she was in the room?"

"I know you must think I'm nuts, that's it's all in my head," Mortimer whispered, his words broken. "But she was there and she spoke to me. Like she has since everything went wrong. She told me . . . she told me that Myra, that thing in there, is wicked . . . not natural."

North's hand found Mortimer's shoulder, a steadying grip. "Mortimer, I know this is difficult, but –"

"North, you heard her, Myra!" Mortimer interrupted, his voice rising. "You heard her! What she said!"

North shook his head, calm but firm. "No, Mortimer. She didn't say a word. She just sat there."

But Mortimer wouldn't hear of it. His face contorted, his voice rising. "No. No." His fingers curled into fists, knuckles white. "That thing in there spoke of the dead woman I saw. Called it her handiwork." He spat the word as if it tasted foul. "And Edna - my Edna – a senile bitch, it said." His eyes, wild and pleading, sought North's. "It heard what my Edna told me. How could it know, if Edna's only in my head?"

North's face paled, the implications of Mortimer's words sinking in. He glanced back at the locked door, then grabbed Mortimer by the shoulders. "We need to go back to the kitchen," he said firmly. "Come on."

They made their way down the stairs, Mortimer's legs shaky beneath him. The kitchen, with its warm light and familiar smells, felt like a safe haven after the nightmare of Myra's room.

North guided Mortimer to a chair, then went to a cabinet and pulled out a bottle of whiskey. He poured a generous amount into a glass and handed it to Mortimer.

"Here," he said, pulling up a chair beside Mortimer. "This might help."

Mortimer grasped the glass with unsteady hands and took a long swig. The whiskey burned its way down his throat, but the warmth that spread through his chest was comforting.

Ellie and Anevay, who had been sitting at the table, looked up in alarm. "What happened?" Ellie asked, her eyes moving between North and Mortimer.

North made a slight movement, a silent request for patience. He waited until Mortimer took another sip of whiskey before he spoke. "Feeling any better?"

Mortimer nodded, taking yet another swallow of whiskey. "I apologize. My mind must be . . ."

North cut in. "I overheard you speaking to someone in your room last night."

Mortimer lowered his eyes, embarrassed. "I'm sorry. Ever since this all began since I lost my Edna, I've been seeing her, conversing with her. I must be losing my mind."

"No," Ellie interjected. "No, you're not losing your mind. I'm no expert, but sometimes we develop coping mechanisms for difficult situations."

Anevay nodded in agreement. "It's like a way to protect yourself."

"But it was so real," Mortimer replied.

"I can still hear her voice, smell her perfume. It's as if she never left."

North leaned forward, his voice gentle. "Grief affects us all differently, Mortimer."

"But how do I know what's real anymore?" Mortimer asked, his eyes searching the room as if hoping to catch a glimpse of Edna.

Ellie reached out, placing her hand on Mortimer's arm. "The love you shared with Edna was real. That's what matters most."

Anevay nodded. "Maybe these visions are your mind's way of holding onto her memory, of processing your loss."

Mortimer sighed, his grief visible. "I miss her so terribly. I don't know how to let go."

"You don't have to let go completely," North said.

"We're here for you, Mortimer. You don't have to face this alone," Ellie said gently.

Mortimer looked up, his eyes glistening with tears. "Thank you . . . for everything."

The room fell silent for a moment. Then Anevay stood up, her voice soft but determined. "Why don't we all have some tea? I think we could use it."

"Not for me," Mortimer said. "I'm sticking to whiskey."

North smiled. "Good idea."

As Anevay moved to the kitchen, the others stayed seated, the silence broken now and then by the light clink of Mortimer's glass as he topped it off with more whiskey.

"I get what you mean about Edna. But I heard Myra too," Mortimer added.

"Tell them what you told me?" North urged.

With a steadying breath, Mortimer recounted the scene, his voice gaining strength with each word. When he finished, all were quiet.

Anevay was the first to break it. "Mortimer has no ties to Myra. Yet, he heard something. This . . . this isn't normal. We have to do something."

North's frustration evident was evident. "But what? We can't just -"

"Her skin condition," Ellie interrupted, turning to Anevay. "Could it be causing . . . whatever this is?"

Anevay frowned, her medical training clashing with the impossible situation they found themselves in. "I've never seen anything like it," she admitted. "The patches, The patches, the way they seem to move... it's unlike anything I've encountered."

"Could the pregnancy be behind this . . . this strangeness?" North pressed. "We're in uncharted territory here."

Anevay drew in a sharp breath, frustration evident. "I don't know. It's possible, I suppose. Pregnancy can trigger all sorts of changes, but this . . . this goes beyond anything I've seen or read."

Mortimer set his glass down, the whiskey having steadied his nerves somewhat. "What if," he began, his voice measured, "what if . . . and this is gonna sound crazy . . . what if it's not the pregnancy causing the condition, but something else?"

The others turned to look at him, their expressions a mixture of confusion and dawning realization.

"What do you mean?" Ellie asked, her voice tentative but curious.

Mortimer leaned forward, his words barely escaping his lips. "What if whatever is causing the skin condition . . . whatever that thing is . . . is some malevolent force . . . something purely evil."

The room seemed to tighten with his words. North gripped the back of Mortimer's chair, his fingers turning pale as they clenched the metal frame as if he could anchor himself in a world that was rapidly losing its shape.

"That's not . . . no, that's not possible," Anevay murmured, though the tremble in her voice betrayed her. "And that 'thing' is a human being. You're not making any sense."

"Is it?" Mortimer countered, taking another sip of whiskey. "Is it a human, or now, something else? We live in a world where almost everyone has disappeared. Where I see my dead wife, and she talks to me. Where strange lights draw people away. Are we really in any position to say what's possible and what isn't?"

Silence wrapped around them as they sat with his words. The tick of the kitchen clock seemed unnaturally louder than before, an unwanted reminder of time pressing on.

"If that's true," North spoke, the burden of his thoughts visible in the tightness of his brow, "what does that mean for the other pregnancies?" His gaze shifted to Anevay, his eyes wide with worry. "Could that same . . . force . . . come after you and Ellie?"

Anevay's hand instinctively rested on her growing belly. "No. That won't happen." But the certainty was gone from her voice.

Ellie, steadier now, responded. "Whatever affected Myra hasn't touched us."

"Our pregnancies are normal," Anevay added, though it sounded more like an attempt at reassurance. "We don't have any of the symptoms Myra showed."

"But can we even be sure that is Myra upstairs?" Mortimer pressed. "Can we be sure that what's locked in the room upstairs is Myra? Or . . . is it some kind of creature, an entity that . . ."

North's hand hit the table with a loud crack, cutting through the tension. "Enough. This isn't some horror story. We need to focus. Protect her and the baby she's carrying. And where the hell is that old man? Why isn't he here helping us?"

All eyes turned to him. His body was tense, his jaw clenched, but the determination in his expression seemed to pull them all back from the brink.

Anevay, her resolve bolstered by her training, was forceful. "North's right. Whatever's happening, we have a responsibility to that child. And to Myra, if she's still . . . in there."

Ellie sighed. "But how do we do that? "But how? How do we protect ourselves and that baby when we don't even understand what's happening?"

***

The nights that followed at Brower's stretched long and dark, suffocating Mortimer in their stillness. Every creak of the building seemed to magnify in the silence, his heart frantically thudding in the void. Yet none of this compared to the most terrible sound - the one that should not have been there, clawing at his sanity like a starving rat. A voice, hers, oozed through the walls, a voice that only he could hear, a voice that spoke his dead wife's name, calling to him, a presence that defied explanation.

At first, it was indistinguishable, like the wind outside or the rain pattering on the roof. But as time passed, the voice grew louder, its edges sharper, insinuating itself into his thoughts. Myra's voice, was unmistakable, yet wholly out of place.

"Your Edna was never real," the voice hissed, sending Mortimer's mind spiraling. "She was just a figment, a vessel meant to keep you in line. You were always destined for much worse, Mortimer. Much worse."

He pressed his pillow against his ears, squeezing his eyes shut in a desperate attempt to drown out the sound. Still, the words found him, seeping through the very air.

"Didn't it ever strike you as strange?" Myra's words coiled tighter around his thoughts. "Why did she disappear so easily, leaving you all alone?"

He shook his head, sweat slicking his forehead.

No! No! This can't be happening!

He refused to believe it. But as he fought the thoughts crawling through his mind, he felt as though his sanity was slipping, leaving him adrift in something incomprehensible, dangerous.

"She never belonged to you," the voice cackled, her laughter cutting through the room like ice. "She was an illusion, a false memory implanted to keep you docile."

"No," Mortimer muttered, his voice muffled, weak. "That's not true. Edna was real. She was my wife. We had a life together."

But Myra's laughter echoed, tearing at him with each mocking note. It was a laugh that scraped against his sanity, leaving bloody gouges in its wake. The seed of doubt planted by her words, once a mere speck, began to grow, twisting around Mortimer's last grip on reality. He knew this torment was only just beginning.

"Poor, foolish Mortimer," Myra's voice softened, cruelly. "None of this is what you think it is. The truth is right in front of you if only you'd open your eyes."

Night after night, Mortimer struggled against the constant torment. He tried to drown out the voice with the hum of old tunes, whispered prayers, anything that could silence the words gnawing at his mind. But nothing stopped it. The voice was relentless, a constant barrage of doubt and cruel insinuations.

And then one night, something inside Mortimer broke. He flung his covers aside and stormed into the hallway, his feet pounding against the cold floor. The corridor seemed endless, filled with nothing but closed doors and shadows.

He found himself in front of the locked door - the source of his torment. Without thinking, he banged his fists against it, over and over, desperate to silence the voice.

"Shut up! Leave me alone!" Mortimer's scream tore through the building, shaking the stillness.

The sound of other doors opening echoed down the hall. North appeared first, his hair tousled from sleep but his eyes were sharp and awake. Behind him, Ellie and Anevay, their expressions serious and drawn.

"Mortimer?" North's voice was careful. "What's going on?"

Mortimer turned to them, his face wild, breath heavy. "Can't you hear it? Myra's voice! She won't stop! She keeps saying these horrible things - about Edna, about everything."

The three exchanged a glance, one filled with sorrow and concern. Anevay stepped closer, her tone gentle, but firm. "Mortimer, there's no voice. No one's saying anything."

Mortimer shook his head fiercely. "No, you don't understand. I can hear her. She's right here, talking about Edna, saying she wasn't real!"

North placed a steady hand on Mortimer's shoulder, guiding him back toward his room. "Come on, old friend. Let's get you back to your room. You need rest."

As they helped him back to bed, Mortimer saw the looks in Ellie and Anevay's eyes.

They think I'm losing his mind. Maybe they're right. But that voice... it's so real.

Alone again, Mortimer stared at the familiar darkness of his room. His eyes wandered toward the chair in the corner, and there she was - Edna, sitting quietly, her silver hair shining in the dim light from the window.

"Edna," he whispered, his heart swelling with both disbelief and hope. "You've come back."

She smiled, though it was a smile touched with sadness and something Mortimer couldn't quite place. "I'm always here, love. You need to listen carefully. She's not right, Mortimer. And neither is the baby she's carrying."

Mortimer sat up, his heart caught between disbelief and the haunting familiarity of her voice. "What do you mean, Edna?"

Edna's eyes met his, and for a moment, Mortimer saw something unknowable in their depths. "She's evil . . . the devil's work. You know what has to be done, Mortimer. But do you have the strength to face it?"

Mortimer hesitated before asking what he had been afraid to voice, a question that had been lurking in the darkest corners of his mind. "Are you telling me I have to . . . kill her?"

Edna's image wavered slightly, her form dimming like a memory slowly fading. "If the opportunity presents itself."

With that, she disappeared, leaving Mortimer alone once more. The room plunged into a deafening silence, broken only by the sound of his ragged breathing.

When the dawn broke, Mortimer sat motionless. The events of the night played over and over in his mind - Myra's voice, Edna's warning, his own mounting dread.

I know the others think I'm losing my grip on reality.

Yet, as the first light of day crept across the room, something shifted within Mortimer. He knew he couldn't dismiss the feeling that had taken hold.

Whatever's happening here, whatever force brought us all together, it's trying to tell me something. But what?.

As he heard the others stirring, their movements marking their daily routines in this strange place. A decision crystallized in his thoughts. He would bide his time, watching and learning, readying himself for whatever might come. Edna's words echoed in his memory - if a chance arose, he would seize it without hesitation.

25 More rituals

The light in Brower's Hall was thin, seeping through narrow windows and casting elongated shadows along the floor. Every morning, just as dawn broke, North would take his place outside Myra's door, one hand gripping the rifle, the other holding a small key. Ellie stood beside him with a tray of breakfast. They carried out their ritual in silence, the only sound the click of the key in the lock and the soft creak of the door opening.

"Morning, Myra," Ellie would say gently, setting the tray down on the dresser, beside the untouched one from the night before. Myra, once full of life, now sat still, her eyes distant, haunted by a sorrow she could not escape. She mumbled to herself, pulling at her hair, and sometimes hurled insults or curses in their direction, her words sharp and bitter.

"Let's get this done," North would urge, his voice low, his gaze steady. His duty was to protect Ellie, to ensure everything stayed in control. The rifle was a constant presence, a reminder of the silent dangers that lurked within their thoughts.

As they made their way down the corridor, Myra's steps faltered, her frail body moving with difficulty. Ellie kept a steady hand on her arm, guiding her gently. North followed closely, his watchful eyes fixed on Myra, ready for anything. Inside the bathroom, Ellie helped Myra to the toilet and the bath, while North stood guard, never breaking his vigilance. Every twitch of Myra's hand, every movement, was closely tracked, his gaze sharp, waiting for the slightest sign of something deeper, something darker hidden within her illness.

"Let's get you cleaned up," Ellie said with quiet efficiency, her hands quick but gentle. Myra's skin was pale, her fingers raw from constant pulling at her hair. She murmured under her breath, her words faint and fragmented as Ellie washed her.

"She's getting worse," Ellie whispered one morning, her eyes meeting North's with concern. North's expression did not change, though a muscle in his jaw tightened.

"Doesn't matter," he replied. "The child is what matters." His eyes shifted to Myra's rounded belly. "She just needs to hold on."

After the morning ritual, North and Ellie would escort Myra back to her room, the silence stretching between them. At midday, North would stand guard again, this time escorting Ellie as she brought another meal. They placed the tray down, the sound of the dishes ringing in the quiet, and retrieved the untouched breakfast.

"Eat something," Ellie urged, her voice soft, but Myra rarely responded. She would pick at her food, her mind distant, her eyes fixed on some far-off place. As the days passed, she became more withdrawn, her words increasingly incoherent. Her hair came out in clumps, and her scalp was sore and bleeding. Her skin turned a grayish hue, dry and cracked, like a shell that was slowly wearing away.

"She's losing her mind," Ellie said one evening as they left Myra's room. North's face was stony.

"It doesn't matter," he repeated, his voice hard. "The baby is all that matters." His words were a repeated refrain, as though he was trying to reassure himself as much as anyone else.

The weekly medical check-ups were the worst. North and Mortimer would escort Myra to the infirmary, their grips tight as they held her flailing body. Anevay would be waiting, her hands steady, her face calm.

"Hold her still," Anevay instructed, her voice even. Myra would kick and scream, her face wild, filled with a strange fury. North and Mortimer held her down, their expressions grim, determined. Eventually, Mortimer created a harness, rigging it from ropes, so they could restrain Myra more easily during the examinations.

"Shh, Myra," Anevay murmured, working quickly, her focus entirely on the task. Myra's anger eventually gave way to sobbing, her body shaking as Anevay continued her examination.

"She's deteriorating," Anevay remarked one day, as they strapped Myra back into the harness. "She won't be able to last much longer."

"It doesn't matter," North answered, his eyes hard. "We just need to keep her alive until the baby comes."

But it wasn't only Myra who was deteriorating. Mortimer, too, was slowly unraveling. Myra's voice followed him, even when she wasn't there, filling his thoughts with her madness. At night, as he lay in bed, her words echoed in his mind, persistent and cruel.

"They don't need you," she whispered one night, her voice a thread weaving through his dreams. "You're nothing but a relic, an old man waiting for the end."

By day, he tried to push her voice away, focusing on his duties, ensuring everything in Brower's ran smoothly. But her words dug deeper, wearing him down. His hands, already trembling with age, shook more, betraying the unease that now lived within him. He found himself glancing over his shoulder, half-expecting to see the spectral form of his late wife, Edna, or worse, the sinister apparition of Myra. In the quiet moments between tasks, he would sometimes catch his reflection in a mirror, seeing not the resolute man he once was, but a ghost of himself, a hollow shell, besieged by the whispers of a mind going mad.

***

The days slipped into one another, their routine predictable yet oppressive, interrupted only by the slow unraveling of Myra's mind. Even as they carried on with their duties - tending the gardens, caring for the animals, patching the barn roof, foraging for supplies - Myra's deteriorating state loomed over them. Her presence in that locked room became a constant, unsettling thrum, a fragile balance they teetered upon.

At first, her wild outbursts had filled the house with anger and accusations, but those fiery eruptions had faded into muttered incoherence. Then, there was only silence. A silence more unnerving than her raving. It felt as if Myra had withdrawn into a place they could never reach, her mind constructing a world beyond their understanding.

When she did speak, it was in fractured phrases, disjointed words that hinted at horrors they dared not imagine. "The light . . . it burns," she would cry out, her eyes fixed on a point none of them could see. "They're coming . . . can't you hear them?"

Her hands, once nimble and sure, now fidgeted with an anxious fury. She tore at her remaining hair, forming matted knots that reflected the chaos within her. Her nails, broken and jagged, scratched furrows into her skin, red streaks mapping the course of her descent.

North watched her with a distant calm, his thoughts consumed only by the unborn child. Her agony was simply the price to be paid.

Ellie and Anevay spoke often, their voices hushed, their concern deepening with each conversation as they tried to find solutions.

"She's losing her mind," Ellie said, barely holding back the tears. "We can't keep going like this."

Anevay's face was taut with worry, but her voice remained firm. "I know. But what else can we do?"

Mortimer, who rarely joined their conversations, had once chimed in, his expression hard. "She's nothing but a burden now. And don't forget what she did to Anevay."

Ellie's eyes clouded with sadness. "That wasn't her. She didn't choose this, Mortimer."

His gaze was cold. "Maybe not. But that doesn't change anything. North is right. We need to think about what comes next. We have to look ahead. She's nothing but trouble wrapped in sickly skin."

A harsh edge crept into Ellie's voice. "Is that what your nightmares are telling you?"

Mortimer held her stare, but the intensity in his eyes dimmed, replaced by a shadow of something haunted. He clenched his jaw, sealing the grim truth he couldn't bring himself to speak aloud.

One evening, as they gathered around the kitchen table, North introduced a plan that had been forming in his thoughts.

"Once the baby is born, we let her go," he told them, his voice steady and unmoving. "We release her."

Ellie gasped, her eyes widening with alarm. "You can't be serious. She won't survive out there."

North's expression remained hard. "That's not our concern. The baby is."

Mortimer agreed without hesitation. "It's the safest option. She's a danger to all of us."

Ellie turned to Anevay, searching for support, but found only uncertainty in her face.

"You can't agree with this," Ellie begged.

Anevay sighed, her resolve faltering. "I don't want to, Ellie. But maybe this is the only way. If this is supposed to be a 'divine reset' we have to start somewhere."

Ellie's tears fell freely now. "It's wrong. You know it's wrong."

North's face held no sympathy. "It's what has to be done. For the child."

26 *The key*

Mortimer had been wrestling with it for some time, the madness creeping in that fateful night when Myra's voice first slithered into his brain like a venomous snake. Her words infected him, slowly eroding his mind, each day dragging him closer to a breaking point. He knew he had to act. Edna's lingering whisper - "If the opportunity presents itself" - played endlessly in his mind, a deranged prayer urging him to purge the rot that had overtaken their fragile existence.

The plan took root in his psyche, festering like a sickness. He envisioned the final act: a swift slash across Myra's throat, blood warm against his trembling hands. Then, he would pull her lifeless body into his room, staging a scene that would tell a lie he needed them to believe. He'd drop the key in plain sight, a breadcrumb for the others to follow. His bed would look like a battleground, the sheets ripped and tangled as if from a fierce struggle. When they rushed in, lured by his frantic cries, he'd spin the tale. Myra, wild with madness, must have stolen the key from North during her bath. Her bony fingers nimble enough for such a trick. He'd recount how she crept into his room, desperate, and wielded a knife. His defense would seem the only option.

It's believable.

He convinced himself.

One night, as the others slept, Mortimer lay awake, staring into the dimness above him. The knife he'd taken from the kitchen pressed against his thigh, cold and silent. He waited, tracking the slow march of time, until the moonlight pooled on the floor.

"What are you waiting for, old man?" Myra's voice cackled through his skull, sharp as broken glass. "Afraid of a little blood?"

He ignored her. Or tried to. But her laughter lingered like a sickly-sweet scent that wouldn't dissipate, a constant reminder of the grinning darkness just across the hallway.

Mortimer slid out of bed, his joints protesting every move. The hallway before him stretched out, a tunnel of faint glimmers of moonlight slicing through the gloom. He knew North would be in a deep sleep, his rifle close by, and the small key resting in his belt pouch, within reach but undisturbed.

A soft sound broke the stillness near his feet, a gentle meow. Mortimer's heart jolted in his chest as Shadow, the cat, wound itself around his legs, nearly tripping him.

"Goddamn it," he muttered, shaking the cat off. "Not now."

Shadow let out another wistful meow before slinking away into the shadows, leaving Mortimer to gather his nerve once more. His resolve, though shaken, was firm. This had to end - for Edna, for what little remained of his sanity.

North's door was ajar, a thin wedge of darkness. He pushed it open slowly, his fingers trembling as they gripped the metal. North's form was a motionless lump under the covers, his snoring steady. Mortimer reached for the belt pouch that hung on a pair of jeans draped over a chair, his hands unsteady with age. The key slipped free, and he backed out into the hallway.

The door to Myra's room loomed before him, the key sliding into place with a faint click. He stepped inside, the moonlight spilling across the bed where Myra lay. She was barely a shadow of herself now, a skeletal figure propped against the pillows, her skin mostly patches now, colors red and white. Beneath it, dark shapes moved, visible for a moment before sinking back out of sight. Her eyes fixed on the knife in his hand, but there was no fear.

"Well, well," she rasped, her voice brittle. "Looks like the old man finally grew a pair." There was no fear in her voice, only a weary acceptance tinged with something else.

Amusement?

"I've been expecting you, old man," she continued. "Took you long enough."

Mortimer's throat tightened. "I don't want to do this," he croaked, hating the tremor in his voice. "But I have to. You know I have to."

Myra's laugh was hollow, a sound that sent a chill through him. "Of course you do. It's all part of North's grand plan, isn't it? Kill the monster, save the child, rebuild what's left. But you're wrong, old man. So very fuckin' wrong."

She leaned forward, Mortimer catching a whiff of something rotten, like meat left too long in the sun. "The baby won't survive your butchery," she hissed. "No matter. It was doomed from the moment it quickened in my womb. North's plan is a joke, a fairy tale for grown-ups too scared to face reality. If you kill me now, you'll only be ending my suffering. Oh, and the future? It died along with everyone else."

His grip on the knife faltered. Myra's words struck a chord deep within him, a truth too heavy to bear. His hand dropped to his side, the blade slipping from his grasp.

"I can't . . . I can't," he stammered, stepping back. "I can't do it."

Myra sighed, a weary sound like wind through a graveyard. "Then we're both stuck in this nightmare. But hey, at least you spared me the indignity of dying by your shaky hand. Small favors, right, old man?"

Mortimer turned and stumbled out of the room, his legs shaky. He returned the key to North's pouch, with clumsy fingers, then stumbled back to his room. He collapsed on his bed, the knife still in his hand, and stared at the ceiling. The darkness pressed in, a suffocating blanket woven from guilt and despair. He prayed for sleep, for oblivion, but his mind was a storm-tossed sea of emotions.

As the first gray fingers of dawn crept through the window, Edna appeared in the corner chair. Her ghostly form shimmered, insubstantial as smoke. "Oh, my dear," she moaned in disappointment. "You missed your chance. The evil will live on, all because you hesitated."

Tears burned his eyes. "I couldn't do it, Edna. God help me. I couldn't kill her."

Edna looked away, sorrow deepening in her expression. "You had the chance to end it, to bring peace. Now we're all condemned to carry on with this suffering."

As Edna faded, leaving him alone in the growing light, Mortimer felt his failure pressing heavily against his chest. He longed for it all to end, to break free from this unrelenting nightmare, but there was no escape. The day ahead stretched endlessly, and Mortimer knew with a deep, unbearable certainty that peace would forever elude him.

From down the hall, Myra's laughter drifted angrily. The nightmare persisted.

27 The children

The first contraction hit Ellie like a wave, sudden and powerful, forcing her to clutch the counter's edge with all her strength. She had been in the middle of preparing dinner, the familiar routine of chopping vegetables a comforting distraction from the anticipation that had been building for weeks. Now, as the pain ebbed away, she glanced down at the half-sliced carrot, wondering if the moment had truly arrived.

"North," she called, her voice steady despite the tension building in her body. "I think it's time."

The sound of hurried footsteps echoed through the hallway. North soon appeared in the doorway, a look of excitement and fear on his face. "Are you sure?" he asked, even as he instinctively moved to her side.

A small smile played at the corners of Ellie's mouth. "As sure as I can be about something I've never experienced before."

Anevay entered the kitchen, her own pregnancy nearing its end. "Let's get you to the infirmary," she urged, her nurse's training taking over despite her condition.

As they made their way up the stairs, Ellie felt a sense of surrealism swept over her. Ellie felt a strange detachment, as though she were watching the scene unfold from a distance. This place, once filled with books and students, was now their fortress, their home. And soon, it would witness the birth of their future.

The enormity of it settled on her like an unseen force, adding to the strain of each step.

Mortimer appeared, his face lined with concern. "It's happening?" he asked, falling into step beside them.

North nodded, his arm steady around Ellie's waist. 'It's time."

In the infirmary, transformed months ago into a makeshift delivery room, Ellie found herself on the bed as the contractions grew stronger and more frequent. The change had begun, pulling her forward with unstoppable momentum.

The hours slipped by in a whirlwind of pain, effort and encouragement. Ellie clung to North's hand, her grip fierce, while Anevay worked efficiently despite her own discomfort, guiding Ellie through the process with calm authority.

As dawn broke, painting the sky in hues of pink and gold, a cry pierced the air – strong, defiant, and full of life. Anevay held up the squirming, red-faced infant, tears glistening in her eyes. "It's a boy," she announced, her voice thick with emotion.

As morning light filtered through the windows, bathing the room in soft warmth, the sound of new life broke through—the strong, vibrant cry of a newborn. Anevay lifted the wriggling baby, her eyes shining with emotion. "A boy," she announced, her voice catching.

Ellie collapsed, utterly drained but filled with joy. North leaned down to kiss her, his face streaked with tears. "You did it," he whispered. "He's perfect. What will you call him?"

"Adam," she gasped, her smile radiant. "For a new beginning."

As Anevay tended to the baby, Mortimer stepped closer, his expression one of quiet awe. "May I?" he asked, his voice low.

Ellie nodded, and Mortimer approached, gazing down at the tiny face in her arms. "This is what we've been waiting for," he said softly. "The future is in our hands now."

Just a few days later, during a routine checkup of Ellie, Anevay suddenly winced, her hand flying to her abdomen, eyes widening in surprise. "I think," her voice strained, "my time has come."

What came next was a rush of movement and emotion, a flurry of carefully controlled chaos as they made ready for Anevay's delivery. Ellie, though still tender from her own recent childbirth, moved with surprising elegance. Her body remembered the rhythms of labor, guiding her through each task with a quiet competence. She moved swiftly, gathering clean towels, and donning the whites, gloves, and mask, as though it were second nature. In the brief pauses between contractions, her mind wandered back to those nights of quiet anticipation, when she and Anevay had exchanged their fears and hopes in whispers. Those conversations had been their lifeline, a way to brace for the inevitable. Yet now, faced with the rawness of it all, Ellie realized words could never have fully prepared her for this moment.

She cast her eyes over the checklist Anevay had written, the paper worn at the edges and dotted with smudges from anxious fingers. Every item on the list seemed to hold their entire future - sterile scissors, clean blankets, the precious antibiotics they'd salvaged from long-abandoned hospitals. Ellie took a steadying breath, reminding herself that she knew what to do.

Anevay's labor advanced with a speed that seemed to take even her by surprise, as though her body had long awaited this moment. The contractions came, one after another, building in intensity, drawing her deeper into the fierce and consuming process of bringing life into the world. The pain was intense, but Anevay remained grounded, her medical training helping her navigate each wave of agony. Between the contractions, she would glance at Ellie, her voice steady, a lifeline of calm amid the storm of their shared experience.

"You're doing fine," she reassured, meeting Ellie's gaze with both professional calm and deep affection. "Remember the checklist. Step-by-step . . . just like we practiced."

Ellie followed her instructions with care, her hands moving in sync with Anevay's guidance. The room buzzed with urgency and expectation, every breath and movement a preparation for the new life about to arrive. North was close by, his expression focused and full of wonder, clutching the rifle as if it were a talisman.

Anevay's grip tightened as another contraction hit her. Her breathing quickened, but her resolve remained firm. "Almost there," she groaned, more to herself than anyone else. "Almost there."

With one final push, the room was filled with the small and insistent cry of a newborn. Ellie moved quickly to cut the cord, while North, his large hands uncharacteristically gentle, wrapped the baby in a soft towel, cleaning her with slow, tender movements.

North cradled the tiny child with great care, his eyes bright with unshed tears. "A girl," he said softly, his voice filled with quiet wonder. He brought the baby to Anevay. "We have a son and now a daughter."

Anevay reached out, her fingers trembling as she touched her daughter's cheek. "Hello, little one," she whispered, her eyes glistening with tears of joy. "Welcome to our strange and beautiful world. You will be called Eve."

The rest of the day passed in a haze of joy and exhaustion. Mortimer took up his new responsibilities without hesitation, bringing food and water, and even learning - after a quick lesson from Ellie - how to change diapers with surprising proficiency for someone more accustomed to mechanical tasks. North added cooking to his routine, preparing simple but nourishing meals for the group.

As evening fell, a sense of peace descended. The two newborns slept soundly, unaware of the hope they now carried in their tiny forms.

Several quiet days passed, but then, one night, a scream cut through the stillness - raw and filled with pain. It came from the locked room where Myra was kept.

North jumped to his feet, his face drained of color. "It can't be. It's too soon."

But Anevay was already moving towards the stairs. "Babies don't follow our schedules," she said calmly. "They come when they're ready."

When they opened the door, the air was thick with the scent of rot, and something else - fear. Myra lay on the bed, her frail body twisted in pain, her eyes wild and glassy.

Anevay stepped forward, but Myra's voice lashed out. "Stay back."

"Myra, I'm here to help," Anevay said softly. "Your baby is coming."

Myra let out a harsh, bitter laugh. "Help? You can't do anything."

Despite Myra's defiance, Anevay readied herself for the birth while North stood by the door, a quiet storm of worry brewing within him. Ellie hovered nearby, doing what she could to support Anevay.

Myra's labor was violent, her wails filling Browers. She thrashed and fought, her words spinning into chaos, half-muttered warnings spilling from her lips. "They're coming," she gasped between contractions. "Can't you see them? They're all here."

Time dragged on, the tension thickening with every passing minute. Anevay worked tirelessly, setting aside her own exhaustion, her focus locked on safely delivering Myra's child.

As the early morning light crept in, something indefinable stirred in the room. Myra's cries swelled, and then, without a moment's notice, everything fell silent.

In the ensuing quiet, a new sound emerged — the faint, mewling cry of a newborn. Anevay lifted the child, a girl with a crown of dark hair and eyes that seemed too aware for one just entering the world.

"A daughter," Anevay said softly, moving to place the child in Myra's arms.

But Myra did not reach for her. She lay still, her arms limp at her sides. Her eyes, for the first time in what felt like ages, held a clarity, fixed on the infant with a mixture of dread and acceptance. "She's not mine," she said, her voice soft, almost disbelieving. "She was never mine."

Before anyone could react, Myra's body went rigid. She took in a deep, rattling breath, her gaze sweeping the room.

"You're all going to die," she spoke, her voice eerily calm, "and become nothing but fading visions."

With that, her eyes fluttered shut, her final breath slipping quietly from her lips. Silence filled the room once again, save for the newborn's soft cries.

Mortimer appeared in the doorway, a tentative smile playing on his lips until a voice caught him off guard. "Bring her to us."

He glanced around, searching for some sign that the others had heard it. Their faces showed nothing.

"Bring her to us," the voice urged again, clearer this time, ringing in his mind.

Anevay checked for Myra's pulse, then looked up, her expression somber. "She's gone. What do we do now?"

Ellie, though tears shimmered in her eyes, spoke with quiet resolve. "We go on as always. We adapt. We endure. We love."

She moved closer to Anevay, her eyes resting on the newborn. "Whatever Myra thought, whatever brought her to this point, this child is innocent. She's ours now. Part of our family."

North took a deep breath, his eyes shifting from Myra's lifeless body to the tiny girl cradled in Anevay's arms. "Ellie's right," he affirmed. "She's one of us. She's part of the future we've all been working toward."

Mortimer, who had been watching silently from the doorway, stepped into the room. "I'll take care of Myra," he told them.

Anevay looked up, a question in her eyes. "Are you sure? It's not an easy task."

"I can handle it." He chose not to share the voice that lingered in his thoughts. His smile was gentle. "You should all rest. You'll need your strength for these little ones."

As they left him to tend to Myra, each person was lost in their thoughts, her final words lingering in their minds, But with each step away from her still form, they moved toward something brighter, something yet to come. And the heaviness began to ease.

***

The infirmary was thick with the metallic scent of blood, layered with something even darker that Mortimer couldn't quite name. Myra lay there, lifeless, sprawled in a pool of red, her face frozen in a mask of agony and fear. Mortimer moved with a quiet sense of purpose, reaching for a stack of towels and a thick blanket from a nearby cabinet. He started to blot the blood from the floor, then gently around her body. Carefully, he placed the saturated towels upon her still form and wrapped her body within the thick blanket. A creeping unease settled in the pit of his stomach. It wasn't merely the gruesome sight before him - though that alone could haunt the sturdiest of souls - but the persistent whisper lodged in his mind. Soft as silk, yet chilling as the grave, it repeated with eerie calm: "Bring her to us. Bring her to us."

He pushed the thought aside, struggling to ground himself in the grim task at hand.

There's no voice. It's just exhaustion. Nothing more.

But he wasn't sure he believed it.

He finished the task, the blanket forming a cocoon around Myra's frail form. Mortimer found no tears in his eyes. "Goodbye,

Myra," he uttered quietly, his voice hollow, as if the words were slipping through him unnoticed. He bent to lift Myra's body, surprised at how strangely light she felt; whatever had taken root inside her had drained her of all substance, leaving behind a fragile shell.

He carried her out of the room, down the stairs, acutely aware of the others watching him but refusing to meet them. Outside, the night greeted him with a chill, brisk and biting, the wind stirring the leaves in restless calls of night creatures. He walked steadily, though her body seemed to grow heavier with each step, his muscles burning with the effort. His breath came ragged, his grip slipping as her form thudded to the ground. "Damn it." His strength was failing him, and he gave a resigned sigh. He grabbed her ankles and began to drag her the rest of the way.

The voice in his head grew louder, more urgent now. "Hurry. Bring her to us. We're waiting."

The trees stood before him, their branches extending like bony digits, clawing at the sky. The shadows between them pulsed with a strange energy as if the very darkness were alive. As Mortimer pulled her further into the woods, the darkness pressed in, feeling almost alive, drawing him deeper.

In a small clearing, he stopped. There, waiting, was a pack of dogs, but not in any familiar sense. These were beasts born of nightmares, their fur blackened and matted, hanging in clumps from their skeletal bodies. But it was their eyes that carried the true horror - they glowed, a deep, menacing red, more like coals than any natural fire. The pack remained still at first, watching him with an intelligence that sent a chill coursing through Mortimer. These were no ordinary animals.

At first, the pack remained still, a collection of tense muscles and vigilant eyes. They spread out around him, creating a quiet circle that left no room for escape. The leader, a creature of bone and rage, stood on a moss-covered rock, observing him with a keen awareness.

But he moved forward, compelled by something he couldn't name until he reached the edge of the clearing. "Here she is," he said panting, releasing his grip on her ankles. "Take her."

For a long moment, all was still. The dogs watched him, unblinking. Then, with terrifying suddenness, they descended. Their jaws snapped and tore at Myra's body, shredding the blanket as if it were nothing. Mortimer could not look away. The sounds - flesh ripping, bones breaking - pierced through his mind. He wanted to look away but he found himself unable to do so. Each sickening sound carved itself into his mind, the wet, tearing sounds, the splintering of bones. It was a relentless echo that would linger long after the darkness of the night had faded. He understood these noises would follow him long after the night ended.

And just as swiftly as they'd come, the dogs retreated into the shadows, leaving behind nothing but scraps of cloth and dark stains on the ground. Mortimer stood there, trembling, the bile rising in his throat.

What have I done?

Then, the voice returned, unexpectedly soft. "You've done well. She's with us now."

Whether that brought Mortimer any peace, he couldn't say. He turned, his legs heavy, his steps faltering, and made his way back to Browers, not daring to glance back at the clearing where the dogs had disappeared into the night.

***

The infirmary was alive with quiet purpose. Anevay, Ellie, and North tended to the three newborns, allowing a rare sense of calm to settle. Ellie and Anevay sat side by side, each holding their baby, while North gently rocked Myra's daughter, coaxing the child into a peaceful slumber.

"What should we name her?" Anevay asked softly, breaking the stillness.

All eyes turned to North, who gazed at the small bundle resting against him. His face held a quiet storm of emotions - wonder mingling with a deep sadness, joy intertwined with uncertainty. He spent a long moment looking down at the infant as if seeking answers in her delicate features.

"Hope," he said at last. "She's hope, despite everything. A chance for a better tomorrow."

Ellie and Anevay exchanged faint smiles, their tired faces momentarily brightening. The room felt lighter as if they could finally breathe in the possibility of brighter days ahead.

But the moment quickly shifted as something caught his eye. His hand trembled slightly as he adjusted the baby in the light. "What's this?" his voice tight with worry.

He motioned for the others to come closer, pointing toward a spot on the baby's arm. "Look," a finger hovering over Hope's tiny arm.

Anevay and Ellie moved in closer. There, on the infant's skin was a small, translucent patch, almost glimmering, as though a piece of her had been replaced with living glass.

Anevay let out a breath. "She got it from her mother."

Silence fell over the room again, the earlier warmth fading like a distant memory. They exchanged uneasy glances, unspoken questions and fears passing between them. The tiny mark on Hope's arm suddenly no bigger than a fingertip, suddenly seemed to represent all the unknowns of their new world.

28 Visions

Back inside Browers, Mortimer described the scene in stark terms, his voice trembling slightly, painting a picture of horror. "I brought her to the forest's edge, a broken thing," he croaked. "I meant to lay her to rest, but the dogs came. Wild, hungry things. They tore her away from me and disappeared into the dark, like shadows that swallowed the night." His words were a cobweb, spun from lies and fear, and they were caught in it, helpless flies.

North offered a thin lifeline. "At least you're okay," his voice a gentle hand on Mortimer's shoulder. "Rest now, old friend. Morning will bring a new day."

Mortimer managed a weak smile.

When he finally collapsed onto his bed, he lay there staring at the ceiling. The night played over and over in his mind like a wound that wouldn't close. He could still see those black dogs, their teeth tearing into Myra's flesh, her body twisted and broken. The scent of blood clung to him, heavy and real. Her weight was still in his arms, though she wasn't there. Bones snapping, the dogs growling - it all stayed with him.

Exhaustion dragged at him, threatening to pull him under. Then, something shifted in the room. He heard it. His eyes snapped open. She sat there, in that chair by the window. Edna. Her outline blurred by the dim light, but unmistakable. She looked different. Her hair was down, her hands moved restlessly in her lap, her face pale, eyes fixed upon him with an intensity that spoke of hunger or madness or both. He didn't know whether to feel fear or comfort.

"She's gone, love," her voice barely rose above the quiet.

He sucked in a breath, slow and ragged. "Yeah. It's done now."

Edna's expression changed, something close to sorrow weighing her down that made Mortimer's stomach churn. "You think so. It's just begun. What she carried - it's not gone. It's here. Taken root, deep in the heart of one who remains. The world is forever dark."

His eyes shut tight, trying to blot out the images rising inside him, the things he'd been a part of. He wanted it all to end, the memories, the endless nights. The walls crept in around him, narrowing, suffocating.

"You did what you thought you had to," Edna's voice came again. "I don't blame you for it, love. The hardest choices always leave marks."

He forced his eyes open, focusing on the cracks running through the ceiling. They formed patterns that his mind twisted into grotesque shapes. "There wasn't any choice," he told her, his words more for himself than Edna. "I couldn't do it."

Her form seemed to waver as if caught between worlds. "Nothing's ever over. The darkness isn't gone. It's only waiting."

The room grew colder, and he fumbled his way under the covers. One tear slipped free, hot and unexpected, tracing a path down his cheek. It wasn't just grief. It was a weight of guilt that pressed him down, squeezing the air from his lungs. He stared at

Edna, wanting to reach for her, to feel her hand one more time. But she was out of reach now, far away.

"Sleep," she whispered, soft as the wind. "You'll need it for what's coming."

Mortimer felt the pull of sleep at the edges of his awareness. He closed his eyes, though peace wouldn't come. His thoughts, still haunted by the uncertain shadows of the future. As he slipped into a fitful sleep, Edna's words were somewhere far behind him.

"The world is forever dark."

***

The greenhouse took on a different life at night, the air heavy with the fragrance of damp soil and flourishing greenery. Anevay found Ellie there, her silhouette gently illuminated by the dim overhead lights, fingers buried in the dirt as she planted sunflower seeds with quiet determination. The soft hum of the ventilation system was the only sound accompanying her shallow breaths.

"Sunflowers at this hour? It's quite late," Anevay's voice was gentle, barely disturbing the quiet. Her tone carried a soft understanding, as though she had uncovered a secret rhythm Ellie had woven into a new nightly ritual.

Ellie glanced up. Her smile was small but sincere like a delicate sprout breaking through the pavement.

"Been a busy day. Still so much to do. Never enough time," she said, her fingers gently pressing the seeds into the earth as though they held the answers to unspoken questions. "And you're still up."

"I've brought something for you." Anevay reached into her pocket, fingers curling around the worry stone. Its familiar contours, worn smooth by countless touches, felt like a symbol of their shared journey. As she held it out to Ellie, the stone seemed to carry the essence of all they had endured together.

"I think," Anevay spoke softly, "it's time this found its way home."

Between them, the stone gleamed dully, a bridge spanning the chasm of loss and hope that defined their new world.

***

In the years that followed Myra's death, life at Browers fell into something like routine, though the memory of what had come before still drifted in quiet corners. The children, Adam, Eve, and Hope, grew rapidly, and each day they were schooled by Anevay for at least four hours in the old ways. But even as they thrived, outside of what Anevay taught them, they learned the new ways, the ones born of necessity. For the dangers around them were never far from mind.

Adam, the oldest, had North's quiet about him, that way of holding the world at arm's length while keeping it in view. He followed North close, learning the things a man needed to know: how to track, to shoot, to watch the land. He split his time with Ellie too, tending to the plants, knowing the animals in the barn. Eve, sharp and curious, stayed near Anevay, soaking up every scrap of knowledge about medicine. Her hands were steady, her mind quicker than the others. And then there was Hope. Fragile, the illness clinging to her, a quiet shadow. Her skin carried the mark left by her mother, spreading slowly but surely. Anevay worked at it day and night, but it was like trying to hold back a tide with bare hands.

Ellie spent her days moving through the familiar rhythm of tending the greenhouses, and the barn animals. She was their center, her hands keeping the wheels turning, her quiet work giving them all food and some small comfort. North stood watch, the rifle slung over his shoulder, eyes never still. Those mangy dogs, with their glowing red eyes, haunted him. He patrolled each day, the edge of the forest always in his sight, ready for what might come.

Anevay divided her days between instructing the children and assisting Ellie while managing the infirmary. She gave the children their weekly checkups, her sharp mind, and steady hands catching every detail. She kept careful notes, a ledger of their growth and well-being. Hope troubled her most, the sickness lingering, a problem that stayed out of reach no matter how hard she tried to grasp it.

Mortimer, meanwhile, remained focused on maintaining and upgrading the facilities at Browers. His primary concern was the power system. He salvaged batteries from other facilities, rewiring controllers and mending monitors, ensuring a steady pulse of energy flowing from his labors. Without his deft touch, darkness would creep in, and the world would grow quiet. Adam occasionally joined him, learning about wiring and circuits, and helping to document procedures for a future that felt always uncertain.

As the years passed, visions of Edna had faded, though the memories stayed with him. He had accepted the silence that accompanied her absence, pouring himself into his tasks. Yet,

Hope's condition kept him at bay, her presence stirring something deep within him that he couldn't quite name.

As for North, the ghostly remains of a life once lived, had long since faded into the void. Those routines that once defined his existence - the cherished memories of his childhood, his father's steady presence, the solemn visits to his mother's grave, and the imaginary conversations he held with her as he grew - all had been consumed by the relentless march of time. He did think back to it, but only once, and found it darkly amusing - those past rituals, now as foreign as ancient hieroglyphs. A grim smile twisted his lips, for he understood with brutal clarity that in this new world, this silent wasteland of ash and bone, he had merely exchanged one set of hollow routines for another, equally meaningless. The earth cared not for the habits of men, living or dead.

***

Over the days, North and Mortimer became close. On one day, each took a break from their tasks, finding themselves sitting next to each other on a splintered bench that sagged beneath their weight. The wind, dry and steady, stirred the dust at their feet. Neither man spoke for a long time. They didn't need to. The silence between them was as old as their friendship, as familiar as the lines on their hands. They watched the world burn its colors into the horizon, each lost in thoughts they rarely shared.

"Your father," Mortimer began, his voice a gravel drawl that cut through the stillness, "you never really talk about him."

North looked up, the lines in his face deepening as if those words had scratched at something raw. "No," he said after a moment, "not much to say about him. Was a hard life for him, losing my mother."

Mortimer nodded, chewing on the silence for a bit. "Must've been hard. Him, losing her like that."

North's eyes, steady and dark, settled on the fire. "It was. But I don't remember him ever breaking." His voice was calm, but there was a quiet crack underneath, a fissure that time had worn thin. "He looked at me, you know. This person that had taken his whole world away. Never held any anger toward me. It was always as if it was time to get on with things. He never stopped moving me forward."

"He pushed you into teaching?"

North shook his head. "Was a teacher himself. Elementary school. He didn't push. Didn't have to. He showed me. Every day, he'd get up, and work. Never missed a beat. Grief didn't stop him. He wasn't a man who took to weakness, not even in himself. Education . . . I think it was his way of keeping me straight, keeping me from drifting off into something else. He thought if I had my mind set on books, on things that mattered, I'd stay out of trouble. And I did. That's where I acquired my passion for books. And eventually, my passion to be a writer."

Mortimer snorted, leaning back in his chair. "That's nice. He did his job then."

"Job?" North asked.

"His job as a father. Raising you the right way."

North glanced up. "He sure did. You know . . . every day I used to think about him, go over the memories in my mind. It was my way of making sure I'd never forget. But all that stopped when the end came. Turns out, I can never forget him, what he did for me." He paused. "What about your father? He was strict, wasn't he?"

Mortimer stared into the dim light, as if the past was sitting right there in front of him, waiting to be spoken. "Strict doesn't even cover it," he said, voice low. "He was a hard man. Believed in rules, in order. He had this way of looking at you like you were never quite enough. Like no matter what you did, it wasn't ever going to satisfy him. He had a belt for when you stepped out of line. I guess he wore it more than he should've."

North let that hang in the air for a moment, his hands folded between his knees. "That makes you the way you are?"

Mortimer shrugged, a bitter twist in his mouth. "Suppose so. You get raised like that, you learn quickly how to keep your head down. Or you fight back, but that wasn't me. I took it. Took it and did what he wanted. Made me hard too, in a different way."

North shifted in his seat. "Funny how that works," he muttered. "Two men, same goal . . . keeping us on track. But they went about it so differently."

Mortimer huffed out a breath, shaking his head. "Your old man, he might've been quiet, but he had sense. My father, he was all rules and no reason. Just anger wrapped up in something he thought was righteousness. Didn't care how it affected you, as long as you obeyed."

North's gaze stayed ahead watching the wind carry the dust about. "I think my father was scared," he said quietly. "Not of me. Of what would happen if he didn't hold it all together. He lost my mother, and maybe he figured if he let go, even for a second, everything would slip away. So he just . . . tightened his grip a little."

"Fear will do that," Mortimer said. "Make a man hold on to what he can control."

North nodded, a sad smile playing on his lips. "Maybe. But I always loved him. I tried to understand the grief that consumed him, to take some of it from him if I could."

Mortimer turned to him, his eyes filled with a quiet understanding. "And perhaps, in doing so, you gave him a reason to hold on. A reason to keep fighting."

North looked away, the vastness of the desert stretching out before them. "I hope so," he said. "I hope so."

The wind gusted slightly. Mortimer shifted in his seat, and for a while, neither man spoke. The quiet settled in around them, not unwelcome, but thick with the past, with fathers and the lessons they left behind.

North's voice broke the silence once more, soft and steady. "We're both still here, though."

"Yeah," Mortimer said, a trace of something softer in his voice. "We are."

***

There came one evening, as the sun sank low, casting shadows that stretched like fingers across Browers when North summoned the group for their daily meeting. They gathered around the table in the kitchen, a small island of light in the encroaching gloom.

"Everyone's here," North stated, his voice cutting through the stillness. "Let's get started."

Ellie spoke first. "The greenhouses are thriving. We're looking at a strong harvest this season. There looks to be enough rainwater to sustain us. The animals are healthy, and we have supplies to see us through the winter."

Anevay followed with her update. "The children are doing well with their lessons, and they're growing stronger every day. Adam and Eve are in good health. As for Hope, we're managing her condition as best we can. I've been trying out some new treatments, but it's a slow process."

Mortimer shifted in his chair, a slight ease in his posture. "The new batteries are in. I've rewired the controllers with Adam's help. Power should hold steady now. I'll keep an eye on it. Just need to clean the solar panels up on the roof."

"Think you can manage that?" North asked, a hint of worry threading through his tone. "None of us are getting any younger. I worry about you."

Mortimer chuckled, the corners of his eyes crinkling. "Your concern is duly noted. This work is an old habit now, second nature. I'll manage just fine."

North's gaze swept the table, resting on each person, one after the other. "Good. We're making headway, all things considered. Still, we cannot afford to let our guard down. The dogs grow bolder, creeping nearer to the perimeter. Vigilance is necessary."

Ellie's hand found North's arm. "We will stay vigilant. We are a team. We'll look out for each other."

As the meeting broke up, Mortimer retreated to his workshop in the basement, a realm steeped in the whir of machines and the sharp scent of oil mingling with cold metal. He had a few tasks yet to finish before nightfall. Engrossed in the work, he navigated the cluttered space, tools in hand, while memories danced at the edges of his mind. The image of Edna, nestled in that corner chair, flickered back into view, her words echoing faintly in his thoughts. He shook his head, casting the recollection aside, and returned to the present task.

Anevay moved softly through the upstairs rooms, checking on the children. They lay in peaceful slumber, unaware of the world outside.

Later that evening, Anevay and North met in a quiet corner of the greenhouse, gazing upward at the stars dotting the sky. North's rifle rested across his lap, his eyes scanning the darkness beyond the glass.

"I worry about them," Anevay admitted, her voice barely a wisp. "The children. Especially Hope."

North's grip tightened on the rifle. "We'll protect them. You're doing the best you can with Hope."

"But her condition is clearly worsening. Her skin is red and irritated. I've applied another ointment I made, but when I asked her if it hurt, she just smiled and said no. Her bright eyes met mine as she asked if it would ever go away. She's such a sweetheart."

"What did you tell her?" North asked.

"I told her I wasn't sure, but I'd find a way to make it better."

North offered reassurance. "You will."

That night, Mortimer lay in his bed when a sound stirred him. It was faint, a whisper that seemed to drift through the stillness. He sat upright, heart hammering in his chest. "Edna?" Silence answered him. The room was barren, the chair in the corner empty. He settled back down, the whisper fading into the quiet.

Eyes shut tight, he sought sleep, but a heavy dread remained, an unwelcome specter refusing to depart.

Days rolled onward, the rhythm of life maintaining its relentless march. Children, with their endless energy, filled the air with laughter - a bright flame cutting through the heavy cloak of uncertainty. Their hours were woven from play and learning, each second a testament to their spirit and innocence. Ellie and Anevay toiled, unwavering in their commitment, their resolve a quiet yet potent force propelling them forth. Hands never stilled, spirits never dimmed, they faced the trials with poise and strength.

North, ever watchful, kept his gaze fixed on the horizon. He moved with purpose, each step deliberate, as if attuned to the subtle tremors of the world around him, always prepared for whatever may come.

Meanwhile, Mortimer immersed himself in his work, the relentless grind of machinery offering a distraction from the unease that crept through his mind like smoke. The rhythmic clatter of metal striking metal filled the space, drowning out the whispers of uncertainty. Yet, beneath it all, an undeniable sense of foreboding clung to him, an awareness that something significant loomed in the distance, out of sight, poised to alter the course of all things.

***

The sun rose slow, low over the horizon, its warmth sliding across the kitchen, casting long shadows through the high windows. The group gathered for breakfast, the rich scent of fresh bread, eggs and bacon, and coffee filling the air. Mortimer sat at the head of the table, a small smile curving his lips, content in the moment.

"Today's the day," he announced. "I'll be up on the roof this morning to clean the solar panels."

"Want some help?" Adam asked.

Mortimer smiled. "No, son. You've got your studies. I'll manage."

Adam met his gaze and returned the smile.

North, across the table, raised his eyes, a hint of worry creeping across his face. "Are you sure that's wise? We're both not as young as we once were."

Mortimer let out a low laugh. "Speak for yourself, North. I'm still plenty young."

Ellie glanced up from her plate, worry flickering in her eyes. "Please be careful, Mortimer."

"Always," he replied, a wink punctuating his words. "Done it a hundred times. Today will be no different."

The group finished their breakfast, the usual routine of chores and tasks ahead of them. North's concern lingered in the back of his mind, but Mortimer's calm demeanor and confidence seemed to ease his mind if only a little. As everyone moved on to their daily duties, Mortimer began to ready himself for the job ahead.

He grabbed a small broom and a bucket with some cleaning fluid, his hands sure. The metal stairs up were steep but he climbed like it was nothing, each step the same as it ever was, his mind set on the task. At the top, he pushed open the door, stepped onto the roof where the panels spread out in every direction, shining in the morning sun. The wires and boxes lay scattered, a mess to some, but to him, it all made sense. He stood there a moment, the wind tugging at his shirt, his eyes roaming the panels as if deciding where to start. It was a moment of calm, a breath before the plunge into the day's tasks.

Then he saw something, something off in the corner of his eye. Movement, far out at the edge of the roof. His heart jolted in his chest. He squinted into the light, trying to make it out. A small figure, a girl, standing where no one should be. It was Hope, her red, blistered skin unmistakable. The sight of her was a shock, something cold settling in his gut. He stared, not believing, not sure if he was looking at fear or something close to awe.

How can she be here?

Questions ran wild through his thoughts, each one pushing harder than the last, as he stepped forward, cautious, drawn to her like something inevitable. The roof beneath him felt wrong, and unstable, as if the ground itself was giving way underfoot. Mortimer's mind worked quickly, tension pulling tighter with each breath, as he moved toward the edge, toward Hope, toward whatever waited there for him.

"How did you get up here, little one?" he asked.

Closer now, Hope didn't stir, her eyes locked on his, hard and cold. Her small hand reached out, and Mortimer felt a calm come over him, like something settling. He reached too, his fingers just shy of touching hers, but when he tried to take hold, his hand slid through hers as though she wasn't there at all.

A vision!

The revelation was both electrifying and disorienting, causing his balance to falter. In that split second of confusion, Mortimer stumbled forward, his foot catching on the edge of a panel.

Time seemed to slow as he teetered on the brink. His arms went wide, fighting for a hold that wasn't there. Gravity took him, and with a scream that tore through the air, Mortimer plummeted from the roof. The sky and the ground became one spinning mass until his body hit the ground, hard, with a sickening thud.

Ellie, bent over her plants in the greenhouse, caught a blur of something at the edge of her vision. Her heart sank as she turned to see Mortimer's crumpled form lying on the ground below. Panic gripped her, her voice trembling with urgency as she called out, "North! North, something's happened to Mortimer!" Her plea shattered the delicate calm of the day, cutting through the air with a desperate cry for help.

They ran. When they reached him, what they found was wrong, twisted. Mortimer's body lay in a heap, bent and broken, blood creeping slowly from the back of his skull. His breathing was ragged, each gasp pulling him farther away.

North dropped down beside him, his face ashen and taut with fear. "Mortimer, stay with us," he urged, his voice breaking under the weight of impending loss.

Mortimer's eyes opened slowly, those clouded eyes pale and lifeless, like stones worn smooth by years of river water. For a moment, something passed through them, a shadow of the man he once was. "North . . . Ellie . . ." His voice cracked, dry like leaves caught in a gust of wind. "I can't feel anything . . . It's like I'm floating." He paused, his breath thin and uneven. "I'm sorry . . ."

"Don't talk. Save your strength," North replied, trying to keep his voice steady though he felt something shatter inside him. He'd seen death before, too much of it, but this was different. This was Mortimer. "Save your strength, my friend. You've got more to do today." The lie tasted bitter on his tongue, a hollow reassurance that neither of them believed.

North looked to Ellie, his eyes wild with a desperation he couldn't quite hide. "Get Anevay. Now!" The words came sharp, cut with fear and the truth they were both too late to outrun.

Ellie ran, heart pounding like a drum, returning with Anevay close behind, breathless and wide-eyed. But the sight that met them stopped them dead in their tracks, as surely as if they'd run into an invisible wall.

North held Mortimer's body in his arms, his shoulders shaking with sobs pulled from some deep place in him, uncontrollable. The morning sun, indifferent to their grief, cast long shadows painting a scene of loss that none of them would ever forget.

Anevay knelt beside them, hands trembling even as her instincts took over. She pressed her fingers to Mortimer's throat, searching for a pulse she knew she wouldn't find. His skin already cooling, the life slipping away like air from a punctured tire, leaving nothing but the shell of a man they once knew.

"He's gone," she whispered sadly.

North's sobs fell to the silence, a silence so profound it seemed to have weight, pressing down on all of them. Shadows of what had been and what would come settled around them like a storm already passed. In that quiet, Mortimer's death became real, a change in the world so sudden it hurt to think of it. They were islands of life in a sea of absence, and one more light had just gone out.

Ellie set her hand on North's shoulder, her tears falling. "He was a good man. He did what he felt was always best."

North, his face streaked with tears, answered in a voice worn and broken. "He did."

They sat in the quiet, the world a shifting ground beneath their feet. The future, once steady and clear, brightened by the light of the children, now seemed clouded and confused. The loss had scattered their world into fragments, and they were left to piece it together in the dark. But there was something beneath it all, a pull, a quiet tension that waited as if the world held its breath for what came next. It wasn't just sorrow. It was the quiet promise that what had ended here was giving way to something else. Something new.

***

The sky was bruised and swollen, purples and yellows smearing together like an old wound. The sun was dim, its light weak, trying but failing to cut through the heavy layers of clouds. Wind swept over them, cold and sharp, dragging the smell of rain behind it, pulling the last bits of warmth from the earth. The small group stood at the rise, braced against the elements, the task before them pressing down like a weight none of them wanted to carry. Above, the heavens gave no comfort, only watched with indifference.

North's hand engulfed Adam's tiny fingers, feeling the boy's warmth like a lifeline in this cold, dead world. Ellie and Anevay stood close, each holding onto a child, as if letting go would mean losing them to the wind. Eve, with her wild hair and wide eyes, clung to Ellie's leg, cautious, unsure. Hope, true to her name, stood quiet and firm, her gaze far ahead as though she could see past the present, something none of them could touch.

Something's coming. Something's always coming.

At the top of the hill, Mortimer's grave was marked by a sorry-looking cross, just two boards tied together with wire, already starting to creak in the wind. It stood, holding its ground against the land that was always looking to take it back. North planted his feet, feeling the damp earth suck at his boots as if it wanted to drag him in with Mortimer. He cleared his throat, and the sound was dry and coarse, barely more than a whisper over the wind.

"Mortimer was a good man," North said, his voice low, scraping. "He kept us safe. He did what he had to do, made this place run so we could sleep at night, so we could dare to dream of a future."

Ellie and Anevay's eyes glistened like rain-slicked glass, their sorrow a living, breathing thing that seemed to fill the air like fog. Adam looked up at North, his young face full of things he couldn't yet name, death being one of them. But its finality somehow coldly seeped into his being. Eve whimpered soft, like a small thing caught in the dark. And Hope, peeking out from behind Ellie's legs, her eyes dry and watchful, with a calm that didn't fit her age.

North kept his eyes on the cross. He spoke to it as if Mortimer could still hear. "He carried things none of us understood. He made choices that kept us here, kept us alive. We owe him. And we'll carry on because of him."

He stopped, the wind taking his words, and when he spoke again, it was for Mortimer alone. "There were ghosts, always. The ones we hold in the back of our minds, never letting us go. But I remember the times he'd talk about the world before, the world we lost. There was sorrow, deep and enduring in his voice about what happened. Yet, when we talked about the future, there was always hope in his eyes, an unwavering optimism. I'll miss him. He's with his love now. With his Edna."

He turned to the others, his eyes moving from one to the next. "We'll keep it going. We owe him that. We'll dream of a future because he believed in one." His words were met with silence, but the silence was agreement, a promise in the quiet that followed.

Anevay shook with quiet sobs, and North held Adam's hand tighter, drawing whatever strength he could from the boy's presence. "May he find peace," North's voice cracking like thin iced, "May his soul keep watch over us, because God knows we need all the help we can get in this world of ours. Rest easy, old friend. You've earned it."

The wind picked up, a low whistle through the trees, and North felt something in it, a presence he couldn't name. Mortimer, maybe. Watching. He didn't know if it gave him comfort or if it made him wary.

The sky opened up then, rain falling soft and steady, mixing with the tears. They stood there a moment longer, the rain drumming a quiet song, before they turned, one by one, and began the slow walk back to Browers.

Ellie and Anevay walked ahead, their heads bowed against the rain. North and Adam followed, their steps heavy with the burden of loss. Hope, led by Ellie, craned her neck to look back at the grave, her face unreadable, something in her eyes that made North uneasy. As her gaze reached the edge of the trees, a small smile flickered across her lips, a thing that seemed strangely out of place.

At the top of the hill, the black dogs showed themselves, long and lean, their eyes burning like coals in the fading light. They moved with a steady intent, drawn toward the grave, their hunger plain in every step. Hope's grin widened, a secret curve to it that no one else caught.

North watched them, his voice calm though carrying something darker. "There's something about those dogs," he said, "they're more than shadows."

He noticed the shift in Hope's grin, barely perceptible. A strange unease crept into him, a sense that things weren't right. "Hope," he asked, his tone careful, "what do you see out there?"

She shrugged. "Just the night, Papa. Only the night."

North glanced at her, unsettled. Something wasn't right. He'd have to keep an eye on her. There were truths locked behind those eyes. But for now, all he could do was wait and wonder what might come crawling out of the dark when no one was looking.

29　For the ages

Fifteen years or so had passed since the great undoing, the years shaping the land and the few who remained. The fields thrived, greenhouses tended by Ellie and Eve's steady hands. Adam, now a strong boy of fifteen, had taken up the role of protector, North's old rifle resting sure in his grip. His hands, hardened beyond his age, knew every groove in that stock like it was an extension of himself. And Hope, sweet irony of a name, bore her affliction with a quiet grace that wounded them all. Her skin, a patchwork of raw, reddened splotches, told a tale of survival that not even they could fully grasp.

North, once a man of formidable presence, shuffled through Browers like a ghost of his former self. The children called him Papa now, and the cane in his grip was a scepter, the last emblem of his reign in this broken kingdom. Eighty years behind him, his body had turned against him, every joint stiff and grinding. Yet his mind remained sharp, a blade honed on years of hard living. Each morning before the sun, he rose, fumbling with pen and paper, filling out his lists like a man clinging to life's last anchor. He kept track of every morsel, each tally mark a whisper of their thin grasp on survival. His logs, etched in shaky scrawl, captured the mundane and the unspeakable.

At dawn, North began his rounds. A slow, deliberate march through the bowels of Browers, checking what still worked, what sputtered and groaned under the weight of time. It was a routine forged in desperation, a comfort born of necessity. In the stillness of those moments, when the burden threatened to crush him, North closed his eyes and tried to remember the world before. But those memories, too, were slipping away, like sand through an old man's fingers.

One of those mornings, during the familiar slog, North saw him. Through the doorway's thin light, the old man sat on a bench, draped in a trench coat, a hat pulled low, the empty leash still clutched in his hand.

Hmmm . . . didn't trip the alarm . . .

"Adam!" North called, his voice trembling with age and astonishment.

Adam, nearly as tall as North, was beside him in an instant. "What is it, Papa?"

North pointed a twisted finger at the figure. "Look. It's him. The old man. From the café."

Adam's eyes widened. "Stay here, Papa. I'll get Ellie and Anevay."

"No, no," North's voice was thin. "Help me to him."

Reluctantly, Adam wrapped his arm around the frail man's shoulders, the old weight of him leaning in, and they made their slow way outside. Ellie and Anevay appeared from the dim corners, their faces shadowed by both dread and wonder.

Halfway to the bench, North stopped. "Thank you, Adam. I'll go the rest of the way alone," he told him. "You can go back."

Adam hesitated, gripping his North's arm. "Let me go with you," he pleaded.

North shook his head. "No. This is something I have to do myself."

Adam stepped back, worried for North, but did as he was told and returned to Browers where the others had gathered.

Ellie's voice was low as she spoke to her son, explaining the old man's past. "He brought Papa here. He won't harm him."

"But what do we know about him? Does he have a name?" Adam asked.

Ellie glanced at the old man on the bench. "Names don't matter to him. He's a shadow, a passing thing. He's been around longer than we can imagine, yet he's as fleeting as a breeze through open fields."

They watched in silence as North hobbled toward the bench, the old man's eyes, ancient and knowing, settled on North as he eased himself onto the bench, breathless and weary. "Time hasn't been kind to you, has it?" the old man mused. A wry smile played at the corners of his mouth. "But then, it isn't kind to anyone. Not even me. You'd think I would've known better, considering I'm the one who set it all in motion."

North managed a soft chuckle, brittle as it was. "It's been long," he replied, each word carrying the burden of what he had witnessed and endured, of all he'd done. "Too long."

The old man's eyes softened. "You've done well, old North," he said, and there was a warmth in his voice that made North's chest tighten with an emotion he couldn't quite name. "You found your father's strength within you, that resilience you once thought was beyond your reach. And look what you've built with it – this place where humanity can again begin anew."

North's sigh was deep and weary, carrying with it memories of countless sleepless nights. "It wasn't easy," he admitted.

"It wasn't supposed to be," the old man said, his voice far away. "What was it your father used to say? Ah, yes . . . 'Buy the ticket, take the ride.'" He offered North a smile, one that held both sorrow and pride. "Well, old North, you've had quite the ride. But even the longest journeys have their end."

North closed his eyes, a sense of peace washing over him. "I'm ready. It's time for me to go."

"Yes. But before you can rest, there's one more thing you need to do."

North exhaled deeply. "What's that?"

"You need to get your family ready. Three women and their children will be here soon. And after them, others. Tell your family not to fear. What you've built here will carry on."

North's voice was barely a whisper. "But I am tired . . . so tired."

"We all are." The old man smiled, a rare and fleeting expression.

And then he was gone. Just like that. North, alone on the bench, took a long, slow breath and began the walk back. When he reached the others, they surrounded him, their faces drawn, full of questions. Adam rushed to his side, supporting him as he made his way inside.

"Papa, what did he say?' Adam's voice was urgent.

North met his eyes, a sad smile playing on his lips. "He said my time's up. I'll be leaving soon."

Adam's face crumpled, his voice cracking like thin ice. "Where are you going?"

North's smile was delicate, a pale echo of the robust grin that once lit up his face. It hovered on his lips but failed to reach his eyes, which held a distant look, already staring into a world beyond their own. "With him," his voice soft but clear, nodding towards the now empty bench. "With the old man. To a place where I can finally lay this tired old body to rest." He hesitated, his gaze sweeping over the faces of his family, lingering on each one as if committing them to memory. "But before I leave, we've got work to do. Three women and their children are coming. Our little community here is about to get a whole lot bigger."

Ellie's hand found North's arm, her fingers curling into the fabric of his shirt as if she could keep him tethered to this world through sheer force of will. "We'll be ready," she told him, voice firm, though a tremble pulled at her mouth. Her eyes, usually sharp with purpose, were now wet with what she could no longer hold back.

Anevay wiped at the tears in her eyes. "We'll start the preparations." Her thoughts already strayed toward the work, the steps they'd have to take. "We'll do what needs doing."

Ellie and Anevay shared a look, an understanding that needed no words. They'd known this moment would come, spoken of it in the still hours of the night when the truth was easier to bear. But knowing and being ready were two different things. North had taught them to keep on, no matter the loss, to salvage what could be saved, to make something out of the broken world left behind. It was the craft of survival, the shaping of lives from the wreckage.

North's smile widened, and for a brief instant, he seemed the man he used to be. A tear ran the course of his weathered cheek. "You've come so far," he said, his voice catching. "I'm proud of you all, proud of what we've done together."

They gathered close, this family born of hardship, pieced together by the cruel twist of time. Survivors in a world that had lost its color, where the days stretched thin. And as the sun fell, casting its fading light over Browers, the air turned soft, false in its quiet. They knew better. The night would bring something new, and in this place, nothing new came without a price.

***

The days came heavy with work. Ellie and Eve tended the greenhouses and animals without pause, hands always moving, eyes on the crops and the beasts. They worked like they were trying to outrun time, knowing new mouths would soon need feeding. Adam spent his hours with the guns and supplies, counting each bullet and ration, not letting a single item slip past his care. Anevay, always quick and steady, busied herself in the infirmary, preparing for the injured or sick that might come. And Hope, careful in her movements, took up the task of mending clothes and sorting blankets, her fingers working slow but sure.

North, though age had worn him down, set to his tasks like a man who knew his time was measured. He poured over his logs, writing down each step of the day, planning for the things that hadn't come yet but would. His mind was a long way from the present, already looking toward the future he'd never see.

One evening, the family sat together around the table, the quiet hum of their talk broken by North's voice.

"I want you all to know how much you mean to me," he started, his voice trembling with heartfelt emotion. "You've made this a home. When I'm gone, I need you to keep it that way. Look after one another. Take care of those who'll come. Build a community that will thrive long after I'm gone."

Adam reached across the table, taking North's hand. "We will, Papa. We'll make you proud."

North nodded, a tired smile on his face. "I know you will, son."

***

The night closed in over Browers, a thick and unrelenting thing, wrapping the old place in silence. Inside, nothing stirred save for the low murmur of machines long settled into their age. North lay still, his breath shallow, each rise and fall a reminder of what little remained. His cane stood by, patient and silent.

Sleep tugged at him, heavy, when he saw the figure at the foot of his bed. The old man stood there as he had before, familiar and distant, wrapped in shadows that seemed to breathe on their own. North's eyes cracked open, recognition stirring in their depths.

"You've come," he murmured in a dry rasp.

The old man gave the smallest nod. "It's time, old North."

North shifted, pain digging deep into his bones. The old man offered his hand, and North took it, the strength of another flowing through him. He swung his legs over the side, feet meeting the cold floor with a finality that settled somewhere beyond words.

"Where are we going?" North asked, his voice stronger now, bolstered by the old man's presence.

"To a place where peace awaits," came the reply. There was more in those words, something unspoken.

North's hand reached for the cane, but the old man stopped him. "You won't need it." And there was a tug in his mind, something half-forgotten, a memory brushing against the edges of consciousness. It was as if the old man had uttered these words long ago, in some forgotten moment.

With the old man's hand steadying him, North rose. They walked side by side down the hallway, the walls dim and receding, memories leaking into the space between them. Time became fluid, slipping from one moment into the next, past and present mingling until they were the same.

North broke the silence with a voice soft as a child's. "Will I see them again? My father? My mother? Will I finally be able to meet her? To talk to her? There's so much I want to ask her, to tell her." He paused, swallowing with difficulty. "And my Uncle? And Mortimer?" His words stumbled slightly as he added, "And my students . . . the ones who disappeared on that last, terrible day? I want to tell them that I am sorry for what happened. How their lives were cut off so short."

The old man turned, his eyes glinting with something like light. "Oh, my friend. You'll see whoever you want to see. That's how it works."

North frowned as a lifetime of questions surged within him. "Will they be real? Will they know me as I was, or as I am now?"

The old man chuckled, a sound low and rumbling. "Real enough. As real as anything here. And they'll see you you. But how they see you . . ." He trailed off, gesturing vaguely. "That part's yours to figure out."

The air thickened, a strange calm settling over North as they moved. With each step, a curious sense of detachment enveloped him, as if he were gently casting off the weight of his mortal existence, shedding layers of his former self.

At last, they stepped out into a wide-open space, boundless and still. There was no light, no dark, just a place where everything waited. North breathed it in, trying to grasp the shape of where he was.

"Where is this?" he asked in awe.

"It's a passage," the old man spoke. "A place where worlds meet. You'll see things here that you couldn't before, truths that have eluded you."

As they walked on, North saw shapes in the distance, figures moving against the stretch of time. Some stirred memories, faces from lives long gone. Others were strangers, blurred by what couldn't be known.

Among them, three women emerged clear. Each with a child at her side, their steps calm, faces lit by something unseen. They turned toward North, the children close to their mothers, their expressions quietly bright.

"These are the ones I told you of," the old man said. "They'll find their way to what you've built, looking for shelter, for something better. But it's on you to guide them."

A sense of purpose welled in North. "How?"

The old man's hand rested on his shoulder, firm and gentle. "Don't you remember?"

But North couldn't. The memory was just out of reach.

The women and children drew closer, their steps barely there, as if they were part of something greater, something North couldn't quite understand. One of them, her face worn but strong, lifted her eyes and met North's. Her gaze widened, something shifting in her like she was seeing far beyond what lay in front of her.

"I see it," she said, her voice sharp in the stillness of the barren landscape. "His face in the light. We have to follow."

A calm came over North, like a tide slowly rolling in.

"I remember," he said. "I'm the old man in the light. Their guide

"That's right," the old man replied. "Your last gift to the world you're leaving."

"Who will greet them?"

"Adam. They will see your face in his, and he will welcome them."

North knew what was needed, with a kind of surety that was both steady and wild. He turned to lead the women and their children towards Browers. Towards sanctuary. Towards a future he'd never see but felt deep within him.

They were on their way to Browers, the distance shrinking with each step, and North saw what lay ahead. Adam stood there, welcoming them, but then the world around him transformed. Time blurred, the past and present tangled, fading like old scars. North felt the years fall from him, worn down by struggle and pain, swept away like dust in the wind. His eyes searched, and found the old man, standing with a quiet smile as if he'd known all along.

"The ride is ending, but theirs is just beginning," the old man told North. "You've given them a chance. That's all I ever hoped for."

North's eyes clouded, the old man fading into a soft glow. He closed his eyes, peace settling in him. When he opened them again, the old man was walking beside him, leading him onward.

The years fell away, and North felt whole. He looked back, hoping to see Browers again, but it was gone.

He closed his eyes for the last time, letting the old man lead him further into a realm of wonders.

30 Legacy

The day they buried North began with a sky so blue it seemed almost indifferent. Ellie stood by the door, watching the children gather, though they weren't really children anymore. They huddled together, and their voices fell low, almost like they didn't want the day to hear them.

Anevay joined her, offering a quiet presence. "It's time," she said, her hand resting on Ellie's shoulder.

Ellie took a deep breath, steadying herself, though her heart moved like a storm inside. "Let's go," she answered, her voice calm where her thoughts weren't.

They walked down to the lawn, where North's body lay, wrapped in a simple blanket. The children moved aside, giving way without a word, their eyes all on her. Ellie felt it, something unspoken waiting for her, thick in the air.

She faced them - no longer the children she once knew - and waited. Adam, Eve, Hope - stood together, their expressions solemn but composed. They had grown up in this world, shaped by loss, though Ellie still marveled at how much of it they'd endured.

This is what he's left behind. The fruit of his labor, his grit, his endless faith in a future he'd never see.

"We're here," Ellie began, her voice clear, cutting through the quiet, "to say goodbye to someone who wasn't just our leader or our Papa. He was the one who showed us the way when the world disappeared before our eyes."

As she spoke, her thoughts wandered back to those early days at Browers. The fear that gripped them all. The endless stretch of not knowing what came next, clinging to hope so thin you couldn't tell if it was real. But North had been there, unmoved, holding them together when everything else fell apart.

"Papa believed in us," she said, looking at each face around her. "He believed we could rebuild, that we could create something new and beautiful out of the ruins of what was lost. And look at us now."

There was a ripple among them, heads lowering, hands clasping tighter. A silent understanding passed between them, a wordless grief shared by all.

"As we say goodbye to Papa," Ellie went on, "we don't just honor him with what we say. We honor him with what we do. We'll keep going. We'll keep building, growing, like he always wanted. That's how we remember him."

She stepped back then, nodding to Adam, Eve, and Hope. They moved forward, lifting North's body with care, lowering him into the ground. Ellie felt something rise up in her, heavy and sharp, almost too much to bear. But Anevay's hand found hers, squeezing tightly. Together, they watched as the first handfuls of dirt were scattered over the blanket.

Adam took the shovel and did the rest. Eve and Hope planted flowers, small and fragile, but alive. As the last bit of dirt was pressed down, Ellie spoke once more.

"Papa loved John Keats, a poet from the time before," she said softly, unfolding a piece of paper. "He read his words every day. I'll end with some of those words now . . .

Forlorn! the very word is like a bell
To toll me back from thee to my sole self!
Adieu! the fancy cannot cheat so well
As she is fam'd to do, deceiving elf.
Adieu! adieu! thy plaintive anthem fades
Past the near meadows, over the still stream,
Up the hillside; and now 'tis buried deep
In the next valley-glades:
Was it a vision, or a waking dream?
Fled is that music: -Do I wake or sleep?"

Ellie stood by the mound of fresh dirt, her connection to North's grave something she didn't need to speak aloud. Anevay beside her, hand resting firm, not a word exchanged. Adam and Eve were near enough to be felt, their presence solid like the ground underfoot. But Hope was already gone, her shape swallowed by the horizon.

When night fell over Browers, Ellie returned to North's room. His presence still lingered in the stillness, in the chair pulled up to the desk, in the worn spines of books along the shelves. She sat there, her hands running across the desk's smooth surface.

How many decisions had been made here? How many problems solved? What futures had passed through his mind?

Her fingers moved without thought, opening the drawers. It felt like crossing a line that shouldn't be crossed, an act of trespass. Yet something pulled her forward, a force she couldn't name, driving her hands to sift through what had been left behind. Beneath old lists and papers, her name sat on an envelope.

Her hands shook as she tore it open finding three documents inside. On the first, North's handwriting, so familiar and steady, filled the page.

Ellie,

If you're reading this, then I've finally taken that last journey. Don't grieve too much for me - I've lived a full life, fuller than I ever could've imagined in those dark days after the divine reset.

I'm leaving you in charge. I know you don't think you're ready, but trust me, you are. You've always been the heart of this community, even when you didn't realize it. The others will look to you now, not just for leadership, but for hope.

I've left in this envelope two other documents. Read them both to the group. And Ellie - now that our community has grown, others may be on their way. Keep watching. Keep believing.

Thank you for everything. For your friendship. For your support. For your steadfast commitment to our shared vision. I couldn't have done any of this without you.

Take care of them. Take care of yourself.

North, Papa

Ellie read the letter once, then again, and a third time. North's words ran clear in her mind. She folded the paper slowly, and placed it in her pocket. The other papers lay untouched on the desk as if she weren't ready to face them just yet. But what they carried called to her, quiet but insistent.

She breathed deep, thoughts and memories thick inside her. Her hand hovered over the next page, hesitating. Then, with a breath let out, she picked up the first sheet and her eyes began their path across the lines.

The paper was aged, yellowed some, but still sharp with what it meant. Their early days at Browers came alive again as she read, as sharp now as the day North had written it. "The Eleven Tables," he'd named them, a nod to old laws that had once governed men. But these weren't set in wood or stone; they were in ink, now fading, time gnawing at what even the strongest hands once held firm.

She paused at the sixth rule, a smile touched her lips. "Be wary of the unknown . . ." it read. How many times had they encountered the unknown?

Every moment of every day.

The seventh and fifth rules lay bare what they'd built together: "Never give up hope . . ." and "Be strong . . ." Simple words that had shaped their community, guided their actions, and ultimately led them to this moment.

But the eleventh rule caught her and made her throat tighten. North's bold hand had written it, underlined twice: "Never ever forget the mothers . . ."

Ellie laid the paper down, her fingers resting gently on it. Sacred, in its way. North's words, his last to them, seemed to breathe on their own. A bridge between what was and what would come, a map to steer through the waters they had yet to cross.

Her eyes tracked North's handwriting again, slow and deliberate. The thought came to her without effort, clear and settled.

This will be the foundation of our law. Not just rules to be followed, but a way to live.

It stirred something deep in her, a quiet sense of what was to come.

With a deep breath, she reached for the last document. She reached for the final sheet. Whatever North had left them, whatever he had poured into these words - wisdom, caution, a trace of hope - she knew it would guide them forward. The crumple of the paper in her hands sounded loud in the still air of his office. She began to read. The script was no longer the sure, steady hand she'd known. The lines wavered, uneven, fragile. The sight of it undid her. Her eyes burned and the tears came, unasked for, warm as they slipped down her face. Each drop that hit the page smeared the ink, blurring the words as if North's last message was fading into her sorrow.

My Dearest Friends,

Permit me, a former professor and humble writer of tales, to guide this missive with a heavy heart and trembling hand. Once, I envisioned our shared tale as a masterpiece, a saga to inspire and enchant future generations, a ballad sung in the halls of heroes. Yet, time, the insidious thief, has stolen the vibrancy from my pen, leaving but shadows of memory.

Let us speak truly of our journey, a path marked by both sunlight and shadow. Mortimer, a steadfast companion, was torn from us in a storm of fate, leaving a void as vast as the empty sea. Anevay, a guiding light in our darkest hours, her courage a warm hearth against the cold. Ellie, with a heart pure as morning dew, bore our burdens with a grace that humbled us all. And then there was Myra, a shadow cast across our hearth, her spirit a tempestuous sea. May the sun now warm her troubled soul.

Our children, the bright flowers that sprung forth amidst our trials, brought laughter and renewal. Their spirits, like the morning sun, chased away the shadows of despair. Their laughter was a melody that lifted our weary hearts, a reminder of the innocence and hope that still thrived amidst the trials of our journey.

As the years have passed, I find myself reflecting on the bonds we have forged. These bonds, tempered by the fires of adversity, have become unbreakable chains of friendship and love. Each of you has left an indelible mark upon my soul, a witness to the strength and resilience of the human spirit.

Now, as dusk descends upon my days, I offer this as a parting gift, a token of gratitude for your presence in my life. Though my strength wanes, my heart remains steadfast. May our paths converge once more in the halls of eternity, where friendships forged in fire shall forever endure.

With deepest affection,

Papa

Ellie lowered the letter, a faint smile touching her lips. North's words lingered with her, their meaning sinking deeper than she'd expected. She'd never given much thought to his stories before, never made the time to read them. But now, seeing his hand so clear in this letter, different from his usual notes, she felt a pull, a need to know the rest of his words, the ones he'd spun into tales.

She eased into his chair, the leather worn smooth from years of use, letting his voice settle in the quiet. The room held still, save for the steady pulse of the old clock. Through the windows, thin shafts of light cut across the dust, and the air seemed heavy with the weight of all that had come to pass. The world had shifted so far beyond what it once was, yet here, in this small space, time dragged on, indifferent to it all.

Papa, I hope we'll meet again.

***

The next day, they came. Three women stood at the edge of the campus, each with a child by their side. Weariness marked their faces, uncertainty etched deep. Adam was the first to approach and welcome them, and one of the women spoke, noting the resemblance to an old man she saw in the light that guided them.

"It's our Papa," he said, a wide smile breaking the solemnity of the moment. "Welcome home."

Eve, Ellie, Anevay, and Hope embraced them, their arms open wide, inviting them into the warmth and safety of Browers. The community grew, just as the old man had envisioned. The newcomers carried tales of survival and loss, yet they also bore the weight of hope and resilience. Together, they began to forge a new future upon the foundations laid by North, with his eleven tables and blessings.

As the seasons turned, generations sprung to life, and the compound flourished. The greenhouses brimmed with bounty, the barn thrummed with life, and the infirmary was always a place of healing and comfort. Children, once strangers, now roamed the fields together, their laughter rising like a vow of renewal in a world reborn.

And at the heart of it all, the memory of North remained, a guiding presence that would forever shape the community he had helped build. His spirit infused their daily lives - the checklists, the stories told over meals. He had been their anchor and protector. In his absence, they honored his legacy, ensuring Browers remained a haven of hope and resilience.

***

Time flowed onward, as it always does. One day, Adam found himself easing onto a bench outside Browers, his knees protesting with a familiar ache. The toll of age did not sit well with him, yet he accepted it as inevitable. The late afternoon sun stretched shadows across the campus, which pulsed with the energy of a vibrant community. Laughter of children danced on the breeze, mingling with the whisper of leaves and the distant murmur of everyday life.

His gaze wandered to the small graveyard by Browers, where four graves rested under a blanket of flowers. A slow smile touched his lips. His eyes moved back to the building. There sat Hope, surrounded by her children and grandchildren, their skin a patchwork of translucence and shadow, a genetic legacy as visible as any family heirloom. Adam watched them, the old pull stirring in his chest, that feeling he'd carried for so long it seemed part of him, like the stone in his pocket his mother had given him.

Then he turned his gaze to the other children at play. Their laughter rose and fell like the wind through the trees, a sound both close and infinitely far. He watched their energy, a wildness that stirred something long dormant within him, a time when his own body had known such freedom. Yet the memory fluttered just beyond his reach, like a name forgotten, and he marveled at how the simplest joys could slip away, rendered alien by the slow march of years.

He took a long breath, the air carrying the rich scent of late summer and enduring memories. Time had drawn its lines across his face, each crease a story, each wrinkle a truth grasped. His hair, once dark as night, now gleamed like silver in moonlight, and his body felt fragile like the pages of an old book turned soft with age. Yet his eyes, those eyes - still bright, as if they had consumed all the tales life had to offer and remained hungry for more.

"Grandpa," a voice broke through, pulling him from his reverie. He turned to see one of his grandsons, a boy of ten with eyes alight, racing toward him with the wild abandon of youth. The boy landed on the bench beside him, breathless from his run. "I saw something yesterday," he exclaimed, his eyes wide with excitement and a hint of fear.

Adam smiled, a warmth spreading through him as he regarded the boy. There was something in the child's face that echoed his own youth, that blend of awe and trepidation that comes with glimpsing the unknown. He leaned in, his voice soft.

"Oh? What did you see?" he asked, an invitation to share.

"A big black dog with red eyes," the boy whispered as if the very utterance might conjure the creature. "It was just outside the fence, but then the adults chased it away."

Adam's smile dimmed slightly, replaced by contemplation. He rested a hand on his grandson's knee. "They come and go, but if you remain strong and watchful, there's no need for fear," he replied, weariness threading through his voice. "Remember Great Papa's eleven tables. What's number ten?"

"There will always be dogs," the boy replied with a frown. "But why do they come here? What do they want?"

Adam sighed, his gaze wandering back to the children, their laughter a distant hum. "Sometimes the world beyond our sanctuary sends reminders of what lies beyond. It tells us to shine light into the shadows, a lesson to never take goodness for granted."

The boy mulled over this before asking, "Grandpa, why do you sit here every day? You're always on this bench, just watching."

Adam's smile returned, but it was a sad, wistful smile that spoke of years of waiting and watching. His eyes turned toward the horizon, absorbing the essence of a life rich with memories.

With a quiet certainty, he simply said, "I'm waiting for the old man."

ABOUT THE AUTHOR

Philip **Mazza** is a novelist with a boundless imagination, captivating readers with the epic fantasy series *The Harrow Saga*. Born in New York in 1959, he earned a degree in Business from LeMoyne College and an MBA, later holding leadership roles in human resources and operations. Now a professor at the Madden School of Business and Economics, Philip dedicates his time to his students and writing. *At the End of it All* is his sixth novel. He and his wife enjoy travel and continue to live in upstate New York.

www.ingramcontent.com/pod-product-compliance
Lightning Source LLC
Chambersburg PA
CBHW030250270626
47156CB00021B/301